Brothers Gone Before

Brothers Gone Before

A Civil War Story

Kent Gramm

RESOURCE *Publications* · Eugene, Oregon

BROTHERS GONE BEFORE
A Civil War Story

Resource Publications
An Imprint of Wipf and Stock Publishers
199 W. 8th Ave., Suite 3
Eugene, OR 97401

www.wipfandstock.com

PAPERBACK ISBN: 979-8-3852-4536-9
HARDCOVER ISBN: 979-8-3852-4537-6
EBOOK ISBN: 979-8-3852-4538-3
VERSION NUMBER 03/27/25

In Memoriam

The men and families

of the 2nd, 6th, and 7th Wisconsin,

19th Indiana,

24th Michigan

Volunteer Infantry Regiments

Army of the Potomac

Iron Brigade

We are springing to the call
Of our Brothers gone before,
Shouting the battle cry of Freedom;
And we'll fill the vacant ranks
With a million free men more . . .

—"The Battle Cry of Freedom,"
George F. Root, 1862

War is in many respects brutalizing, but the fortitude
and moral courage to bear up cheerfully and manfully
under its discipline is ennobling. Some men, it makes,
and more, it ruins.

—Rufus Dawes,
Sixth Wisconsin Volunteer Infantry

Contents

The Young Soldiers

The Johnny Soldier

Vernon would never forget the sunny Sunday morning when everything changed: when a soldier entered the back of their church—a recruiting officer wearing a new blue uniform and high boots that struck loudly on the wood floor.

A few evenings later, as his older brother sorted through the mound of belongings he would take along—it seemed for the twentieth time—and the lamp cast his shadow dark and wavering across the low slanted ceiling, Vernon asked, "Forrest, aren't you frightened to go to war?"

The sandy-haired older brother put down the shirt he was refolding with the same habitual care he used when putting dry goods on the shelves in the store below them. He smiled the gentle smile that Forrest thought was usually a little too patient. "Sometimes I feel more afraid than I ever have of anything." He hastily added, "But when you know you're doing right, you don't feel much of anything most of the time."

Vernon regarded his brother carefully. He was tall: he would be an easy target. "Why do you think it's the right thing, Forrest?"

"You don't believe going to war is right, do you?"

Vernon shook his head. "Why should we do anything about those crazy Southerners? Let them go! Let them go to hell if they want to."

"Come, Vern; we don't have to talk like everybody else."

"Well, we don't have to sign up to go into the army like everybody else, either! Why is it our fight?" Vernon hesitated, then continued, "I've thought a good deal about this. Charlie and George and I have talked it over."

The Martens brothers—George two years older than Vernon and Charlie a year younger—had been friends with the Mikelson boys for as long as Vernon remembered. They were the next family down the road when the Mikelsons still had their farm. Now the Martens often came into town and of course traded at the Mikelson's store. People liked the fresh smell of clean shelving and the sanded floor; there was always something new and interesting—boxes of hats, candles, pots and pans, and lots of things to waste time over and use as excuses to talk about the news. Quite a few of the older fellows and a good many married farmers said the war had been started by rich Easterners over rich men's interests, and the Easterners ought to fight it out if they wanted to. Let the Southerners do what they pleased, and let the New Yorkers do what they pleased, and let us here in Wisconsin stay out of it. But then there were those who said that if the Mississippi River were closed by the Secessionists and we in Wisconsin and Minnesota couldn't get our goods and crops to market, then we'd feel this war right soon.

The last time she and Vernon had walked together, Nancy Parker had spoken as if she assumed he would be leaving next year. She said she would knit socks for him and the other boys. But Vernon had decided that the war was simply foolishness, and Forrest knew it.

Staring down at his seated brother, Forrest looked a little strange in that flickering half-light—somehow older, and pale. "It might be wrong for you, Vern, but it is right for me to go. Where would we be without the United States of America? Father and Mother might have starved in Norway. We wouldn't be alive at all! Someone in this family needs to do his duty toward our country."

Vernon frowned immediately. The older brother sat down and that quiet smile came again. "Vern, to me one reason is the same as another, because to tell you the truth, I don't understand why I am going. I simply must go."

"They'll miss you," Vernon muttered. "More than they'd miss me if I went."

Three days later the table where Forrest's pile of clothing had rested was clean and empty. The chair over which Forrest always draped his trousers and shirt was bare.

Finally the first letters came. Two arrived together:

May 6, 1861
Camp Randall
Madison, Wisconsin

Dear Brother Vernon,

I've never been so happy in all my 18 years. The other boys are fine company—they say and do things that Mother and Father would never let us do at home. You remember what Father said at the train station: "Now, Son, remember that war brings temptations. You stay away from the girls who hang around soldiers!"

Well, when our company got off the train in Madison there were rows and rows of pretty girls dressed in red, white, and blue, waving flags and wanting ever so badly to kiss us. And of course we must oblige. We do everything in the line of duty. The girls of Madison think we are the bulliest boys! We told them we'd whip the Rebels in a couple of months and be home kissing them again on the Fourth of July.

There was a band waiting for us at the station, and it began playing as we got off the train. After we had done with kissing all the girls we could reach, the whole company got into line very smartly and marched past the band as it played "Yankee Doodle." All along the streets people stood cheering and waving flags.

Our company, the La Crosse Light Guards, has become part of the Second Wisconsin Volunteer Infantry Regiment. The other companies are bully. The Grant County Grays have splendid uniforms and I hear that the whole regiment will be supplied with such uniforms by the State of Wisconsin. You know how girls like boys in uniform. A couple of us are planning to go into town as soon as they let us have some free time—when we get our uniforms, that is!

I can't tell you what it's like to be with one thousand good Wisconsin boys ready to go out and teach the rebels a lesson. You should see us!—ten splendid companies in all!

It's too bad you are only 17. There won't be another call for volunteers because we are going to whip the rebs this summer, but if you ever have the chance to go into the Army—change your stubborn mind and take it! If it comes before you're 18, why, then, lie about your age. God will forgive a little lie if it's for the sake of your country.

Something's up! Our corporal is rounding us out of our tents.

I'll write and tell you what it is tomorrow.

Your Brother,
Forrest

May 7, 1861
Camp Randall

Brother Vernon,

What a pretty row the boys had last night! Our company was not involved, but some of the rougher sort of fellows in the other companies left camp last night and made a lot of noise in the city.

Now I fear the citizens of Madison look at us in a different light. I think if some of the boys want to go off and have a good time, they needn't do so at the cost of making enemies of our friends. We'll have enemies enough when we meet the rebels. You needn't get roaring drunk and smash windows to have fun.

Our Company was turned out last night to go find those rowdies. Of course, some of our boys took the opportunity to roam about a bit on their own.

Some of the boys are writing home saying that all we do during off-duty times is read our Bibles, gaze at pictures of our loved ones, and converse soberly on the state of the country. This is a great joke. It is true that some of the boys do that, but not many. We have all kinds of entertainments that are a bit more uproarious. Wrestling and boxing are frequent pastimes; some of the boys play cards; singing is popular. The patriotic songs are our favorites. When we turn all these energies on the rebels, won't they howl!

But when I write to Mother, don't you think I say most the same thing? She must think we are reading our Bibles, lest she worry that her son is being corrupted by Army life. And Father would come here himself to straighten us out! And surely after all, we are a Christian Army even if we are imperfect and young and foolish, and we shall do God's work in spite of ourselves if necessary.

Well, little brother, eat your potatoes and grow up—and come join us before the war is over!

Your Brother,
Forrest

The night of fiddling and dancing at the Tollufson's barn began with a disappointment. Vernon, with Charlie Martens along for support, called at the Parkers' house on First Street down along the river, on Thursday evening. Vernon had never asked a young lady to permit him to escort her anywhere, and most of the week leading up to Thursday was an eternity of worry. He and Nancy Parker had been friendly since their days in the lower grades. Only recently, Nancy seemed to be on his mind all day long.

Nancy was a very cheerful, smart young lady, a strawberry blonde with freckles and clear blue eyes. Vernon had never thought of her as pretty, but recently everything near her had become beautiful. The house on First Street was now strange and almost forbidding, whereas it had always been ordinary up until now. Nancy used to laugh like any other girl, but now there was something different in the sound. A strange and strong lift would swell in Vernon's chest when Nancy came into the store with her family. Vernon had begun avoiding her. At the same time, he felt a fierce possessiveness: he wanted to defend her and stand between her and the whole cruel world. He could not understand how Nancy could talk and laugh with anybody else, when he was quietly sorting things along the shelves in plain sight.

But they had always had an understanding. It was clear to everyone. Vernon knew beyond a doubt that he and Nancy were matched. When he and Charlie stood at the Parkers' door on Thursday evening, it ought to have been the most natural thing in the world. But her brother Edward came to the door. Vernon's confidence fell a little. Edward was a big man, six years older than Vernon, and reputed to be one of the smartest young attorneys in the county. He had studied at the University in Madison, then read law in Milwaukee. Considered a most eligible bachelor, he should be married to somebody in Milwaukee or Madison by now, Vernon thought irritably. It was about time he cut the strings to home, a man of his age.

"Well, Charlie Martens and . . ."

"Vernon Mikelson," Vernon said a little curtly.

"Oh yes, Vernon." Edward Parker smiled a smile that Vernon did not understand. "You've grown a little since I saw you last."

"We see you've grown a little something, too, since last we laid eyes on you," Charlie said. Vernon drew a little breath of relief. This is why Charlie was along. He always knew what to say. Edward now wore a full moustache, reddish blond like his close-cropped hair. It looked very military, and Vernon experienced a mild distaste at the thought. Then it occurred to him that his brother Forrest did not merely look military; he was actually in the army fighting for the Union. A twinge of sadness took all the irritation out of Vernon.

"Well, I'm only here to talk to your sister Nancy, if I may. It will take but a minute."

"Of course, Vernon," Edward said. Vernon felt that by his friendliness, Edward had somehow drawn him into his power. Edward turned and called, "Nan! Someone here to see you!" He turned back to the boys on the porch. "Come in?"

"Thank you, but we can't stay," Charlie said as Vernon took a step toward the door.

"No, we mustn't," Vernon said, stopping abruptly. He noticed a flicker of amusement in Edward's mouth and eyes. Vernon felt his face grow warm.

But then Nancy came to the door. Her presence was always light, like an angel's, Vernon thought, his heart lifting again. He couldn't help grinning like a fool. "Good evening, Nancy."

"Vernon Mikelson, and Charles Martens! To what do I owe this full-strength visit?"

"I'm here to ask if I may escort you to the Tollufsons' on Saturday," Vernon blurted out. He had perfected and practiced the line all week, but instantly regretted having loosed it so fast. Now there was nothing else to say.

"Oh, no! Not for the world, Vernon!" She put her arm through her brother's. "Not as long as Eddie's here. I simply must have his company until he goes back to Milwaukee next month!" She smiled up at Edward and laughed. "But I'll save at least one dance for you, Vern!"

He took that away from the brief interview: she had used his familiar name. He looked at Charlie ruefully. "At least she called me 'Vern.'"

Charlie seemed to find it all amusing. "She's not going to marry him instead of you, VERN."

Vernon flushed again.

"Vern, you take these things too hard. She just wants to be with her brother as much as she can. Who knows when she will see him next. For all anyone knows, he's enlisted in the army and will be off to the war."

Vernon started breathing faster. "She's at the age when she needs to think about serious things."

"Like marrying you, no doubt."

"Yes, now that you mention it." The thought of Edward going into the army put a frantic feeling where all the other feelings had been. He went on quickly. "And no doubt she will dance with everybody else but me on Saturday. That's just what she's like."

"There's plenty of fish in the river, if that's how you feel, Vern."

"I'm not particularly interested in fish. I want an angel."

"Angels are the worst."

"What?"

"Take my word for it: you'll be in hell if you marry an angel. A girl is just a girl and that's the way it ought to be."

"What do you know about girls?"

"Enough to know they're only human."

"I don't want one that's only human."

Charlie scratched his head bemusedly. "You understand that you aren't making any sense, don't you?"

Vernon shrugged. "I don't care."

*

Miss Parker indeed saved the next to last dance for Vernon. Because the brother had reserved the last waltz, the last minus one had significant meaning. Or should have had. But Vernon found it difficult to concentrate. The barn was decorated with bunting and flags, and large, painted posters saying "For the Good Old Flag," and "On to Richmond," and "Death to Treason!" Worst of all, Edward Parker was wearing a uniform. He had not only enlisted, but was a captain raising a company for a regiment that would leave Milwaukee in a month.

Nancy of course also danced with everyone else, not excluding Charlie and George Martens. Vernon couldn't help noticing this out loud. "I am only being cordial, Vern!" she said as the band played "Listen to the Mockingbird." "Some of the boys will be going away to war, and how could I be cold to them? Like my brother," she said as her eyes misted. "I do love my brother, Vernon! Edward is so brave!"

The Marten boys caught up with Vernon on the way home.

"You left before the last one?" George said.

"I just came out and kicked around."

"You must be in love," George observed.

"Do you know what? I hate this foolish war, and I haven't even been in it. I'm never going to join up. Hear me, Charlie and George: I'm never going to be fool enough to join this war for fools. The rebels are fools and the abolitionists are fools, and the government are fools."

"Your brother," George said. "Is he a fool, too?"

Vernon looked away.

June 12, 1861
Second Wisconsin Infantry Regiment
United States Volunteers
Camp Randall

My Dear Brother,

Yesterday we were mustered in, which means we are officially soldiers of the Republic. The feeling is unlike anything else. I am now in the Army of George Washington and the great patriots before us. Again the enemies of Freedom and Union are at the gates, and again the loyal youth of the farms and villages answer the call, with their lives if necessary. It is Lexington and Concord again. What a splendid thing it is to go in for something larger than yourself, Vern, and be willing to give all. When you ask most of the boys why they are in, they will say, "For the Old Flag," or "For Old Glory." Tears almost come into my eyes as I write. You can't know what the flag means until you are in the company of boys who will bleed for it. I love the Church, Vern; but sometimes I think I love my country the same way.

Some of the boys are in for the excitement, of course, and some just to get out of staying at home. There are a few abolitionists, but few of us care about the Negro Question. Many of the boys will say, "I'm not fighting for Africans. Free the slaves, and soon they'll be up here working us out of our jobs. Do you want them living on the next farm?" I've never seen an African. I don't believe the President means to free the slaves, but to preserve the Union. If we let the

Southerners have their way over us, soon we'll all be slaves, and the old United States of America will be nothing more than a big plantation growing tobacco and cotton.

One thing has turned out differently. We all came in with the understanding that our term of enlistment would be three months. Well, the President has called for three year volunteers—actually, three years or the duration of the war. The Governor asked all of us to enlist anyway, for three years instead of three months. Some of the boys were unpleasant about it, but I don't think anybody left for home. We all enrolled, and most of us cheerfully. What difference does it make? It's in our hands to end this war, and we mean to end it this summer whether our enlistment is for three months or thirty years. We all know that our own bravery is what will end this war, and we cannot begin by being afraid of the sound of "three years." We'll be home for harvest in any event.

The military routine is the same every day except Sunday, when the Chaplain convenes us for prayer and hymns, Scripture, and a patriotic sermon. At daylight during the week a cannon is fired to wake us, and we must rise, dress, and present ourselves for roll call. Roll call takes some time. Then we have one half hour to wash and generally ready ourselves and our tents before drill, which is at seven o'clock. After drill we get breakfast, each company together. Then we march back to our tents and by this time it is eight o'clock. At that time the officers drill, then the company drills together at 9:30. This is a long drill, and it lasts until dinner time at noon, when the drum beat calls us to the meal. Father would be quite displeased to know that one of the favorite table graces is:

> Oh thou who blessed the loaves and fishes,
> Look down upon these old tin dishes.
> By thy great power those dishes smash.
> Bless each of us and curse this hash.

At 2:00 we engage in sword drill, with wooden swords; then musket and maneuver drill between 3:00 and 5:00. Supper is shortly after five. When we are finished we must get polished up for dress parade, which lasts until sunset. From that time until nine we, as some of the boys say, "study military tactics"—which usually means talk or sing or write letters or play whist with somebody's new deck of cards. I am happy we won't have to stay in camp very much longer, but for now it is a novelty and not too hard to endure.

We have the best officers in the world. Our Captain is Wilson Colwell, a man you would follow anywhere. (You know a Captain is commander of a Company.)

The Colonel of the Regiment is Park Coon. There is nobody better than he is at handling ten Companies. Nobody is more fervently for the Union. Some complain that he is a political appointee rather than a military man, but he is completely confident of his abilities and so are we. We aren't professional soldiers, and only a civilian can understand us properly.

Our military man is the Regiment's second in command, Lieutenant Colonel Henry Peck. He was several years at West Point. A more intelligent man I have never seen. You should hear him talk! He knows more about movements, and strategy, and military history, and about Napoleon's Maxims, than any man alive.

Colonel Coon and Lieutenant Colonel Peck are the best of friends. Together they are agreed, and have said to us, that all they want is for us to live up to their soldierly standards.

The Regiment's Major is Duncan McDonald. We have Scots, English, Germans, Norwegians, Irish, various others, as well as native-born Americans like us. The American Union is truly the hope and mirror of the whole world.

We have an Adjutant, too. I am not certain, Brother, of what an Adjutant does, but I am sure he will do it well! The Quartermaster sees to it that we are properly supplied at all times.

The Regiment has—can you believe it?—three surgeons. Only a thousand men, and three surgeons! I think I am beginning to understand what is meant by Government wastefulness. If father knew that his taxes support three surgeons for one thousand men, he would be waiting to see the Governor tomorrow! (He would approve of our having a Chaplain.)

One aspect of Army life you need not envy is drill. Every day but Sunday is drill, drill, drill. You probably do not know, Brother, that War is not simply a matter of learning to shoot a musket and then running at the enemy in a crowd. We must learn to move in Company, indeed in Regiment, as one man. We advance at a walk shoulder to shoulder. That is how an enemy is attacked. You must present a solid front of muskets and bayonets, and break the enemy's lines.

Imagine how difficult it is to have a thousand men advance at exactly the same speed, with nobody out ahead of the others, and nobody lagging behind. A thousand men! And then—try to imagine—suppose you want to move a little to the left. Not much, mind you—just perhaps fifty feet. What do you do? You have to execute a maneuver. Everyone must turn obliquely to the left on command at exactly the same time, and keep walking. Imagine what happened the first time we tried this! You have never seen so many men bumping into each other at once, and so much laughing—and a bit of cursing, mostly from our officers—and men knocked to the ground; and the whole lot of us stopped in one milling mass.

Well then, suppose you want to move more sharply to the left or right, or suppose you want to turn the whole Regiment at right angles to what it was? Remember, you have not only one line of men, but usually two lines, in a regimental front.

And worse still, Brother: Suppose you are marching in a column down a road, and you have to get out of a column into a battle line. Or—let me give you a very difficult problem indeed: Suppose you are advancing in a double battle line, and you come to a stream with a small bridge. You have to turn the battle lines into a column, and then on the other side of the stream you have to come out into lines again. Imagine!

These maneuvers are still mysteries to us, and to the officers. But no doubt we will master them.

The citizens of Madison have had about enough of us. Some nights ago a crowd of the boys tried to break into a brewery and make off with a few barrels, but the owner met them with a blazing shotgun. It is well that we have not been issued anything more deadly than broomsticks and wooden muskets. Nobody was hurt at the Battle of the Brewery, but we have worn out our welcome in this city, I fear. They know most of us are sound fellows, but the few men of the rougher, baser sort spoil everything.

We are beginning to wonder when we will go East. Rumor has it that the rebels are at this moment surrounding the Capital. We are all eager to go to Washington and pitch into them.

I will write to you from the East next time, Brother. Give Father all the help you can.

For the Union,
Forrest

The weather turned warm suddenly in mid-June, as so often happens in Western Wisconsin, by-passing spring nearly altogether. Farmers were working hard during daylight hours, and the store was nearly empty all day. Nels sat over the account books but hardly turned a page. Vernon thought his father was worried about the slow business, but there never seemed to be an occasion to say anything to the silent man.

One afternoon when crates of goods and barrels of rice, flour, and sugar were delivered, Vernon and Nels worked together. It felt good to be doing something, even if it was only lifting barrels off the wagon and wheeling them into the store. It seemed to make Nels forget whatever was bothering him, enough to be humming an old Norwegian tune. Vernon took the iron claw to one of the crates as his father turned a barrel into its new place near the front of the store. The lettering on the glass cast shadows across Nels's face, and he seemed to fall into reverie again.

Vernon quickly said, "You know, Father, business isn't so bad for this time of year."

Nels looked up, surprised. "Who said business is bad?"

"Well, I . . ."

"Business is plenty good for this time of the year. As soon as it rains, we will have trouble keeping up with all the people who will come in. That is why I have ordered all this. Who is saying business is bad? Is Mother worried?"

"No, no, Father. I thought you were worried."

"I? Worried? Nonsense! Not when there's nothing you can do about it."

A good while later Nels asked his son to go to the post office and see if there had come a letter from Forrest.

This time, a letter was waiting.

June 23, 1861
Camp Brady
Harrisburg, Pennsylvania

Dear Brother,

We are in camp in the capital of Pennsylvania, only a day away from Washington.

We came all the way by rail. Indiana and Ohio were flat and uninteresting, but Pennsylvania is beautiful. It is rolling, like the gentle hills of Wisconsin, but there are mountains here, too. I remember Father saying that when he first travelled to Wisconsin from Norway, the scenery of Pennsylvania reminded him of home. Around Harrisburg we saw neat, well-kept farms owned by Germans, as you see in Wisconsin. I am thankful that the stain of Rebellion never will come to this prosperous, tidy, pretty countryside.

In Chicago we stopped to change trains and we were given a military escort. In Toledo we were served breakfast by the pretty girls of the community. Brother, you must become a soldier. In Cleveland—how we now love Cleveland!—we paraded through the city with positively hundreds and hundreds of the most beautiful women I have ever seen. I think after the war I am going to settle in Cleveland! Many little girls were dressed in white, with red, white, and blue ribbons in their hair and on their dresses. They cheered us, waving flags. Let us never wonder what we are fighting for! You should have seen another stop in Ohio that night—dozens of lovely young ladies turned out, and fifty of our boys (I do not say whether or not I was among them) left the cars and exercised the maneuver of advance, and kissed with impressive vigor these ladies who—and you must not ask how I know—kissed back with fine patriotic fervor!

A man was knocked off the train here in Pennsylvania while he was lounging on top of his car. One felt the need for air in the cars, which were dusty and hot. This man, I have heard, was killed, but I do not know if it is true. It feels strange to know that one of the fellows who grew up with us in Wisconsin, and lived with us during those days in Madison, is now dead, and in such an inglorious way, before we have come face to face with the enemy. I grieve for the sake of his parents and loved ones.

We have been issued arms, finally. Unfortunately, we did not get the new Springfields, but instead got old Harper's Ferry Muskets. They are not rifles but smoothbores, which means they are no good at all at a range over 75 or 100 yards. But Vernon, these are deadly things at short range. They fire not only a musket ball, but three buckshot with it. And the ball is .69 caliber! A big weight of lead! We shall make ourselves felt with what we have.

We have been issued the muskets and 40 rounds of ammunition because they expect trouble as we pass through Baltimore. You know eastern Maryland is full of Secesh, as they call Secessionists here. But we will get through and relieve Washington, if we have to shoot our way through!

Next time from Washington!

Your Brother,
Forrest

"What is the matter with Father, do you know?" Vernon had left the store and gone out behind the house, where Mother was hanging up the laundry. Annabel had stopped pinning sheets on the next line and was listening, but Vernon felt that this was too important to be stopped by worrying about what his sister overheard. It was hot and windy, and the bright sheets billowed out like clouds or flapping flags.

"Wrong? Nothing is wrong with your father, Vernie. He's a tough old *Nordmann.*" She resumed pinning up a pillowcase but couldn't help asking, without taking the clothespin from her mouth, "Why do you ask if anything is wrong with Father?"

"Anybody can see it," Annabel said. "I know what he means."

Vernon looked at his sister, and despite his wish to tell her to be quiet this once, he felt a pang. He didn't know why. Maybe he was proud of her knowing what Vernon knew.

"Yes," he said. "We can see it."

"He's worried about Forrest," Annabel said matter-of-factly to them both, and went back to her part of the clothesline.

"He most certainly is not," Mother said. "He knows that God will take care of your brother. Whatever God wants to happen will happen. If it is God's will . . ." She stopped and cleared her throat. "Everything happens for the best."

"I know, Mother," Vernon said carefully. "I know God's will shall be done. But there is something wrong with Father. I am doing all the books now, Mother. Father gives them to me to tend, not as if he is teaching me responsibilities but as if he doesn't care. I wait on most of the customers. He leaves when customers come. He sits all day, Mother!"

"Oh, let us not carry on," she said, giving a significant look toward Annabel. But the girl had been watching.

"I'm twelve years old now, Mother. And I belong to this family, too."

"There's nothing wrong with your father that a little rest won't cure."

"Rest," Annabel repeated.

"Mother," Vernon said insistently, now. "What about yesterday? There has never been a Fourth of July when Father did not come along to hear the speeches. He didn't even stand at the window to watch the parade! And last night—well, you know."

"He sat upstairs alone while we were out," Annabel supplied.

Vernon now felt afraid but at the same time he wanted to press for an answer. Mother's face became the picture of battle—a struggle between self-control and agony. He knew she would not hold it in.

"Your father needs rest, children. His heart is not so good any more. That is why you have to do more and more, Vernon. You will have to keep on with all you are doing, and I am afraid you will have to do even more."

"What is the matter with Father's heart, Mother?" Annabel held a clothespin tightly in each fist.

"It is just weak. He can't do so much any more."

"He acts so different," Annabel said. "Not just quiet." She stood looking into her mother's light blue eyes. "Is he afraid he's going to die, Mother?"

Vernon wanted the conversation to stop. He put his hands into his pockets and involuntarily backed away. He did not like Mother being upset. He hoped she would let the matter go.

But she didn't. "He's afraid that he will die before Forrest comes back." She lifted her apron to wipe her eyes. Then she said, forcing the words at first, "But he is a tough old Norwegian, I said. We will get by, and he will be all right."

"I'll try to help, Mother," Vernon said quietly, ready to go back inside.

"I know you will, Vernie. And you too, Annie. It will be all right. Everything will be all right. We are getting more help with the store, anyhow."

Vernon was not sure he had heard correctly. "What was that? More help?"

"Yes, your father and I have decided to hire another young man to help out. To kind of take, you know, to take—"

"To take Forrest's place," Annabel finished.

"*Ja.*"

Vernon turned to go inside. "I can do it all," he said quietly but insistently. "We don't need anyone else."

"Vernon!" his mother called. "We don't mean you can't do the work of two men. But you can't do your work, and Father's work, and . . ."

Vernon nodded. He knew it was right. He hadn't thought of it before. He wondered how they would pay an outsider. Would this new person live with them, too? He walked toward the back door.

Annabel had come up and was pulling at his sleeve. She said quietly, "It's Forrest. Far is worried about Forrest. I know it. If only he could come back, everything would be all right. Far would get well. Can't he come back?"

"I wish Forrest could come back right now," Vernon said. Everything would be different. But Forrest was a thousand miles away. The sheets flapped violently in the hot wind.

July 4, 1861
Camp Peck
Virginia

Dear Brother,

I am sorry not to have written to you from Washington. I thought it best to write to Mother and Father, and send Annie a little something. And we expected to stay longer in the Capital City.

I think I wrote of fears as to our reception in Baltimore. A Massachusetts regiment had marched through a while before and was attacked by stone-throwing Plug Uglies. The Massachusetts boys fired back—sending Secessionists screaming all through eastern Maryland and, no doubt, the whole South. Perhaps that is why we saw no Plug Uglies. On the contrary, we were cheered by crowds of people.

The Second Wisconsin Volunteer Infantry has the distinction of being the very first three-year regiment to arrive in the Capital. The few others to arrive before us were three-month regiments. I believe that this is an omen of our Regiment playing an important part in the War for the Union.

We are in the land of treason. We marched out of Washington City and crossed the Potomac two days ago. Now let the Secesh army boast of taking the loyal Capital!

You can see we have named our camp "Camp Peck," in honor of our second in command. Lt. Colonel Peck is Colonel Coon's backbone in military matters. He has a noble black charger to ride, and though he does not look the part of a soldier in every respect (he is both youthful-looking and balding), he cuts a fine figure on the gleaming stallion. I think he rides as well as can be expected. He always gives his opinions on the minutest details among the men and is always approachable. We are in awe of his military knowledge. He knows words and maneuvers that I fear we shall never master, should the war last a whole year!

We still believe Colonel Coon to be the right man in the right place, though some of course murmur and complain. I am told he is a little arrogant, in that he often does not speak to soldiers when addressed, but I believe he is merely trying to discourage familiarity toward officers. This is, of course, a regiment of civilian volunteers, and I wonder whether he is not being a bit too officer-ish, but I am sure he knows best. And he has high standards for his regiment.

We truly love and admire our Captain Colwell. I think he is the best of the entire regiment. He is always sociable, though never brash or too familiar. He has a smile for everyone, and would give his boots to a man who needed shoes. He was in the iron business for a time, and founded a bank in La Crosse, though he is only in his thirties. He was elected Mayor in April but chose to enter the Army instead—as you may have heard, for the information is famous. We find his advice always sound and practical, though often not quite what the regimental command requires. I think that an officer who is with the men on a daily, almost hourly, basis, and stands the test of the soldiers' respect and affection under those close circumstances, is a great man and a good man.

Just when we thought we were going to whip the rebels by ourselves, we found that we were to become part of a brigade. A brigade is made up of four whole regiments together—and is a huge group of men, almost an army itself. We are brigaded with three New York regiments. You should see them! The 79th N.Y. is full of Scotsmen, and they call themselves the Highlanders. Can you believe it—they wear Scotch kilts! Even their everyday trousers are plaid. They make our plain Wisconsin gray look drab, but I hope we will be ready for business.

The 69th N.Y. are Irishmen. They have a regimental flag of Irish green, complete with the Harp of Erin. You should hear them speak. We are not close by them in camp, but our boys try to make excuses to slip out and visit them just to listen to their talk. We have our own Irish in the 2nd, but not hundreds!

One of their companies is made up entirely of firemen. Vernon, they wear their felt hats and fire coats and red shirts from the fire house! Captain Colwell says they will make good targets for the rebels.

We have learned more about some of the other Captains in our Regiment. Randolph, of Company H, is a temperance man. He is not much enjoyed by his company. Recently he drew the company's ration of whiskey, a gallon, and assembled his men as if it were going to be passed among them as usual. Instead, he poured it out on the ground. Imagine the sorrow among those poor Wisconsin men!

Allen of Company I is called Long Tom. We hear he is a good man. He seems to know his business. His men say they will follow him to hell or Richmond, which are about the same, just as our Company says about our Captain Colwell.

The brigade commander is General William T. Sherman, a small unimportant-looking man I have seen only once, and from a distance. There are rumors that he is not completely sane, but there are always rumors. I would rather not have a mediocre man in command of the Brigade.

We were disappointed to hear that the Brigade, rather than the Regiment, is the important unit in armies. So we wish we were better-prepared in our drills and maneuvers as a regiment before having to join a full brigade. But under Coon and Peck, things will be all right.

The rebel army is at a place called Manassas along Bull's Run Creek, which is not far away. We wanted to go fight them today so we could win the war on the Fourth of July, as is proper, but the politicians and the high-up generals are slow, and cautious, and want to have everything just right beforehand. So I suppose we'll sit here for another week or so before we pitch into the traitors. I hear there is a multitude of them, but we'll lick them no matter what.

Every day carriages of ladies and politicians come down from Washington City with picnic lunches and look at us. I suppose when we go down to Manassas they will follow along and watch the battle, for the entertainment. It surely will be entertaining to see whether the rebels can run as well as they can boast.

You don't write anything about Father. Only Mother and Annabel, and a little about yourself. Vern, you might as well forget about Nancy Parker, if things are as you say. There are a lot of nice girls about. Is Father all right?

Forrest

Everyone in town knew about the great Battle of Bull Run, which had been fought seven days ago now. There had been no word from Forrest.

Surely he had been in the battle. Vernon had heard that the government printed a list of everyone killed, and he took his horse all the way to Hudson to get a copy, or to look at one. Forrest's name had not been on it, but a man at the newspaper office had told him that the list was no good. There must be mistakes, misspellings, and furthermore, men who had been wounded in battle would not be reported as killed, but might have died afterward. Vernon looked at the man, who was not a great deal older than himself. He was cocky, but not so much that he didn't let a little concern for Vernon and his family show through. That was just how newspapermen ought to be, Vernon thought. He liked the smell of the place. But when he turned to go, he realized that all he could tell his family is that they would simply have to wait for a letter.

He slept past his usual rising time the next morning because he had gotten in so late and so tired. He hadn't even wanted to eat anything. He had slept like a stone, and the voices downstairs seemed unreal and far away. Suddenly he sat up. A woman weeping! He jumped out of bed and pulled on his trousers. There must be a dozen people downstairs. Loud sobbing, and quiet voices. It wasn't Father's voice, though he must be there. It was Mr. Martens.

Why this weeping? What has happened to Forrest?

He stumbled down the stairs. Father, Mother, Annabel, Charlie and his father and mother. Charlie's mother was weeping. Vernon stood on the bottom step, fumbling with his shirt buttons. Mother looked at him and said, "You must go after him. You go with Charlie, Vernie."

"What's happened? Is Forrest all right?" Instantly he regretted blurting out the question, for it raised a louder sob from Emma Martens. Vernon's mother left Mrs. Martens' side and came to Vernon, taking him with both hands by the shoulders.

"Vernie, George Martens has run off to join the army. You and Charlie go and stop him before he gets on the train in Hudson. It will kill his mother and father."

Vernon looked at Mr. Martens, who appeared to be simply confused. He had been talking quietly all this time, but not to anyone. Now he looked at Father. "What is happening to the country, Nels? Everyone is going crazy. Everyone goes out to be killed. There is no sense in anyone any more." He looked at his son, Charlie, who was struggling with some thought.

I know what Charlie is thinking, Vernon said to himself. *I know him well enough. George had told him he was going, and made Charlie promise not to tell. Now Charlie is tortured for not having broken his promise.*

"Charlie, I'll go with you," Vernon said. But then he thought: *I can't go.* "Trygg is worn out from yesterday," he said helplessly to Father. "I can't ride him all the way to Hudson again today!"

Father nodded tiredly. His face was drawn and almost white. "You have to take Bestemann. I haven't ridden him hard all summer. Take him."

"Go, Vernie!" Annabel cried.

"You must bring something to eat!" Mother said. "I will get it while you put your boots on."

"Oh please hurry," Mrs. Martens said, still sobbing into her handkerchief.

Vernon and Charlie rode as hard as they had ever ridden, until Charlie's horse threw a shoe and began to favor the leg. Vernon rode ahead on his father's big black horse.

As he rode along the river coming into Hudson, Vernon heard the whistle. In another minute steam was visible over the woods on the Minnesota side, and then he could see the locomotive coming out of the trees. It was going slowly, making the turn onto the bridge across the St. Croix.

Bestemann was lathered along his neck in a way that Vernon hated to see, but they had made it. He leaped from the horse and tied him, then waded into the crowd spread out along the platform. "George!" he shouted. "George Martens!"

A hand sprang out from behind him, seizing Vernon by the back of his shirt. It was George, carrying a large carpet bag. "Vern, they sent you to fetch me back?"

"They did," Vernon said, panting. "Am I glad I got here in time!"

"Well by jingo, I'm not!" George said. "They should have sent Charlie. What's the matter with Charlie?"

"He came. Threw a shoe. Back about four miles."

"Vern," George said, his dark eyes very intense, "on behalf of my family, I thank you for what you have done. But I can't go back. Not now. Not after I ran off and came here with these boys."

"I know," Vernon said.

"You know?"

Vernon nodded. "I know I can't talk you into going back, and I'm not big enough to force you back. But I had to do it."

"Yes. They're probably beside themselves."

"Your mother is sobbing hysterically, and your father—"

"Don't tell me what is only torture to hear, Vern! Not if it won't make any difference anyway. You have to tell them I'm as old as your brother, Vern. Tell them that."

Vernon looked at George as though transfixed.

"Tell them that, Vern. I am old enough and I absolutely must do it. Tell them I could not stay at home. I'm going to Milwaukee and joining that regiment Ed Parker has a company in."

Vernon looked up.

"Yes, Vern. Tell them that. Tell them we'll take care of ourselves. We'll come back just fine. You know Lincoln has called for more men, Vern. Tell them that, too. Oh Vern, I just couldn't stay home after Bull Run!"

Vernon had nothing to say. He looked at the train pulling into the station. Huge blasts of steam blew out over the tracks and shot across the platform. George slapped him on the shoulder.

"You should come too, Vern. You come out this winter. I'll save you a place in the company."

George turned nervously toward the train. He looked comical in his too-small Sunday suit. The Martens hadn't gone to church often in the past few years; that much was plain. And he didn't look old enough to be a soldier. He straightened his black hair and pulled his cravat back into place. "I have to go, Vern."

"They don't want you to go, George. I have to tell you that. And I think everyone is going crazy. I had to tell you that too."

"I know. But you come too. Come out when you turn eighteen. I have to go. Wait! Take my horse back. See her?" George pointed back to the line of horses tied along the street. Vern recognized George's bay. He nodded.

"See?" George said. "It's all the way it's supposed to be. I didn't know what to do with old Perky. I even thought to just let her loose and hope she'd find her way home—back to the farm. Now you can take her, and Charlie can ride her. Things are just right."

"I'll take her."

People were crowding onto the train, and the two were being pressed along with them. "Oh, Vern," George said, reaching into his coat pocket. He took out a white, monogrammed handkerchief. "Give this to Nancy Parker, will you? Tell her I'll take good care of her brother!"

"What?"

George stepped up onto the high iron step. "Give it to her for me, Vern. Tell her I'll take care of her brother!" Vernon angrily lunged back through the press of people and burst out behind the crowd. George was gone, into the train.

"You might go to hell, George Martens. I don't care if you get shot tomorrow!" He threw the handkerchief onto the planks of the platform. "And I'll be damned if I ever sign up to go into your damned regiment!"

He stalked back to George's horse, swallowing bitterly. He pulled the rein and slipped the knot, and tugged the bay hard, not caring if George was watching through one of the open windows.

July 23, 1861
Camp Corcoran
Washington City

Dear Vernon,

You will have seen the newspapers before getting this letter. What shame and humiliation! I can hardly write. But I have to tell someone, and you might as well know the true story. Who knows what the battle reads like in the newspapers.

Twenty-four of the boys are dead. I can hardly get that into my mind. Three in our company. We left them dead on the field. We left 63 of the boys lying on the field wounded, and we ran off. And with those 63 are another 65 gone to rebel prisons. Maybe they'll be paroled or exchanged instead. But our friends are dead, and more are dying, or under the knives of rebel surgeons. Now I know why we have three surgeons. Three aren't enough. Vernon, I don't know what will happen to the Regiment if we have another battle like this, and lose so many boys killed and have so many wounded. We were only one thousand, and to lose 150 almost seems to destroy the Regiment.

But we weren't cowards. I haven't told you, but the one thing I have been afraid of all along is whether I would be a coward. You don't know before you "see the elephant" whether you'll run or not. I was so afraid of being afraid that I couldn't write it in a letter. But we were all thinking about this above everything else. I didn't run.

You know our brave Colonel Coon and Lieutenant Colonel Peck? Before the battle they put on red shirts to show their bravery. They weren't afraid of being more visible than the rest of us. What brave officers! we said. Well, they didn't have to worry about being visible. When the firing started they were gone. If it hadn't been for our brave, true Captains, and for General Sherman, who kindly stayed with our Regiment, the Second Wisconsin would have fallen apart. Coon and Peck are contemptible cowards! Peck, with all his military theory, is nothing but a talking mouth. And Coon, with his high standards! Hypocrite! It is said that Coon was on brigade staff duty during the battle but I don't believe it. He and Peck used their fine horses to carry them back to Washington before we even fired on the enemy.

They were asked to resign, and Major McDonald too, who was likewise absent. They complied instantly. Next time our field officers won't be cowards.

I will not tell you any more that our new officers are "splendid fellows," and so forth. But they are tried and true men. They stood the ordeal by fire, and they are solid men, and if the Second Wisconsin is ever heard from again, these three will be in the thick of it. The new Colonel is O'Connor, from Beloit. Our Lieutenant Colonel is from the 1st Wisconsin—Lucius Fairchild, a fine man. And our youngest Captain, Thomas Allen of Co. I, is the new Major. You will see why our officers elected Allen, though the youngest of them.

Back on the 15th of this month—it seems an age ago!—we received orders to cook three days' rations to carry, and to leave behind everything we didn't need, clothing especially. We marched twelve miles that day, and eight the next. On the 18th we came to Centreville, and heard cannonading on the other side of the town. We were ordered forward in support of the troops engaged with the enemy. We had to go three miles on the double-quick in our wool uniforms under the hot Virginia sun. We threw aside our blankets, haversacks, and everything but our knapsacks and muskets and cartridge boxes—and some threw their knapsacks. The haversack is hard to part with. It's a rectangular bag carried on a belt slung over the shoulder, and into it we put everything: razor, toothbrush, letters, pencils, Testament, books, and food. But you have never been in the Virginia sun in July.

We finally came to the fight—or so it seemed to us, who had never been under fire. The battle a few days later made this action look like nothing more than the skirmish it was. We formed line of battle in a woods, but lay down to avoid the shot and shell that was being fired at us by the rebels. We lay like that for three hours, metal whining and crashing over us, sending heavy branches down, and shells exploded close enough to wound three men. The next day one of the three, Myron Gardner, died. He was the first to be mortally wounded in our Regiment. We all tried to see what the wounded men looked like as they were carried off. "Is that what I will look like if I am struck?" is what each man asks himself. They suffer, the wounded, with their torn flesh and agonizing holes. And these men were wounded doing nothing but lying down. I am told that to lie still under artillery fire without being able to do anything about it is one of the severest tests of discipline, especially among green troops, which we were. We endured it.

But that is all we did. We were ordered back to Centreville, and there we made camp—or, shall I say, we made campfires and stacked arms and lay on the ground and otherwise did nothing—for three days.

On Sunday morning of the 21st we were formed up in our Division—a division consists of two or more brigades. I had thought our Brigade was a great army, but now I realized that battles are fought by divisions, and divisions joined together in corps, and armies made up of corps. I had known that, but I had never seen it. What a splendid sight it would be—a division of three brigades in line, each brigade in double line of battle. Thousands of men, perhaps eight or nine thousand, with arms gleaming in the sunlight, and regimental flags flying—all in even lines, steadily advancing.

But that isn't what we saw. At noon we crossed the stream now made famous, Bull's Run, and went after the rebels, who were already retreating. I was aware only of our brigade, and not the others of the division. A major from the staff of the commander of the Army, General McDowell, led us to where we were supposed to go in.

There were lines of other Union troops off to our right, and when we went forward the rebels were already falling back. On our immediate right there was a big stone house where two roads came together. The rebels crossed the road in lines and clusters, and we went after them.

Up ahead on some high ground you could perhaps call a hill was another stone house—the now-famous Henry House, but we didn't know any names until we read the papers afterward—and we could see that the rebels were making a stand there. There were plenty of them; you could make out about a dozen regimental flags, meaning three or four brigades. I could not see far to each side, but I had the impression that we had several brigades, possibly more, ready to attack.

You must understand that what the newspapers say and what a fellow in battle sees are two different things. Battle is confusion, and smoke, and awfully loud noise. But we could see them up on the hill.

Sherman didn't send the whole brigade forward. I don't know why not. We went first, our regiment alone. There was fighting on both sides of us as other regiments from other brigades went forward. It was a shambles.

The rebel flag is easy to mistake for ours, and easy to mistake for a flag of truce. They had the same trouble with us, because our regiment has gray uniforms. Sometimes you don't know whom you're supposed to be firing at, and you don't know whether the fellows firing at you are friends or enemies.

We went forward in line of battle. Never mind what you have read about gallant cavalry charges. An infantry charge is a walk, shoulder-to-shoulder, meant to tear a broad hole in the enemy's line.

You go forward with shells whistling past you, and you don't know whether you will be hit or not. It occurs to you to run and find a place to hide or get down behind something, but your comrades are marching and you must share their fates.

Then the enemy infantry opens. A volley far off sounds like the tearing of a heavy canvas cloth, but close up it's louder than a thunderclap overhead—all the single shots almost in unison, the whole length of the enemy line. You see orange flames from their musket barrels spurting through a sudden blossom of smoke which nearly hides the men behind it.

Instantly the nasty zip-zip-zip *of musket balls is all around, and you hear the sickening thuds of some of them striking your friends. You hear cries, startled exclamations, curses, prayers. But in the excitement you forget to be afraid—unless your legs have already taken you away to the rear. You don't pay attention to the fellows falling and screaming.*

The order is given to halt and raise muskets. We have already loaded. "Aim!" is the command. I shut my eyes. "Fire!" And we all fire together. The next thing I knew, I was lying on my back. I felt that I had been shot. I told you we have big, long, Harper's Ferry muskets. Well, the kick of one of those is terrific, and if you are not accustomed to it and fail to anticipate it, it knocks you down. I looked and saw many of the fellows in the same ridiculous predicament. In front of our line was a curtain of smoke.

I jumped up as the Regiment went forward. The enemy gave us another volley, but we did not falter though boys fell right and left. You know from the newspapers that the rebels were under the General Jackson who is now called "Stonewall" Jackson because his brigade stood like a stone wall. It was those troops we fought.

We loaded as we walked forward; and then the order was given to halt and fire. We advanced, and again we took the fire of the rebels. We were nearly at the top of the hill, face to face with the rebels. They fired at us steadily, and it seemed that we all knew then that we must go back.

We had not been trained in retiring, so we went back in a jumble, falling out of company formation. Part way down the hill our Captains sorted us out—while under the fire of the enemy, you understand—and we went forward again. One of the New York regiments came up along with us this time.

The Henry House Hill is not a narrow hill; there is plenty of room on it for brigades to stand and for brigades to attack. Regiments to our right were joining in the attacks. I had the idea that we were near to the left of our army.

Again we went through the bullets and smoke. "Steady, men!" shouted the line officers behind us. The color guard in the center of the regiment kept Old Glory and the Wisconsin State Flag waving. The rebels fired, and we fired, and as we came near to the crest of the hill again I felt us melting back. At that point it was difficult to see very much through the smoke. I could make out men going back, some staying; but the evenness of our line was gone. All one can do is go back then.

One of the New York regiments came forward through us at that time. We have not learned how to pass one body of troops through another, and so the two regiments became mixed together. That made it impossible to obey orders, because you hear shouting officers from every direction and you don't know which are your officers and your orders.

We went back down and re-formed at the base of the hill, watched other regiments go up, and waited. I cannot recall exactly how long we waited, but some time later we became aware that something was wrong to our right. Then it became clear that we were not attacking the rebels any more, but that masses of our own troops were coming toward us.

The general retreat followed. Another rebel army had managed to join the one we were fighting and had struck our right, forcing it toward us, causing us to bunch up and mingle together. At first everything was orderly. We didn't feel any sense of hurry or even discouragement.

But then panic ran through the army, which was fast becoming a milling crowd. Shouts to the effect that rebel cavalry was riding in among us were everywhere, and we jammed together more because a wagon had overturned on the only nearby bridge over Bull's Run. Carriages of men and women who had driven from Washington to watch the battle added to the confusion.

We all began to hurry toward Bull's Run, crossing it wherever possible, and went up the higher ground behind, which was cluttered with carriages, wagons, abandoned cannons.

We had got back to a stone bridge where a few of our regiment still held together. That there actually was rebel cavalry on the field I can attest to, because about a dozen of them—that's all I saw—made a dash at our color guard to try to take our regimental flag. A gallant fellow from Company C, Stevenson I think is his name, actually fought a rebel with his musket butt and saved the flag.

Captain Allen was in an open field running and shouting, waving his sword at the men, rallying us together. Men from many regiments stopped there, in all kinds of uniforms—our gray, the red pants of some New York regiments, blue uniforms, kilts. There must have been several hundred. We were actually the rear guard of McDowell's army. We formed a ring, eight men deep all around, to defend against cavalry. Cavalry has no chance against massed infantry; only running, disorganized infantry has anything to fear from cavalry.

But again the cry rang out, "Here comes cavalry!" I think it was some idiot making a joke, but the panic of the whole army ran through us, and everyone—myself included—ran like jackrabbits. I looked behind and saw poor Captain Allen all by himself, bewildered, but then running in long strides to catch up with us.

We made our way through a litter of guns, knapsacks, swords, ration boxes, wagons, ambulances, carts, dead mules and horses, caissons abandoned by artillery crews, civilians. And we didn't stop until we got back to Centreville.

There the Regiment was re-formed. We are still pretty well played out, and our grimy uniforms are stiff with greasy dust. These uniforms were not well-tailored; nearly everyone has a split in the seat, where our drawers show through. I imagine the rebels enjoyed seeing us run, displaying our "flags of truce." Some of the boys are nicknaming us the Ragged-Ass Second. (Don't repeat this to Mother.)

Brother, I can hardly tell you what this all means to us. We do not feel beaten, but shamed. We are determined to fight it out with the rebels again. The three month men all around us are going home, but we of course will stay. Now it looks as though we might be staying a long time, perhaps a year or more. This is no three-month war.

I will not look forward to battle again. Before Bull's Run, most of us were hopping for a fight, but now it's different. A fight is confusion and killing and screaming, fear and madness. I don't know whether I should feel courageous or not, Vernon. I didn't run, and I did stop with Captain Allen. But I did these things without thinking. When our line first went forward I lost all sense of danger, and I paid no attention to my friends and comrades who were falling down and screaming. If you have no sense of danger, you aren't courageous—perhaps brave at most, the way an animal that doesn't understand its peril is brave. Courage exists only when you are afraid, and stand to your work anyway.

Some men's knees shake if they have to talk in front of an assembly, some get pale and sick when they have to talk to a girl, and these same men might stand forever facing a line of cannon under a hot Virginia sun. And we men who faced the rebel muskets and cannons on Henry House Hill, we same men jumped up and ran off like jackrabbits when someone shouted that rebel cavalry was coming—and we had been prepared for them. Last Sunday the army as a whole acted like an unthinking animal and so did I. I am beginning to wonder whether I will run next time, or what I will do if ever I am really afraid; and I wonder what I am really made of inside.

And I wonder whether the country can be saved unless we get better commanding generals. McDowell has been relieved of command, and a new "Mac" is in charge, McClellan. I have seen him once already, riding through the camp. (I never saw McDowell.) McClellan looks every inch the soldier. You have confidence just looking at him. If he can't make us into an army and whip the rebels, nobody can. I hope we are more right about him than we were about Coon and Peck.

There is a rumor that our Regiment will be taken out of this brigade and put in another, with other Wisconsin regiments. I hope so.

Last night we sang "Home, Sweet Home" around the campfires, and "Nearer, My God, to Thee." I have never sung a Christian hymn so fervently. We were all near to God, Vernon. May God be near to us!

Your Brother,
Forrest

All the local young men who might have been available to help at the Mikelson's store were either in the army or doing late summer farm work. There would be no relief, no hired help, until sometime in the fall—provided a satisfactory employee could be found. Vernon rose early, worked all day, later than the farmers, and went to bed exhausted. To relieve his boredom, Vernon began to grow a beard for several weeks, found that it did nothing for boredom except make one's underchin itch all day long, and so shaved it off. Not only was he busy all day, including Saturdays, he saw nothing of his best friend. Charlie Martens was also doing the work of two sons and hardly ever left the farm. His mother and sisters came in on their wagon and purchased what little they needed this time of year.

Sometimes Billy Faust and Bodley Jones came into the store with nothing to do, and Vernon welcomed their presence. Billy broke his arm falling from a hay mow near the end of August, and he often drifted around looking for someone to talk to. He would limp into the store (he had given an ankle a good sprain in the same fall), settle against a counter, and watch Vernon come and go. He said he was perfectly satisfied to "keep an eye on things." It should have been unnecessary, because Nels Mikelson was nearly always in the store, but he seemed only half there. He would sit back in a corner, sometimes drumming his fingers over a ledger, or move up to one of the windows in front and watch people going by. He had lost weight, and his hair seemed grayer than it had been only at the beginning of summer.

Billy was called "Billy" even though he would be twenty years old in February. He was a very small young man, slight in build and with a boyish face. His black hair always seemed to have been carefully combed and slicked by his mother. His trying to grow a moustache all summer only served to accentuate his boyishness: it came out very sparse and wispy. He looked like a little boy who had taken a pen to his upper lip, and his evident pride in the effect was amusing to everyone but Billy.

"Going to join up." Vernon had heard this several times over the past few days, so he went on weighing out bags of white beans. "They can't use me at home."

"You're doing us good here, Billy."

"Yeah, well, I suppose I am." Billy examined the back of his good hand. "Next you know, I'll be in charge here."

"No doubt about it. And welcome to it." Vernon looked at his father, wondering whether he understood the boys were only joking, but Nels was gazing out the window as if he hadn't heard a thing.

"I've pretty much decided."

"You know what I think, Billy. When your arm heals and you're useful at home again, you have no business going off to the war."

"They ain't won it yet, you know."

"I know."

"And you know why."

"I suppose I do. It's because you haven't pitched in yet."

"You have it exactly."

"You've coached me, Billy, until I could get it right."

"What does your brother think, Vern?"

"About what?"

Billy wrinkled his mouth in exasperation. "The war! What does he think about the war? I mean, does he like being in the army?"

Vernon straightened up as he tied the small burlap bag. He hadn't thought about this before. "You know, I can't tell." He walked over to a shelf and got another bag.

Billy watched him expectantly. "Well? Is that all?"

"What do you mean, Is that all?"

"You just don't know?"

"Nope."

"Well, what do you think?"

"I expect he likes it well enough." Vernon looked again toward Nels. Then he motioned to Billy. "Billy, I need to get more twine over at Carter's. Come along?"

"Sure. Anything."

The street was parched and powdery. August had been as dry as usual, and there had been little moisture so far this month. Vernon kicked some of the dust, thinking.

"Billy, I don't know how to answer your questions in front of Father."

Billy lifted his eyebrows in surprise, then pressed his lips. "Aw, Vern, I never thought about it, talking in front of your father like that, as if he wasn't there. I am truly sorry, Vern. What a jackass I am."

Vernon walked on. "It's all right, Billy. I don't know what we can do about it. He's always there. He probably knows perfectly well we don't need twine."

"You gonna buy some?"

"Never thought that far. Suppose I'll have to." He thought about it a minute. "Naw. He'll never notice when we come back, one way or the other."

They turned the corner beside the white Presbyterian church, and sat down on the steps.

"I can't say Forrest likes the army, because then Father will think Forrest would rather be where he is than at home. And I can't say he doesn't like the army, because then Father will worry about him more. I guess after all the truth is, I don't know."

"Maybe Forrest don't know, himself."

"Maybe not. He sure enough didn't like being in a battle. I don't hear from him as often any more." Vernon mechanically took out his penknife and absently applied it to the step he was sitting on.

"Hey," Billy said.

Vernon looked up.

"You can't whittle on a church, you fool."

Vernon put the knife back into his pocket. "Getting as bad as my old man."

"I always thought you was considerably worse."

"Thanks, Billy. The main thing I can't say in the store is, this whole war is plain foolishness. It is not necessary. If I say that in front of Father, it sounds like I am calling my brother a fool, and Forrest is not a fool. I just don't understand why he joined the army." He looked down at the small gash in the step. "He talks differently in his letters, more as he goes along. He believes in what he's doing—I can tell without his saying it—like people believe in church."

"Well I believe it too, Vern. We can't let them rebels tear up this country. It's the only country we got, and it's a sight better than any other country on earth."

"Your family came over after mine did."

"We got out of Germany in 1848. I was born there."

"You don't talk like it."

"No I don't. The Southern rebels are like the German emperors."

"Seems all they want is their independence."

"Yeah, Vern, and they want the black man's independence too, and next thing, they'll want ours. They are natural born rulers. And they can go to hell. But they won't take this country with 'em. Not as long as Billy Faust is here to teach them their duty."

"Good for Billy Faust. I hope he wins the war."

"You ain't planning on going."

"Nope. I am not."

Billy looked down the street. "Better go back. Don't take this long to buy twine."

The two walked back toward the store. Neither said anything. Billy was not happy with tense silences.

"Hey, Vern, how's things with you and Miss Parker?"

"There is no such thing as me and Miss Parker."

"I took up the wrong subject, didn't I?"

"Oh, there's no difficulty, Billy. Just no subject."

"Well what happened? You two was for each other since school days, wasn't you?"

"I thought so."

"I see. She makin' time with somebody else?"

"With everybody else. Everybody and his brother."

"You sure?"

"Sure enough. You go in first." Father wasn't sitting at the window any more. Vernon showed Billy through the door, then slapped the frame with his open hand.

August 28, 1861
Meridian Hill
Washington City

Dear Brother,

We've been gadding about the other regiments finding out all we can about our fellow Westerners. Yesterday our old Ragged-Ass Second joined King's Brigade, which has the Fifth and Sixth Wisconsin—and the Nineteenth Indiana. The latter is disappointing because it isn't another Wisconsin regiment, but we are happy with knowing that together we make up the only all Western brigade in this Eastern army.

General Rufus King is from Milwaukee, where he was Editor of the Mil-waukee Sentinel, and has been Superintendent of Schools there. It's fitting for General King to command a brigade of northwesterners against the slavehold-ers. His grandfather, also named Rufus King, was a delegate to both the Conti-nental Congress and the Constitutional Convention, and he was the man who wrote the Resolution prohibiting slavery in the new northwest—of which our old Wisconsin is a part, Brother. It's a distinguished family. His father fought in the War of 1812, and was President of Columbia University. The General shows his heritage, rough-looking but distinguished, though perhaps not quite as military as one might expect. I am told he acts like a plain man, quiet and unassuming. Not what you'd expect from someone of his lineage. I hope he's as good as he ought to be.

He has a good brigade.

I haven't seen any of the officers of the Fifth, but the Sixth is a fine outfit. They aren't veterans like we are, but they'll do. Its Colonel, Cutler, is an old man; he's fifty-some. A crusty, gray-haired fellow with a white beard—who'll tolerate no nonsense, either from his men or from the enemy, is what he looks like. His officers are the best our state can offer. Frank Haskell and Rufus Dawes are the most soldierly men I have ever seen—intelligent-looking and decent. They have a man named Bragg, who has the sharpest eyes I've ever seen, except for Dawes.

The main thing about the Colonel of the 19th Indiana is that he's tall. They call him "Long Sol;" his name is Solomon Meredith. He's a Quaker. You know Quakers aren't supposed to fight. We'll see. Fighting is wrong but rebellion and slavery are just as wrong, so what ought a Christian to do? But we are fighting for others, not ourselves. The rebels are fighting for their own "rights" at the expense of others, and that is wrong.

The Sixth had a little entertainment from the Plug Uglies in Baltimore, but came through all right. There is a company full of North Woods lumberjacks in the Sixth; I don't think any Plug Uglies could stand up to those men. We had the grand opportunity of hearing the Sixth's brass band this morning. What a wretched assemblage of misfits. The music sounded like a funeral march. I trust they'll be discarded like the other unnecessary baggage once we get out of camp.

We should get out of camp soon, and have at the rebs again. The boys are feeling good again, and so am I. "Little Mac," our beloved Commanding General, is a great man. When he rides along the lines in review, we feel like soldiers. And we know that he cares about each one of us, and wants to do the best by us. In turn, we want to do the best by him. Just give us a chance at the rebels, with our George McClellan, and Richmond will have a hundred thousand unexpected visitors.

We have been constructing earthworks to defend Washington; the place we're building is to be known as Fort Marcy. We are fighting the rebels with pick & shovel. I would rather be on the move, even if it's another battle. Surely this camp life will end soon.

Your Brother Forrest

Long after sundown Vernon sat by his window staring at the harvest moon. On the otherwise empty table lay the most recent of Forrest's letters addressed to Vernon. It had been written nearly three weeks ago, and it wasn't full of news, but one phrase would not lie still, and Vernon had read the letter over and over again the last two weeks. "We feel like soldiers," Forrest had written. How was that different? Vernon knew his brother had changed somehow. But how? He wasn't a home boy any more. He wrote from something inside that nobody had seen before. You would think he would write hard, seasoned things, being a soldier. But no, there was an abandon in Forrest that soldiering for the Union had brought out, a thing that a boy growing up in a stolid Norwegian household did not show.

They weren't so different. Vernon had grown up, too, he thought as he looked at the low moon. Smoke from bonfires as the farmers around burned off their stalks had swelled it to what seemed like three times its normal size and made it blood-orange. Vernon's window was open, and he could smell the sweet, dusty smell from the fields. *I have come to a ripeness of my own,* Vernon thought. A few years ago, maybe even last year, he would have been driven into a blue, morbid state of mind by Nancy Parker being untrue to the ideal of their growing love. He might even have wept, before. Now, he would neither mope nor give up. If she were meant for him, then she would come around. If not, well . . .

He would not contemplate his future without her yet. He might join the cavalry. Riding across the smoking fields, through shot-torn woods, sword held at the ready, jaw tight and determined. He could feel the galloping stallion beneath him. Someday they would have to fight the rebels up here in Wisconsin. The Parkers, including Ed, cowering inside their house, would look out and see the National cavalry sweep down the street. She would catch sight of him, officer's straps on his shoulders, next to him an aide carrying the snapping guidon, white, with a red Crusader's cross . . .

"Vernie?"

Startled, he turned. His mother was standing in the low doorway. A flash of irritation went through him.

"Why are you still sitting up?" she asked quietly.

"Me? Oh . . ."

She came in and slowly sat herself down in Forrest's chair. Every once in a while Vernon noticed how tired her movements were. A little more gray around the edges of her light brown hair. Usually fastened behind her head, it was now flowing down behind her old flannel robe. Its dim whiteness seemed to speak back to the moon outside, purer and cleaner. She sighed a long sigh, saying "Ja."

"Why are you awake, Mother?"

"One doesn't need as much sleep when one is nearly fifty years old." She sat and looked out the other window. She usually spoke freely; right now she was acting more like Father.

It began to seem as if she would sit all through the night, without saying anything.

"Mother?"

"You see, this is not good for Annabel."

Vernon leaned forward toward where Mother sat, on the other side of the two beds. "What is not good for Annabel?"

"Oh . . . I don't know."

"Don't know?"

"Well, I mean I don't know what to complain about this time."

"You don't complain, Mother. You complain too little."

"What good does it do?"

Vernon nodded wryly. This is what Norwegians are like. I am probably going to be like this myself, he thought.

She shifted a little in the chair. "Father needs help now. Annabel is afraid all the time. She thinks soon we will be only the three of us—that you will go off to the war. She does not study as well as she should. She sleeps less than a girl of her age should sleep. She tosses around in the bed."

"I'll go to Hudson on Monday and look for someone to help out here. He can move in with me up here, for now."

"Will you, Vernie? I hope you can find someone."

"The harvest is home. There will be lots of boys hanging around the courthouse in Hudson."

"We don't want any courthouse boys."

"No, no, Mother. They sit in on the trials for entertainment, knowing they can be found there for work. I'll find a decent fellow."

"You can't tell what a man is like until you have had him around for a good long time."

"Mother, do you want me to go or not?"

"*Ja*, of course. I just don't know . . ."

"It will be all right, Mother. We'll get through until Forrest comes back."

They sat in silence. Mother didn't seem to be willing to go yet, but she said nothing further. Then Vernon noticed that she was wiping her eyes. It made him feel very impatient. He wished she would go.

"What is it, Mother?"

"Why should I give you my worries? You have enough of your own."

"Mother!"

"Well, how should I tell you that Forrest will not come back?"

"What? What do you mean, Mother? Of course Forrest will come back. The war won't last forever!"

She stood up to go. "Vernie, I just know that he will not come back. I know it as sure as I know anything, as I know the hand in front of my face. That is why I cannot help your Father. We both grieve already. It is all up to you here now. You must get help not for Father, but for yourself."

"I'm all right, Mother. And Forrest will come back."

"No."

She is stubborn, Vernon thought. *She has to be right, even if it breaks her heart.*

"Mother, nobody knows the future."

"God knows the future."

Vernon was about to say, *And God has told you that Forrest will not come back?* But he could not speak that way to Mother. He said nothing.

"What must be, will be," she added. "There is no use worrying over it. But I can't help it. I worry about all of you."

"And we worry about you, and Father worries about Forrest and about Annabel and me, and Annabel worries about you and Father. We have to stop this, or else we will all go mad, Mother!"

"The whole country is mad. Why not us?"

"I think you should go and get some sleep, Mother."

She moved to the door. "At least we don't have to get up so early tomorrow."

With an irritated shock, Vernon realized he had said nothing about tomorrow morning as yet. "Oh, Mother."

"What is it? You are not going to church tomorrow?"

"Mother, you are a pessimist. Yes, I am going to church, but I plan to go with Bodley Jones to his church."

"Why?"

"Well . . ." The way Mother said Why? made the idea seem absolutely foolish. Certainly it was unthinkable to Father and Mother.

"I want to hear the new Presbyterian minister."

"He is not new. He has been there nearly two years."

"Well, that's new for me. I've never heard him."

"*Ja*, well, you never heard the Baptist preacher in town either, and surely you are not about to go listen to a shouting, hairy Baptist, are you?"

"I would just like to see what it's like, Mother."

"What for?"

"Well, why not?"

"Because the Presbyterians don't hold worship services. All they do is listen to sermons."

"Mother, it isn't that I'm thinking of leaving the Lutheran Church."

"I should say not."

"Just tomorrow."

"I suppose you are old enough to do whatever you want. But you have not told me why."

"Oh, all right. Nancy Parker goes to that church." Thunder in heaven, was there no privacy, no respect for persons? Blast it, Vernon thought.

Mother turned, saying, "Huh." Then she turned back. "She is a nice young girl, Vernie. But she is an English girl."

*

Wearing his paper collar and smallish gray Sunday suit, Vernon walked toward the Apothecary where he was to meet Bodley Jones. He had delayed until it was almost too late, hoping Bodley would already be there. Vernon didn't want the Parkers to see him waiting.

Sure enough, there was Bodley's huge form, bending over and peering into the window. Bodley was at least six foot three, and well over two hundred fifty pounds. He worked all over the country and in town doing things that required strength, bringing in good money for his family. His father had worked the mines in Platteville until ruining his back. Then he moved the family up here, all nine children and his wife, in hopes that everyone else could run the farm and raise enough money. Bodley was third oldest, and by a narrow margin the largest.

"Love them colors to the bottles," Bodley said, pointing to the small collection of liniments and solutions. "Someday I'm gonna get me a whole bottle of that limewater. Then I'll smell like a crackerjack, I'll tell you."

"I think you should use that instead," Vernon said, pointing to a light blue bottle of linalool.

"Perfume," Bodley said. "When I get my hair long as yours Vern, then I'll get perfume for my locks." He removed his hat, showing brown hair an even half-inch long all around his large head.

"What happened to you?" Vern exclaimed.

Bodley replaced his hat with exactitude, pulling in back and adjusting in front by the reflection in the shop window. "Ain't gonna work in the feed mill with long hair. Someday the machinery takes a snatch at you, and next thing you know you are mixed up with buckwheat in a big canvas bag. You know what happened to Johnny Smith, don't you?"

"I don't know what happened to any Johnny Smith, Bodley, because there never was any Johnny Smith, and even if there was, I wouldn't believe you."

The young men walked toward the First Presbyterian Church. The doors were still open, and piano music came from inside.

"You are nervous as a cat, Vern."

"That is why you are along," Vernon said, swallowing.

"Then ask me what happened to Johnny Smith."

"Will not." They ascended the stairs, entering the plain white church. There was only a cross up front, nothing on the walls. Pale violet light came from colored windows, but there were no figures on the windows. As they walked to an unoccupied pew and Bodley opened its gate, he bent down and whispered, "Got ground into seed corn and now he's all over the Edgerton's south forty!"

"Take off your hat, by thunder!" Vernon whispered back.

Vernon had chosen carefully. In the same pew, only across the divider, the Parkers were already in their places. Vernon leaned forward and nodded to them. Nancy smiled the brightest smile in the world, and Vernon leaned back with an embarrassing grin on his face. That glad look from her gave him as much of a full-hearted church feeling as he had ever known, and he determined to fill up on Presbyterianism.

However, the sermon was desperately long. Vernon noticed early that Bodley was sweating, although whenever his family was in town they came here and he was used to it. But lately he had been arriving alone some Sundays because the feed mill gave him quarters in town. Mr. Parker owned the feed mill. Vernon stole a glance to his right. Nancy was looking attentively at the minister, as was everyone else.

I'm sick of hearing about the war, Vernon thought. At least in our church, Pastor doesn't talk about the war.

When the service finally ended, Bodley contrived to shove Vernon toward the Parkers. As Nancy descended the steps outside, Vernon caught up with her.

Having just put on his hat, he removed it again. "Nancy!" She turned and stopped, smiling as if she had expected him to catch up. Her blue eyes were as airy as the sky. Standing next to her, he felt like a prince, like a king. He was ready to seize a rearing mount, swing up into the saddle, ride to the sounds of battle.

"Well?" she said, looking at him as someone would who had known him for years, understanding his every thought.

"I wonder how your brother is getting along," he said.

"We hear from him nearly every day. I think he is doing wonderfully well. What about Forrest, Vern?"

Vernon blinked. "Forrest?" He cleared his throat. "I think he is getting on very well too. We don't hear from him nearly so often," he added apologetically. That burned a little. Enlisted men couldn't afford writing materials as officers could.

"Is it true that you do not intend to enlist when you become eighteen?"

Vern wondered who had told her that.

"Yes, it's true."

"Don't you think you're needed?"

He began to feel warm. "I don't think I'm a coward, if that's what it seems like."

"I'm sure it doesn't."

"I just don't think the whole war is needed."

She looked at him quizzically, a little troubled.

"I don't mean that our brothers are wasting their time. I just think—I just think that representative government is inevitable, that nothing can be destroyed by this war. As Jefferson wrote, the truths we hold in this country are self-evident. You don't need to fight for them, and it is useless to fight against them. They will win their way in the world through their own force."

"Do you think people are that wise, or that good?"

"It has nothing to do with people."

The Parkers drew away from the families they were talking to, and it was evidently time to move along. Bodley stood only several feet away.

"Vern," Nancy said earnestly, "I really do hope you are right. I wish I could have your confidence. I am so worried about Eddie."

"I am confident in ideals. It's all a matter of ideals. They are the strongest force in the world."

She nodded silently, uncomprehendingly.

"It was most pleasant to see you this morning, Nancy," Vernon said. She nodded and held out her hand. She had never done that before. Vernon took it in his, made a slight bow, and released her hand. He stood as Nancy and her family walked away.

"If you don't mind me mentioning it," Bodley said, "you are a complete ass."

Exasperated, Vernon could only say, "Thank you."

"Ideals. What a bunch of Guernsey loaves."

Vernon put his hat on. "I thank you again."

"You know, talking about how the war ain't necessary to a girl you want to marry whose brother is in that war is the dumbest, dumb-ass thing I ever heard. Don't it beat everything."

Vernon was still watching the Parkers. "I am so glad I came with you this morning, Bodley." Then he turned and the two walked toward the feed mill.

"Well, each to his own," Bodley said.

Vernon didn't answer.

"Are you really an idealist? I mean, do you really believe what you said about Jefferson and all that?"

"I am an idealist."

"Vern, I'm going to join up. Soon as I'm eighteen in April. I believe in the Union. It ain't an ideal, though."

"No?" Vernon unbuttoned his coat. He was beginning to feel very angry at himself. "What a fool I am," he said between his teeth.

"The Union is just us. We got to fight for it." He nodded definitively. "And yes, you are a fool, all right."

"Well, I'll stick by it, anyway. I am not about to go off and join the army next month."

Bodley removed his hat and scrubbed his short hair with his fingers. "No, I expect you never will." He put the hat on again, plopping its crown with a firm pat of his large hand. "So it looks like I'm going to have to save the Union for the two of us. Next time you write your brother, tell him I'm coming."

October 20, 1861
Arlington Heights, Virginia

Dear Vernon,

It's beautiful down here, Brother. The scenery is hard on war thoughts.

Vern, you must not get so angry about affairs of the heart. Women are unpredictable, I'm told by the fellows here. Not that I would know. I expect to marry one, but never to figure one out. I don't know what Nancy feels about you, sorry to say. As your older brother, I am supposed to have advice for you, but I have none, except to be yourself and don't let her make you into something you don't wish to be. I think this young woman has that ability, or else you have the ability to dream up something that doesn't exist. I just don't want you to be angry or blue, Brother.

Now as for my news, I hate to write these words: We have gone into winter camp. We all thought we'd make another campaign against the secessionist army. I think Little Mac wants us to be ready, and he won't be rushed. He knows his business. He won't throw us at the rebels for nothing, like McDowell did.

But we aren't rid of McDowell completely. This month the army has been organized into corps. King's Brigade is part of McDowell's Division.

You will never guess where Arlington Heights is. It's right across the Potomac River from Washington City. It's the estate of a man named Robert E. Lee, the son of the famous Light Horse Harry Lee, who fought in the Revolution. Unfortunately this Lee is a rebel. So we're camping about a half mile from his mansion, digging the grounds up nicely to prepare for our log cookhouses, stables, and huts. I heard that President Lincoln offered Lee command of all the Union forces, because Lee was once Superintendent of West Point. But the man turned him down, and now where is he? We haven't heard of him at all. Maybe he's been sent down to some southern swamp to watch for our gunboats.

Well, we're enjoying Mr. Lee's hospitality. By December we will have log cabins, courtesy of Lee's trees, with canvas roofs. We'll get sheet iron stoves and we will construct solid mud-and-stick chimneys for them. We'll be warm this winter.

But it feels strange to be in winter quarters. The weather here is still mild. I try to imagine how things are back home. I see the beautiful reds and yellows of the autumn leaves along the blue St. Croix. Perhaps the leaves are already gone at home. Not here. What will we do here until spring?

We have plenty of drill and loading practice, and all of us have picket duty. A picket is a sentinel, keeping watch over the camp, who must stay awake and challenge unauthorized persons. On picket we mostly write letters, play cards, and sometimes doze. A sentinel who sleeps on duty is supposed to be shot, according to regulations, but we are safe here and nothing happens, so the rules are not strictly enforced. One dark night last week one of the fellows shot a calf which had refused to give the countersign.

The Company organized a baseball game the other day. Our side did not fare well, but the activity did pass a couple of hours.

We no longer wear our gray Wisconsin uniforms. The whole Division was issued standard Federal blue last month. The new wool is not as good as our Wisconsin material, except that the trousers seem not to split as readily. It is against the rules, but most of us are keeping our good, heavy gray overcoats for the winter.

Clothing is charged against our clothing allowance. What's unspent at the end of a year comes to us in money. So there is a little resentment at having to pay out the following for inferior goods:

> *pants$3.03*
> *shirt.88*
> *coat6.71*
> *overcoat7.20*
> *drawers.50*
> *socks.26*
> *blanket2.95*
> *rubber blanket1.00*

And so forth. When out of camp, the idea is for two men to tent together: one lays his rubber blanket on the ground, then they use the other two blankets, topped by the other rubber one, over themselves. We each get a tent half, which is a piece of canvas with buttons and holes, so two men can fasten them to-gether and make a pup tent. I vastly prefer our log cabin to a pup tent, which is barely long enough for my height. If I were six feet, I should have to sleep with my face in the rain.

We've also got new muskets. Still not Springfields. At least our new Austrian rifled muskets are not smoothbores, and they can be shot accurately over distances of several hundred yards. But they are heavy and clumsy, and I don't know of any other command that has them, which might make getting ammunition difficult.

We have packed a man with everything regulations demand: rifle, bayonet, knapsack stuffed with spare clothing, coat, haversack, blanket, ammunition, percussion caps, tent half, and so on, and found that the whole load weighs 80 pounds. Whoever writes the regulations doesn't have any brains.

Don't expect to hear from me often during the winter, Brother. There isn't going to be anything to write about. You let me know how the new man is doing, though.

Your Brother Forrest

The new man was Stephen Corbin, a fellow of twenty-four from Ohio. Oddly enough, his dark brown hair was already salted with a little gray on the sides. He was a slender man of average height, always clean and wearing a white shirt, rather sharp-faced except for lips fuller and more expressive than one would expect in a man who seemed always to narrow his energy and attention toward exactly what he wanted to accomplish.

Vernon had not found him at the St. Croix County Courthouse. His mission there had been a failure. But Corbin appeared at the store the following week seeking a position. He had heard that such was available.

"It is my hope to learn store keeping," he had announced. "But it is my ambition to get rich off this war. However, I mean to go about it honestly."

Vernon had been unsure about this frankness, but was thankful to be speaking with someone who did not look at the war as a thing all-important in itself.

Stephen Corbin had been a schoolteacher. Vernon assumed he was a peace Democrat, but Corbin never spoke politics nor referred to the Rebellion beyond what he had said that first afternoon. Why he had given up schoolteaching he also never said, but if his intention was to become wealthy, the reasons were self-evident.

Corbin was a college graduate, having attended Oberlin. He was very quick to pick things up, learning all he needed, or wanted, to know in under two weeks. Vernon wrote to Forrest, "In reply to your interest concerning the New Man, he worked quickly but did not work well as he got what he wanted from us and quit to take a position with Parker's Feed Mill. I expect he will move west in a few months and we will next hear of him as the owner of a bank in San Francisco. We are looking for another New Man." Then he added, "It seems there are only two topics these days, War and Money."

Annabel was suffered to leave off attending school, and resigned her piano lessons, in order to work in the store. Christmas was coming and there was too much to do without help. Mother was in the store more than she ever had been before. Nels seemed to revive a little with snow and cold weather, though he remained stubbornly passive as to making orders and establishing delivery schedules, and Vernon now found himself in the unsatisfactory position of being in charge of the entire family as a work force. Vernon wrote Forrest that there would be little *Jul* this year, though Mother had managed to make *lefse* and a few other Norwegian Christmas things. On Christmas Eve, Vernon cut a tree and the family decorated it in the front room. But the parlor had never been used except for such occasions, for which Forrest had always been present, and the atmosphere was so bleak that the family ate Christmas dinner rapidly and then found work to do.

It was not until after New Year that Vernon received another letter from the East.

December 25, 1861
Arlington Heights, Virginia

Dear Brother,

I hope that at this very time you are all celebrating Christmas, happy over what we have rather than unhappy at not being all together. I hope you are eating julekakke and fattigmand and sandbakkelsen. I'm sure Father is reminding you that we are to be grateful for all the good gifts God gives us, and not quake at the responsibilities He allocates along with them. I am embarrassed to sound like him, but I do believe it.

I am afraid that you exemplify the Prince of Peace better there than we do here. Christmas in the army is not like Christmas at home. The only comfort is that we are defending you at home, so that Christmases can still be celebrated freely in our free land. I am here for Father and Mother, for you and Annabel, and with that I am satisfied.

I sit back and think of Father putting on the Jul log, and helping mother with the cooking that she has never really learned to like. Spare ribs and sausage. I so miss everything, and I would give everything I have here for some lefse and julekakke. Brother, I am not ashamed to say that my eyes water while I think of it.

The only thing that cheers me is the thought of you having to eat lutefisk on New Years Eve. We have salt fish here, and many canned fruits and vegetables, none of which tastes like the real thing; but how you can take fish and make it into the tasteless, clear jelly Father gets sentimental about on New Year is beyond my ken. I suggest that Father send the rebels some barrels of lutefisk and they'll be crying for mercy.

I love all of you at home, and wish I were there. Christmas carols are not the same here. I listen to the Norwegians among us sing the old hymns, and it's almost like home. But it isn't home.

God jul, Brother.

Forrest

Billy Faust, who had been working at the store since the turn of the new year, made arrangements in February for some of the old friends to come to town for Vernon's birthday. There wasn't much to do except drink hot, aged cider around the stove in the store, and quit early so everyone could make his way home through the snow before it got too late. But it was the first time Vernon had seen Charlie since fall, and the first time in months that he had done anything in the evening but work. Bodley Jones was there, and Willie Evans, who lived across the road from the Mikelson's old farm. Bodley could drink a lot of cider, but Willie was having trouble holding his glass and keeping his pipe lit at the same time. It was he who asked the question which was somewhere in the back of everyone's minds.

"So what are you goin' to do, Vern?"

Vernon looked at Willie's weathered face. He appeared to be twenty-five or thirty, though he was only nineteen. Willie was the hunter of the group. He had the perpetually narrowed eyes of a marksman who spent hours looking up at the bright autumn sky from a duck blind. In the winter, he tracked deer and other game across glittering snow. He had been out today. "Well?" he persisted, when Vernon didn't answer.

"I am going to sit here and drink cider, is what I am going to do. And I am going to suggest that you take your feet down."

Willie had his bootless feet propped up on the back of a chair close to the stove.

"I thought I smelt wool," Billy Faust observed, twitching his wispy moustache as if sniffing.

"That ain't all you smelt," Bodley said. "He's been walking in skunk tracks all day, or this boy ain't washed his feet in a month."

Willie took his feet down and felt the bottoms of his socks. "They're right warm." He took another gulp of cider. "Don't care though."

"Well, I can tell you what I'm gonna do," Bodley said. "Only, you boys gotta keep it among just us."

"What you gonna do?" Billy asked, leaning over his knees, cradling his glass in both hands. "Though I reckon I know."

"You know, all right. I'm going to enlist, beginning of next month."

Vernon looked at him in disbelief. "But you won't be eighteen until spring!"

"I know. They don't know."

"You're going to lie about your age?"

"They'll believe me, easy."

"But you can't do that!"

"I look older than some of them recruiting officers."

"That's true," Billy put in. "I couldn't convince anybody if I tried."

"But it's not legal," Vernon objected.

"Vern, everybody does it. Even boys that ain't as big as me," Bodley said. "When Billy has his birthday, we both of us going to go together."

Vernon stared at Billy, open-mouthed.

Billy cleared his throat. "I meant to tell you first. Ol' Bodley's getting too much cider in him and he's spilling the beans." He looked pointedly at Bodley.

"I'm sober as a Presbyterian deacon," Bodley said. "You have to give notice decently and in good order."

"I was going too, Vern. I ain't been keeping this a secret or nothin'."

Vernon blew out a breath. "All right. It's your business, Billy. I knew you were intending to enlist. You haven't made it a secret, all right. But I didn't think this soon. What are we going to do here?"

"You know I thought that through, Vern. Your father is doing very well, I think. He'll be back to his old self by spring, he keeps going as he is. Your sister's back in school already. You won't need me."

"We'll have to get Annabel out of school again."

"Hmmph," Willie Evans said, somewhat thickly. "Think of that, bein' so careful 'bout makin' sure a twelve year old girl gets schooling."

Vernon flared up. "Willie, you know it's important to us here. Just because you never valued your studies—"

"Now we got a hot boy," Bodley observed.

Willie waved it off. "I only mean you can have her out of school helpin' you for a while. Don't hurt nothin'."

Vernon was still angry. "She's the smartest one of us. My sister is not going to be a storekeeper or some farmer's wife. She's going to be a teacher in a university if I have to put her through and pay every penny myself."

"Farmers need wives, Vern," Bodley observed.

"Amen," Billy added.

Vernon sighed. "I mean she's made for books, that's all."

"That's sayin' something, comin' from you, Vern," Billy said. "I got a regular education workin' alongside you these two months."

"I bet none of it stuck, though," Bodley offered.

"Thank you, Bodley. I thank you."

"Well, you can't work cooped up in here all by yourself all the time, Vern," Willie said. "Get her to help you a while. Come out and do some huntin'. Won't be but you and me of the old boys around, once Bods and Billy leave."

Billy looked at Vern. "Gonna come along?"

"I couldn't even if I wanted to. What have we just been talking about? What would happen to my family if I left? Anyway, I don't care one iota about enlisting in the United States Army."

Bodley lifted one eyebrow. "Just what, exactly and precisely, and with a minimum of elaboration, is an 'iota'?"

"He's sayin' he don't particularly care to join up," Billy explained.

"Why not?" Willie asked carelessly.

Vernon did not understand why Willie was asking.

Willie repeated, "I mean, why in blazes not?"

"I just told you why."

"Yeah, well some people right here in this town would say anybody doesn't enlist is a coward."

Vernon carefully put his glass onto the floor.

Bodley held out a hand. "He don't mean nothin', Vern. He's got too much cider in that skinny little body of his."

"I mean plenty," Willie said darkly. "I ain't sayin' you're a coward, Vern. I mean, I don't know as you ain't, but all I'm sayin' is that I am a coward. That's my reason for not goin'."

"What?" Vernon exclaimed.

"You gonna make me say it again? I ain't going because I am afraid to go. I don't want to go out there and get shot. I don't want to go out there and die of dysentery or some other thing that's goin' to kill me sure as a cannonball. I said it. I at least ain't afraid to say it."

"Well I'm afraid too," Billy Faust said. "Kind of. But I'm gonna go anyway. I want to go. I want to see what I'm made of."

"Funny," Bodley said to Willie. "I'd have thought you'd been the first to go, you always goin' huntin' and such. It's just, we're goin' out huntin' secesh."

"They shoot back," Vernon said grimly.

"Yeah, they shoot back," Willie said.

February 20, 1862
Arlington Heights, Virginia

Dear Brother,

There has not been anything to write about except for what I have been writing
to the family. I have not told them what boredom camp life is like, however.
Every day is the same. With the weather becoming a little warmer now (so
soon!), we can hardly stand it.

Reveille comes at 4.00 A.M. and we start drill at 4:30. At seven we have
breakfast. The company drills at 8:00 until 9:30. Then until supper at seven
P.M., followed by dress parade: nothing. Nothing at all. This is boredom. There
has never been invented a boredom like this boredom.

There are times when one is happy with this life. We have concerts, plays,
speeches—and Benjamin Franklin's birthday was celebrated by the printers of
the Regiment giving a gala banquet. But these are all makeshifts, and on the
next day the excitement has worn pale and tepid.

We play whist and chess, and we have had regimental snowball fights,
and sometimes we go out in search of something new to eat, but day after day
there is nothing much to do except get sick. We have lost several men in our
company to consumption and dysentery. Many others in the company have
been given discharges and sent home. This is no way to live.

Colonel O'Connor tries his best to keep us fed and warm and active, and
we appreciate his efforts. He's a good officer. Owl-eyed, a little thin as to beard
and hair, but a decent fellow and a man you like to have as commander.

The most interesting new officer in our camp is an artillery officer named
Gibbon. His Battery B of the Fourth United States Artillery has been assigned
to our brigade. They are regulars, and this Gibbon is quite a soldier. He's a
rather small man, but he has authority and presence. He came through our
camp first in November, recruiting among us for men to fill his battery, which
was considerably down in numbers. I gave thought to transferring to the Artillery, but in the end I didn't volunteer. This man Gibbon went down the line of
volunteers with his sharp eye and picked out his own men. I have never seen
an officer personally do that.

He must have been happy with his Wisconsin men, because he's been
back twice for more. Each time I am tempted, but each time I decide to stay
with my comrades. In the army you build a new family, and you hate to leave
a family twice.

Gibbon was overheard as saying that the volunteers in our regiments
were "the finest material for soldiers" he had ever seen, better than regular
army men. But why should we not be? We are accustomed to working hard for

an honest living, and we respect ourselves too much to act like children. And of course after a long winter with nothing to do we are once again full of fight.

The thing about this Gibbon is that he knows how men think, and what moves them. He has put a little flag on each of the battery's guns, and each flag has either "Wisconsin" or "Indiana" lettered upon it. "These guns belong to your states," he says. "It is your duty to defend them."

You should see the guns. They are twelve-pounder Napoleons—which means they fire twelve-pound shot. They are smoothbores like our original muskets, with no rifling inside to give accuracy at long range. But there is no more useful gun than the Napoleon, we are informed. They can fire shot, shell, canister, and everything. They seldom blow up in your face, and they're sturdy. Furthermore, they're pretty things, considering what brutes they are. They're brass, and shine like gold. Some day perhaps I will go into the Artillery.

We hear that our other armies are doing well, as we sit here. "Unconditional Surrender" Grant has captured two forts on the Tennessee and Cumberland rivers. I wish it would be so easy here: capture two forts, then move down the rivers with gunboats and supplies and men, right into the heart of the Confederacy. But I'm afraid we'll have to slug it out overland between here and Richmond. I wonder what the rebels are doing.

We have reports that they are massing a huge army, twice the size of ours. We are not afraid of them. We have right on our side, and the boys know it. How could I not believe that God will bless us with victory, even though the devil is loose on the other side? I do not judge the rebels, and probably I would do as they are doing had I been born in their place, but selfishness possesses those poor fellows like a disease. "Let my people go!" is what God commanded Moses to say to Pharaoh. Whose people are the slaves, if not God's?

It seems so long since I have been at home among you. I hope the Store is prospering. I want the money I have saved sent here to me, Vernon. I did not tell Father why, but I must tell you. When the boys die of sickness, they are buried right here. I want to be sent home should my time come. I want to entrust the money to an officer for safekeeping, to be used for embalming and transport home. Don't tell this to Father and Mother, but if they do not want to send the money you must persuade them that I need it.

You are eighteen. Congratulations, brother. If we sit in camp long enough, nothing will happen before you feel old enough to enlist, and then the rebels won't have a prayer. But Vern, I have been thinking about it now that I am no longer a boy wild-eyed about Army life. You must stay home and take care of things. I am in earnest concerning that, Brother.

Your Brother Forrest

P.S. The boy who shot the calf on picket duty last fall ordered a bush to halt last night. It did.

Edward Parker returned home as expected in late February, and the reason for his furlough was ostensibly to sign up new recruits. But he had been sent home to recover his health. Mrs. Parker had come into the store and given Billy and Vernon a list to fill, and when Vernon made the delivery at the Parkers' house he was startled by Edward's appearance.

Nancy greeted Vernon at the door, and when he was through carrying foodstuffs back to the pantry she invited him to rest a while in the sitting room. The fire was warm, the low sun shone in the window, and the room was pleasant and inviting. Edward half-reclined on the black horsehair sofa, wrapped in a blue-striped Hudson's Bay blanket. His moustache looked immense because the face behind it, drawn and pale, was so thin that Vernon thought he would not have known it was Ed. What he felt was mostly pity.

"Hello, Vernon. Come in and sit down. I don't blame you for looking surprised by my appearance."

Vernon sat down in a small, straight-backed chair, very uncomfortably, and Nancy seated herself on the black horsehair sofa alongside her brother. She looked very tired, with darkness under her eyes.

"You see, going into the army isn't all glory." Ed's voice was thin, but still elevated above Vernon in the same old way. "You younger fellows sometimes go in without taking thought to what you might get into."

"Vernon says he isn't going in, Eddie." Nancy looked at Vernon with a perfectly bland, blank look.

Vernon cleared his throat. "That's correct. I'm . . . I'm uncertain as to whether I would be doing my best for my family or my country were I to enlist."

"You a Democrat?" Ed asked curtly.

"I suppose so. A loyal Democrat."

Ed smiled bitterly. Vernon continued, with more emphasis, "A peace Democrat."

Nancy looked up at nowhere in particular and said, "I think a little rest would be a nice idea, Edward."

But Edward was sitting up straighter. "I respect your opinions, Vernon. We are fighting for that very right, to express opinions. You wouldn't be accorded that same liberty to say what you believe in the South."

Vernon nodded. He began to feel that the fire was excessively warm. He fidgeted with the gloves in his hand.

Edward continued. "Perhaps you don't believe that. That is your right, as well. You can believe anything you like. But do you know, Vernon, what happens to opinions when you have once been someplace where you know you could be dead tomorrow, or next week?"

"Eddie," Nancy whispered fearfully, taking her brother's arm.

"Vern, what you think before you go to war is all rubbish."

"Eddie!" Nancy exclaimed, dropping her hand.

"I beg your pardon, Nancy. I would never have said such a thing in front of you, except dying men have privileges, and they are excused."

"Oh, Eddie! Please don't talk so!"

He took her hand, but looked steadily at Vernon. "Do you know why I am at home? They say that I am here to bring another hundred men to the brigade, but I am here to die. I had diarrhea for nearly two months. In the middle of that time I contracted typhus. It is killing many men in the Army of the Potomac. I think I am one of only two in our regiment, but it will get worse before spring. I thought I knew what life was, Vernon, but it has all changed."

Edward looked perfectly exhausted, and the unhealthy light in his sunken eyes was frightening, but his voice was clear and sharp. "I understood nothing. I was a good Presbyterian only six months ago, and an American after that. Now, I wouldn't die for the Presbyterian Church. The country of George Washington: if I die, that is what I die for." Without a glance at his sister, he finished, "And I would not hesitate to do so!"

Nancy covered her face with both hands. Vernon stood up. "Edward, I think you are a patriot and a hero," he said with mist in his eyes. "May I shake your hand?" He moved forward but Edward kept his free hand clasped on Nancy's. "I hope you will soon be well," Vernon said hastily. "Nancy, I will find my way out. God bless you both."

Outside, Vernon felt that he had spoken in some kind of delirium. The spectacle of Edward dying, Nancy beside him, made things spin. Why had Edward said those things to him in front of his sister? *What does Edward feel for me, other than contempt? I am his only recruit, perhaps,* Vern thought. *But Edward was in a worse delirium. His brain was not operating properly. Otherwise he never would have said such things. He must be heroic in his own way, Edward Parker; and I must do my own duty, however different, however I see fit.* Settled with that thought, Vernon stepped up onto the sleigh and started the horse back toward the store.

After returning to the barn behind the store and stabling Trygg, Vernon went through the back door and hung up his coat and hat and scarf and gloves. When he entered the store, was surprised to find Bodley Jones there talking to Billy. They stopped and looked at him.

"Did they fire you, Bodley?" Vern asked, smiling. Then a sick shock went through him. "This is it," he said quietly.

Bodley had come to arrange matters with Billy for leaving next week. They would want him to drive them up to Hudson.

"The road's bad up north of here," Vernon said. "The trains might even be stopped."

Billy smiled sadly.

"We been up to see Ed Parker," Bodley said. "Can't stay longer, after talking to him."

"Kind of want to take his place, you know," Billy said.

Vernon stood silently. His friends said nothing.

Finally Vernon had to say something. "I know. I understand what you feel. I just came from the Parker house."

"You have?" Billy said.

"Not to be recruited," Vernon said. "You know I made a delivery. You helped write it out."

Billy looked embarrassed. "Of course. I've forgotten everything in the last fifteen minutes, since Bodley came in."

"War makes everything different," Vernon said.

"Yes. I guess so," Billy said awkwardly.

Bodley laughed. "I know why you was visiting the Parkers. You could have let Billy make the delivery. You wanted to see that girl, Vern."

Vern sighed. "Yes, certainly. I saw her all right."

"Well?" Billy ventured cautiously.

Vernon shook his head. "Nothing works right with me and her any more. Everything I do or say is wrong."

"Aw, Vern, it don't matter," Bodley said. "You don't need to tear loose at the seams over her. There's plenty of girls around here now." Instantly he regretted where his words had gone.

Vernon merely nodded. All the feeling had gone out of him.

"Plenty of pretty girls, too, boy," Billy added. He turned to Bodley, "You just watch. When we get back, ol' Vernon will be married."

"There's only one like her," Vern said softly. "Nobody else is as pretty as she is."

"Yeah, well," Bodley said with a deep breath. "She ain't that pretty, only she acts in a way to make you think she's pretty. Let it go."

"It's her eyes that are beautiful, and her smile, and her thoughts, her soul."

Bodley leaned up against the counter and tossed his fur cap up and down. "Vernie old boy, you could say that of a chipmunk too, if you was as mooney about it as you are about Nancy Parker."

Vernon laughed hopelessly. Then he looked down. "I suppose you boys have to do what you believe is right. It isn't as though you haven't talked about it enough. It's just that there was no reality to it, until now. It makes me think . . ."

"Of your brother, Vern," Bodley said.

"We'll go take care of him, Vern," Billy said.

Vernon sniffed. "Knowing you two, it's more likely that he's going to have to take care of you. God help the rebels, and God help the Army of the Potomac."

"Amen," Billy said, and Bodley added, "Except the rebels part. You going to take us up to Hudson, Vern?"

He nodded.

"Without making a special point of telling anybody, all right Vern?"

"I'll do it. I wouldn't let anybody else do it, long as you're bound and determined to go."

Billy nodded. "Knew you would."

"But why is it that you always have to do the very thing that you most hate to do, instead of somebody else doing it for you?"

"Yep," Bodley said. "That's war."

"That's life," Billy said.

"Now you know why I won't sign up."

"For life?" Bodley laughed, but without mirth. "You don't have any say in that. They slap your behind and toss you out into the world, go as you may."

"We'll get you yet," Billy said. "Before this war is over, you'll be fighting by our side."

"Naw," Bodley yawned. "He's got to stay here. Ain't much choice in that." He looked at Vernon. "You're doin' the right thing. Don't fret about it."

*

On a wet day in March, the snow and ice thawing before its time, Vernon hitched up the sleigh and drove Bodley Jones and Billy Faust up to the train station in Hudson. There was only one other man waiting there, a young red-faced fellow named Anderson, from across the river in Minnesota. Evidently he was going to lie about his age, too. The three got into the same rail car, and Vernon watched them go. They all waved, and Vernon held his hat in his hand for them.

It was a long, long spring. Edward Parker did not recover, but Vernon did not dare to go to the funeral and burial. Nor did he see Nancy Parker in March or April. There was a black wreath on the Parkers' door, and black crepe wound on the two posts each side of the porch steps. What Vernon felt toward Edward Parker was mostly anger.

Annabel left school again to help with the store when spring planting
came around. Nels was better than he had been in the fall, but the old sharp-
ness and activity were gone. Mother was weary most of the time. She said it
was the long, long winter.

April 15, 1862
Virginia

Dear Brother,

*I was glad and sorry at the same time to read that your friends decided to
enlist. By the time you get this they should be with our brigade. I am glad to
have them, though they will probably be in some other Wisconsin regiment.
But now you are rather alone out there, when it comes to the old friends. From
what you say, you are doing a soldier's duty by working day and night in the
store.*

*We are not soldiers but railroad builders and bridge repairers these days.
I suppose all this is necessary, for the Army will surely move this spring, and
we will need transportation not only for ourselves but for our supplies. Did
you know that an infantry division takes up several miles on a road, and that
its wagon train takes up much more than that? We have to carry not only our
food and ammunition, but forage for the horses, spare equipment, medical
supplies, headquarters equipment for each regiment and brigade as well as the
divisional things, and so on. Army mules are what moves this army; when we
can get a railroad or move things on water, matters go more quickly.*

*We know very well what it means to have to use the Virginia roads,
because we have been on them since leaving winter quarters. They are mostly
mud in the spring rains and snow. They seldom corduroy their roads with rails
or macadamize them. What we would give for a good macadamized road
now, with stones to walk across instead of ankle-deep mud to wade in. On the
eighth of this month we had a spring snowstorm—the kind we have in late
April or early May back home, though not as heavy. Rain and very wet snow;
entirely unexpected in this climate. Until two days ago we were almost entirely
confined to our wet tents. It poured rain.*

*King is division commander and in his place Colonel Cutler is com-
manding the Brigade. The Fifth Wisconsin was replaced by the Seventh some
months ago. (They didn't replace the 19th Indiana and make us all Wisconsin;
the Government has found out that brigades all from one state are too much
under the influence of their state governors, who makes demands.) So we are
no longer King's Brigade; we are simply the 2nd, 6th and 7th Wisconsin and
the 19th Indiana. I don't know what if anything they will call us. Cutler is*

temporary; when they give us a brigadier general we will go by his name I suppose.

General McClellan is moving eastward with the army, but we are as yet not part of the movement. Our Division seems to have been created for the maintenance of railroads and for the protecting of Washington. I hope we get into some kind of action soon; I think McClellan will capture Richmond, and we would like to be there.

There is much talk about the great victory this month in Tennessee. The newspapers show that the battle of Shiloh was much worse than ours at Bull's Run. I can hardly imagine it. Perhaps such bloodletting will come to us as well. However, in McClellan we have a tactician and a strategist, and I have the impression that Grant was anything but that at Shiloh. He seems to be the kind who just stays and fights, counting on his re-enforcements to slaughter enough of the enemy to make them quit. I can hardly imagine McClellan being surprised as Grant was, or simply making his soldiers stand and pay his butcher bill. I hope we never see Grant or his like here in the East. Nevertheless, it is encouraging to have a victory for the Union. But did it have to be won in that gruesome way?

I will let you know if anything interesting happens, or if I see your friends. Meanwhile, know that I am doing an honest day's work (for nothing like an honest wage.)

Help Father and embrace Annabel and Mother for me.

Your Brother Forrest

June was a beautiful month, as it generally is in western Wisconsin, with trees coming into leaf and the fragrance of lilac in the air. Every year the Mikelson family went up to the cemetery to plant flowers on Vernon's little sister's grave. This time for the first time Father did not want to go, but Mother said he could not stay home, that he must go. So on a Sunday afternoon the family, carrying two wicker baskets with seedlings and tools and a jug of water, walked up to the cemetery on the hill.

There were quite a few families visiting the cemetery. Some had even brought lunches in baskets. It was the loveliest place in town. Large shade trees, light green with new foliage, stood all across the cemetery's hill. From the crown you could see the Mississippi River. Indians had used the west side of the hill overlooking the river for burial caves. Vernon had crawled into them, though not far, when he was a boy. The town's cemetery, however, occupied the east side of the hill, spreading up onto the flat top.

Vernon watched a family quietly singing a hymn beside a grave. It was one he hadn't heard before, sounding wavery and sad in the open air. He recognized words from the Twenty-third Psalm. The Mikelsons walked on toward the southern edge of the graves. There, under a young maple tree, a small stone was inscribed with the words,

MIKELSON
BABY LAURA
To us the lovely child
Was given
To bud on earth
And bloom in heaven.

Father was first to get on his knees and start pulling up growth covering the space in front of the stone. For a long time they worked in silence, until Annabel spoke to Vernon.

"Do you think she's here, Vernie?"

"She's in heaven, Annie," he answered without conviction.

"I mean, do you think she notices her flowers? Do you think she cares, Vernie?"

"She notices that we do it, somehow, Annabel," Mother said, smoothing a little mound for a blue pansy plant. "If this doesn't make a difference, nothing makes a difference."

"I think I agree, Annie," Vernon said. But he thought, *Only, I wonder if anything makes a difference.*

"She's alive," Father said. "Somewhere, she's alive. Your dear sister is alive, Anna. We are all held forever in the hands of God."

But Annabel was looking at Vernon.

"Of course," he said. He was surprised by what his father had said.

After they finished, they planted pansies, sweet alyssum, geraniums, and morning glories. Mother had watered each small plant carefully with the clay jug of water.

As he looked around again after working on the soil in front of him, Vernon noticed someone kneeling alone up where Edward Parker had been buried. The mound was still new but was covered with grass. It was Nancy kneeling there. "She is a beautiful soul," he thought.

"That's Nancy Parker," Annabel said meaningfully.

"Yes," Vernon said, getting to his feet and looking. But he turned to begin the walk down the hill.

"You have to pay your condolences, Son," Father said, pointing to the girl.

"If you don't talk to her, you will regret it all your life I suppose," Mother added. "We will go back to the house without you."

So Vernon slowly walked to where Nancy knelt, and stood for quite a while. When she noticed him, she stood up and stepped toward him, taking both his hands.

"Vern! How can I thank you enough for coming? Oh, Vern!" Tears came into her eyes. "It is so wrong, Vern! So wrong! How can he be gone? I can't bring myself to believe it. When I go home, I think he's still there. When I read about the armies, I think he's still with them!"

He held her to him, for the first time in his life. Then he nodded toward one of the low wrought-iron benches. "Why don't we sit down." Together they sat for a long time, saying nothing, hand in hand, and the sun went lower in the west. *I have waited for this for years*, Vernon thought, *but not this way.*

As the air became cool, they rose to go back down the hill. Nancy turned to Vernon as they came to the cemetery gate and pulled him to a stop. He was startled by her vehemence and strength. "You must promise me something, Vernon," she said.

"Of course. Anything." He looked at her closely. Her round, freckled face was intense and almost fierce. Her pale blue eyes had the unhealthy shine of her brother's that day last winter.

"You must not join the army, Vern. I could not bear it. We are losing everybody. Everybody is leaving, and I don't know who will come back!"

"They'll be back, Nancy. Our friends will be back." With some anger at himself, he noticed that he could not say this without jealousy. But she was asking *him*, not *them*.

"Promise me, Vernon Mikelson. Promise that you will never go."

He looked into her eyes for a moment. Anything. Absolutely anything. "I promise. I promise, Nancy." He held her again for a long time before they walked on. While he held her, he felt light as air.

This time a long letter came from Forrest, cross-written to save paper. The army was in a new place now.

May 23, 1862
Fredericksburgh, Virginia

Dear Brother,

I've seen the boys, Vern. And they are boys. *I mean the fellows from back home, Billy and Bodley. They're in the Sixth regiment, not this one. So I don't have much chance to socialize with them, but I can talk to them every now and then. Compared to us, they don't know anything, which shows what a winter of drill can do toward making one a soldier. They look like ploughboys more than anything else, even in their uniforms, but we will make them sol-diers, you can bet—and in short order. They're in sound health.*

You are quite alone now except for Charlie, and brother George tells me that Charlie purposes to come out here. I think you should try to persuade him not to, Vern. Some boys have to stay home to take care of things. Don't let him come. We have enough men here.

Earlier today we were reviewed by President Lincoln—the whole Division. But our brigade was singled out for its military appearance and bearing. Lincoln is really as tall as they say, and a little rough-looking. He certainly doesn't look as though he belongs out here with an army; but his presence gave an odd sort of solemnity to this place, and makes us think that we have had an omen of important things to come.

Along with that I have to tell you about a kind of strange thing. You have probably seen the music for the new patriotic song called "The Battle Hymn of the Republic." I gave it no thought at the time, but last October when we were going into camp on Arlington Heights, there was a review of troops at a place called Bailey's Cross Roads. There came a report of the enemy making some kind of movement and the review was suspended. Our Division was ordered back toward Washington.

With our Division a lady visitor was riding at the head of the column. It happened that the Sixth was the first regiment in that column. Though they have a wretched band, they have a singer who is known throughout our brigade, Sergeant John Ticknor. He led in his strong, clear voice that favorite of ours called "John Brown's Body," and the whole regiment would join in on the chorus: "Glory, glory hallelujah, as we go marching on." Now the tune and the chorus, with new words, are famous and sung throughout the North, because that lady visitor was Julia Ward Howe, who has said that hearing the John Brown song that evening, and seeing the review and the army camps, inspired her to write the song.

I think of the song over and over this evening after seeing President Lincoln. It makes me believe that there is purpose in our being here. I don't know that I can say "Mine eyes have seen the glory of the coming of the Lord," but I can almost say, as she writes:

I have seen him in the watchfires of a hundred circling camps

It was our Brigade's singing, Brother, and our army's camps. Many times I have thought, not without anxiety, of her line:

He is sifting out the hearts of men before his judgment seat.

That is how we all feel, Vernon, when we think of battle; we wonder what will be revealed about our hearts. We wonder what we are made of. We don't talk about it much, but I know most of us think about it. The terrible danger, confusion, and excitement of battle will show us what we are. Without this, we could go through a whole lifetime and not know, not ever discover, who we are and what we are made of. War is an evil, but I believe there is a good, a terrible good, that Providence rescues out of it, and that despite all the gruesome horror of it the higher Power and Wisdom makes it turn out according to His purposes, which we will not see in our own lives but which are true and right somehow.

As a Brigade, we have learned something about who and what we are today. It was said that we are one of the finest disciplined brigades in the Union armies. All our months of boredom and drill, drill, drill were not for nothing.

But it is our new commander who has made us realize all this. Do you remember me writing you about that artillery captain of Battery B? Well, he was promoted to brigadier general of volunteers. So these past weeks we have been "Gibbon's Brigade."

We thought King and Cutler were heavy on discipline; they were nothing compared to Gibbon. He has very definite ideas, and he will brook no lagging, carelessness, lack of self-respect, loose discipline. But we are confident that he is doing everything right.

If we throw away articles of clothing on the march we cannot simply requisition new ones as before. Now the replacements are charged against our clothing allowance. Sleeping sentries are no longer tolerated. He had a man sit on a barrel in full sight of the camp all day, right in front of the guard tent, for failing to come to attention and bringing his musket to "present" position on picket duty. Some think it harsh, but nobody is going to let himself be sat on a barrel in plain sight.

The biggest change is that Gibbon has ordered that the whole Brigade be uniformed in the long blue coat of the Regular Army. No more the short jacket. We have light blue trousers. The most distinctive feature is that we all now wear black hats, the left brim fastened up, a black plume on the right, the front adorned with a brass bugle insignia, and a blue braid. Away with the kepi caps that the whole army wears! Some are calling us the Black Hat Brigade—perhaps partly in derision, though it cannot be denied that we look splendid. There are those who complain because this is all charged against our clothing allowance. But I think we now have some idea of ourselves as being different, and more is expected of us. We would look more ridiculous than the other brigades if we ran from battle.

Gibbon treats us with respect. The word in camp is that he still does not think much of us as soldiers, but he has a high opinion of us as material for soldiers. He says we have quick intelligence, and that we listen eagerly during instructions, and then go out and execute the commands with precision and good sense. We are told that discipline and self-respect make courageous and effective soldiers.

But I haven't told you about Fredericksburgh. It is a fine, old, quiet, picturesque town on the Rappahannock River, halfway between Washington and Richmond. It was a lovely sight as we approached it last month, its white church spires and old brick houses, and trees in blossom. And Brother, it has the most beautiful women in the world. I thought the women of Cleveland were beyond compare—but these, these *women, make your heart pound, make your heart sick.*

And do they hate us! They will not even walk under a United States flag. They are perfect to torment, since they are forever impossible for us to have. We noticed that they would prefer to step out into the muddy street up to their ankles rather than walk on a sidewalk under one of our flags. So what did we do? We strung a rope from one side of the street to the other, and hung it all the way across with flags. And what did they *do? They refused to come out at all. Too bad; our little joke deprived us of the sight of these young ladies. We took down the flags.*

You have never heard how a Southern woman talks, Brother. It is enough to drive you mad. The loveliness of their cadences nearly tears you limb from limb—but the rabid nonsense they talk! If we could silence their women, the rebels would go home tomorrow. They are all hatred for the "Yankees," all revenge and blood and God's righteous judgment on us Philistines. Oh, but they are lovely! And ignorant of any world outside of ten miles around Fredericksburgh, Virginia. They didn't even know what Wisconsin is—a city? A country? Really, a State?

When we arrived, all those beautiful women were crying, and all the Negroes were fairly dancing with joy.

We have really "plundered the Egyptians" here, as they say. Some of these shopkeepers, with their fine goods, and foods, and tea and everything else, have been entirely bought out by us. Most of them are too fanatical as secessionists to accept United States greenbacks, and want Confederate notes. And lots of Confederate notes. The prices are outrageous! Well, we were happy to oblige them. I told you that we have quite a few printers in our brigade.

Sadly, we were able to buy out only about three of the stores before the higher-ups sniffed out what we were doing, and the order came down that there was to be no more counterfeiting. But we men in the ranks don't see why these rebels, who made this whole mess, and these planters who live on the sweat of other men, should be given any consideration at all.

Colonel O'Connor is good-humored about all this, but he will not have us shaming the Union or the name of our State. He has a difficult task keeping discipline, and more damage has been done to the property of these rebels than I care to write. (The mother of George Washington is buried here, and some worthless fellows have seen fit to deface the marble monument that stands over her.) But we have come to love Colonel O'Connor, and the approach of his familiar, martial figure is enough to make us think twice about whatever we are doing, wanting to please him. We are proud to have such a man as our Colonel, and he makes us remember we are true Wisconsin men.

Brother, I am partially of a mind to choose one of these lovely Fredericks-burgh ladies and propose to her the benefits of Union, before I leave. Isn't war terrible? But when I consider it fully, I still prefer our good, common-sense, modest Wisconsin girls; and I still go into the field to fight for them.

What would I think if there were rebels in Prescott, Wisconsin writing home about our Sister this way?

Your Brother Forrest

It seemed that Vernon's friends had dropped off the edge of the earth. What he did hear from them came from young men he did not know, from places that did not exist. But there had been no fighting by the Wisconsin regiments this summer, and the Mikelsons, along with the town of Prescott in general hoped that the worst of the war might be over—or at the very least, the worst of this year's campaigning. Though Nels Mikelson had not regained his ability to concentrate on the numbers in the store's ledger books, he was in other respects more like his former self, dealing with his old customers, re-organizing the stock, and suggesting to Vernon what orders should be placed. Annabel would be able to return to school in September. However, receipts had fallen over the past twelve months because, with so many of the young men gone, farms were producing less and struggling to make ends meet. People bought only what they absolutely must have to get them by until things returned to normal.

Vernon was able to take more time away from the business, which meant that he spent long, lazy, deep summer Sunday afternoons with Nancy Parker. She played the piano very well, and two rainy Sundays were whiled away in the Parker parlor. Preferable to Vernon, of course, were clear after-noons when he and Nancy could leave the Parker family behind and picnic or stroll or ride in the country. After each family had returned from their morning church services, Vernon would go calling at Nancy's house. It was always quiet there, as at the Mikelson's home, but the quietness was new and strange at the Parkers', and Nancy welcomed the diversion of a day in the fresh air.

Vernon did not allow the country's tempests to detract from the pursuits of a romantic summer. He spent many weekday hours thinking of Nancy and devising new outings for the coming Sunday. So passed the happiest season of his life.

Toward the end of August, on an oppressively humid Sunday, he called at the Parkers, where Nancy had packed a lunch and was waiting for him. They walked across Main Street, down Elm Street with its small houses and unfenced yards, to the river. There, Vernon had tied the skiff that he and Forrest had used since they were boys to lay trot lines for catfish.

Nancy stepped carefully into the boat and sat in the prow, arranging the full folds of her light blue dress around and under her. Vernon handed her the blanket and the basket, which was filled with bread, cheese, cake, plums, raspberry preserves, and iced water. Removing his shoes and socks, he pushed the boat out from the shore, wading with the soft, sandy bottom coming up warm around his feet. He pushed one last time and deftly lifted himself forward across the skiff's stern, turning so as to seat himself on the bench with his feet suspended over the back of the boat. He reached behind him for a towel, discreetly dried his feet with his back to Nancy, and then put on his socks and shoes. After that he turned and gripped the oars. The current was slow and strong here, but in their favor. He would have to sit up front on the return trip and put his back into the effort, but going out, he could push in a leisurely fashion and allow the current to do most of the work. Nancy held her straw hat against the gentle breeze. They had come here because it would be cooler on the River than in town or out in the country. There would be at least some stir of air.

The Mississippi was not particularly wide here, and it was short trip downstream to Chain Island, really a series of islands joined when the water was low in late summer. There were many exposed, shady beaches now, and it was not difficult to find a place away from others who had come out for the afternoon. Vernon aimed the skiff below the groups of picnickers already setting out their lunches on the upper three islands. It would be farther to row back, but Vernon was not concerned about that. He had worked half his life for an afternoon alone with Nancy on Chain Island, and a little sunburn and backache would not be worth considering today.

Gliding with the current, the skiff did not disturb a group of lazy carp until they were right over the massive fish basking in the warm, shallow water a few yards from the island. Scattering with muddy swirls, the fish roiled away and under the boat, lifting it with their thick bodies.

"Wish I had a carp spear," Vernon said.

Nancy shuddered. "I hate carp. They're so ugly. Those pink lips, and the big scales. Ugh! And they taste so muddy."

"If you smoke 'em, they're not bad. But mostly I just like to get rid of them, to make more room for the other fish. I suppose we shouldn't hold their looks against them."

"Ugh!" Nancy shuddered again.

With a final push on the oars, Vernon shoved the boat hard into shallow water. It stopped with the prow extending over a patch of grassy outcropping.

"Don't get out," Nancy said. "I can jump out. Watch me!" With a hop, she was up on the front of the boat, and then she jumped lightly onto the grass. Vernon was delighted.

"Give me the basket," she said as Vern came forward.

"Oh, no," he said, gallantly, "I can carry it."

"Oh, Vern, it isn't too heavy for a lady."

He picked up the blanket and the basket, and without swaying in the least stepped up to the prow and from it to the ground beside Nancy.

"You've spent lots of time on boats, I see," she said.

"Oh yes. Forrest and I—" something caught in his throat, strangely, and instantaneously an awful look came to Nancy's face. "We used to spend half the summer out on the water. Don't you just love it out here?"

"Oh, yes."

"Look there," he said, pointing to a sand bar visible at the surface about fifty yards downstream. "We used to go to that bar in lower water and spear carp as they came along."

"Oh, how unpleasant."

"Not for boys."

"What did you do with them?"

"Left 'em for the snapping turtles. We'd get back in the skiff and back off a ways, and before long the turtles would be up on the bar after the fish. Then we'd put out lines for catfish and make a fire on the island, down there. There is nothing in this world like catfish fresh caught and fresh cooked out in the open."

"I hate the looks of them, too. I would make a terrible fisherman's wife."

"Channel cats are kind of pretty, except for the faces. They're sleek, and almost silver sometimes. Did you know there are sturgeon in this river?"

"Oh, can't we talk about something besides ugly fish?"

Vernon laughed. "I'm sorry. I'm still a boy, I guess."

Nancy smiled. Then she suggested they find some shade. Vernon carried the basket and blanket, and they walked along the bare shoreline until they came to a place where a large windfall, up by the roots, had left a long, barkless trunk to sit on back from the water.

After they had eaten, they sat quietly watching the river hand in hand, listening to the birds.

"I would like to hear you play and sing some Stephen Foster just now," Vernon said quietly. "I do love your voice."

"It's better out here without anything but the birds and the water to listen to. I think it is such a shame that Mr. Foster is writing all those war songs. They sound so strident and jingly."

"Tinny," Vernon said.

"Yes, tinny. And he can compose such lovely things."

"Southern things, like the 'Way down upon the Swanee River.'" Vernon looked downstream. "Isn't it strange to think that this same water flowing past us will reach armies fighting, perhaps, and rebel country? We could get into the skiff and float downriver, and without further trouble come upon the Confederate States of America. Just by getting into the skiff."

He looked at Nancy and saw that she was not happy with the subject. "I'm sorry," he said.

"Vern, you have to get the idea out of your head. You always bring it up. You promised me, remember."

"I do remember, and the promise stands."

She nodded. "Let it stay far away, Vern. As far away as Egypt."

When Vernon rowed back, the river was glassy still with the deep red of the setting sun sliding across the surface. Going slowly against the current, Vernon reached the landing after the sun had gone and the moon was white and frail in the sky. Down low over the Minnesota sky, the Evening Star shone clear and intense near where the sun had set. The two stood and looked at it wordlessly, the great river spreading past them.

They walked slowly to Main Street, then to the Parkers' house. Vernon felt a terrific excitement verging on trembling. They went through the gate in front of Nancy's house and walked slowly up the path to the porch. Vernon was now almost beside himself. On the steps, as they ascended the first and then the second and then the last, Vernon took and held her hand. They stopped and Nancy turned toward him. He put his other hand to her back and gently pressed her toward him, and they looked deeply into each other's eyes. He lowered his lips to hers and they kissed, gently and briefly. Nancy smiled kindly. "Good night," she said softly. "Thank you for a splendid afternoon, Vern."

He nodded but his throat was so dry that he could say nothing. She walked to her door and went in, looking back once. Vernon felt so light-headed that he reached out to the crepe-wrapped post and held on for a moment, before moving carefully down the steps. "This is where I belong," he said to himself. "Here is my crusade and my glory and my duty. Oh, I love her!" Out in front of the house, he could see the Evening Star very low on the horizon. He thought of a poem he had partly memorized:

Bright star, would I were stedfast as thou art. . .

Awake for ever in a sweet unrest,
Still, still to hear her tender-taken breath,
And so live ever—or else swoon to death.

August 15, 1862
Cedar Mountain, Virginia

Dear Brother Vernon,

We have had a very active summer so far, though with little sight of the enemy. We have been marching and marching, from Fredericksburgh to Chancellorsville and Wilderness Tavern and back, up here near Manassas, and around, and back and forth, in rain, mud, and burning heat. It is all on account of the mysterious Stonewall Jackson, who kept us from joining Little Mac on the Peninsula by threatening Washington. The Government was in panic because of Jackson's army being so close, as you must have read in the papers. Well, our corps has been one of the little Union armies outfoxed by this crafty rebel, chasing him all around the countryside. We never had the pleasure of fighting him, but the other armies did, and came off much the worse for it, as no doubt you have also read.

Eventually he joined Lee's army in front of Richmond, but we never got to join McClellan. (Isn't it odd that the man whose property we camped on last winter has suddenly emerged from nowhere to become the great hero of the Confederacy, along with the wily Stonewall Jackson?) I think the newspapers and the Government have done badly by McClellan. But it must be admitted that Lee is a fighter, and has successfully defended Richmond at terrible cost.

Now, while McClellan and the Army of the Potomac are going to be recalled from the Peninsula, a new army has been formed under General John Pope. We are part of that army. The idea, as best we can make it out, is to advance overland while Lee is busy watching Little Mac depart from below Richmond.

Our general feeling is that if the War Department thinks that Lee will stand still and let Pope move on Richmond, they are badly in need of a little military advice. Already Stonewall Jackson's part of Lee's army is supposed to be somewhere about. What we think is that each side has two armies between Richmond and Washington—we have Pope and McClellan; they have Lee and Jackson—and whichever of the two sides is able to get both their armies together first will be victorious. The two armies acting together will be able to defeat whichever single army they pounce upon.

We have been all over the northern Virginia countryside, and now instead of marching eight and twelve miles per day, we are slogging twenty, twenty-five and even thirty miles in the sun and rain. Stonewall Jackson's famous "foot cavalry" did not do better.

General Gibbon has made us into a fine brigade. At first it was the same as usual, only more of it: early morning drills, forenoon drills, afternoon drills, evening and—honestly—night drills; and still the ceremony of making up the guard and the dress parades. He began whole brigade drills. We thought he was only an artilleryman, but to our amazement he has shown us that he knows infantry drill and maneuvers backward and forward. The brigade is probably the best-drilled, best-disciplined in the United States armies.

But the General has made us believe in it. He has a way of encouraging you by positive rewards for good work, rather than by punishments for failure. Some time ago at an inspection he noticed that three men were especially soldierly in their appearance, in the clean state of their equipment, and their posture. He gave all three passes to spend twenty-four hours off-duty and go blackberry picking. Now every time there is a similar review, every man contends with the others to be the best turned out in order to get one of those passes.

Do you remember how we used to go a-berrying along the railroad tracks? The hot sun and the smell of railroad tar—these things are hard to do without. Not that we are children any more. But to go berry-picking again! Surely this General Gibbon has an unusual understanding of men, how we think and feel.

In addition to the frock coats and all the rest, he ordered us to acquire white leggings—to protect us from the dirt and pests of the march. We have been called the "Bandbox Brigade" by some others because of this, and the fellows want nothing to do with those leggings. Well, one morning the General found his horse neatly fitted out with a set of white leggings. The men thought it was capital fun. Generals don't like to be laughed at, and Gibbon made a vigorous attempt to find the perpetrators. But I think he is not a completely successful actor, and he was unable to entirely suppress his own amusement at the prank.

It is awful about Ed Parker, but you know, with all this marching and all the time in camp, we have lost a lot of the boys. Sick, and sent home, and one thing and another—the Brigade is down to somewhat under 3,000 men.

Our Regiment is still called the Ragged-Ass Second, but that does not express our own opinion of ourselves. We understand that we have been in a battle and the other regiments have not. The others are untried. Perhaps they will make good soldiers; they are nearly as disciplined as we, but only trial by *fire will separate the soldiers from the recruits. I think they are made of the right material. We get along together quite well.*

We call the other regiments the Calico Sixth, the Huckleberry Seventh, and the Swamp Hogs of the Nineteenth. Because an artillery battery has not quite 150 men in it, we call Battery B the 140 Thieves.

We spent the Fourth of July somewhat as we would have at home, with horse and foot races, games, and a sack race. What did you do? I receive your letters and those of the others with great eagerness, fairly tearing them open, and I read and re-read them in camp and on the march. Mother writes often, as you know, and sends things. I am one of the best-shod soldiers in the Company because of her faithful knitting of socks. Some of the men wear their socks and underwear without ever making an attempt to wash the things, and simply throw them away when they are able to obtain new ones. Father never has said much, and when he writes it is usually only stolid advice—but I know what he means.

Since the Fourth it has been hardship and unpleasantness. This chasing of Stonewall Jackson is maddening work, and it does not give us a high opinion of the high command. We have always thought McDowell is a bumbler, and now we are beginning to be unsure of King. I think he was better as a brigade commander than as a division commander.

I long for a Wisconsin summer. The heat here is abominable. I don't know how human beings can choose such a place to live. On one march the Sixth had 150 men fall out from heat exhaustion; fortunately, they all caught up that night. For we have learned that to straggle is to be lost. On one march our regiment and the Seventh and the Nineteenth Indiana together lost 59 men who fell out of line and were captured by Stuart's rebel cavalry. Now they languish in a Richmond prison, and rather than that most of us would choose to be dead. Few members of the Black Hat Brigade straggle, no matter what the hardship.

Today King's Division was reviewed by General Pope. I do not like this General Pope. Most of us think he is a blowhard. He says he is going to be terrible on the enemy; he says "May God have mercy on General Lee, for I won't," and things like that. Perhaps because I am my father's son, I distrust those who talk much. Humility is one of the Christian virtues. Gen. Pope has been signing his dispatches, "Major General John Pope, Headquarters in the Saddle." The joke going around the Regiment is that Pope has his headquarters where his hindquarters ought to be.

I have a feeling that Generals Lee and Jackson will have something to say about our blustery commander and his plans here in Virginia. I am hoping McClellan gets here before it's too late.

Your Brother Forrest
Headquarters under his Tall Black Hat

Vernon made up his mind resolutely, but found he had insufficient courage for proposing marriage to Miss Parker. Perhaps it was lack of knowledge, rather than lack of courage, he told himself as he stared out his bedroom window one morning in September. On the table next to Forrest's letters, two sheets of foolscap lay where Vernon had written proposal exercises the night before. Now and then he had arisen during the night and pencilled another phrase. But this morning they all looked inelegant and ungallant.

After breakfast he lingered over his coffee, and after Father had left the kitchen he asked, "Mother, how did Father propose to you?"

Annabel stood with the dishtowel clutched in her hand, wide-eyed and open-mouthed. But Mother didn't even turn from the sink. "Vern, the words do not matter. All that matters is not to make a mistake."

"Yes, Mother. I . . . It's not that I . . ."

"More than that, I cannot tell you. I do not know how it is done here in this country. You should go and ask one of your friends. Charlie is still here. You should talk to him. You haven't seen him in a long time. Ride out to the Martens' farm this morning. Annabel and I will help your Father today. I have something for you to take to the Martens."

Annabel slowly stepped to the table. "Vernie?"

"Hmm?"

"There isn't something happening here that you haven't told me about, is there? Nancy Parker?"

"Oh, well—"

"Because you know what I think of her!"

Vern stood up with his cup. "She's a wonderful young lady, Annabel. This is up to me, after all."

She looked up at him grief-stricken. "Do you *have* to?"

"I think it is meant to be. I have known it since I was ten years old."

Annabel turned helplessly. "Mother?"

"Anna, go into the pantry and get out three jars of tomato preserves for the Martens. Everything will be all right."

"You can't mean it!" she cried to Vernon.

"Oh, yes, I do mean it. I am slow to decide things, but once I make up my mind, there is no turning back. 'My heart is single,' as it says in the Good Book."

Vernon rode to the Martens' farm and caught sight of Charlie harvesting corn. He was walking behind the wide machine as the "V" of its toothed arms devoured the row. His team plodded along switching at flies, one horse on each side of the row, and Charlie held the implement steady with the sureness of a veteran. Vernon rode Trygg up to the edge of the field, then ran to catch up with Charlie.

"I came to ask your advice, Charlie. I'm going to marry Nancy. And I want you to be best man!"

"I will if you wait until I get back home on leave."

"What? You've gone and enlisted? What has got into your head? Is every man in the country mad?"

"Whoa!" Charlie stood wiping his face with a red handkerchief. "You ain't the one to talk about madness."

"Does your brother know about this? Does your family? What will your family do? Surely you haven't already signed any papers!"

"No, I ain't. But I will."

"I can't believe you are going away, too! It isn't possible!"

Charlie shoved part of the handkerchief into his pocket. "Shouldn't be much surprise in it, Vern. Now, what's this about marrying Nancy Parker?"

"You know how we've been all this time."

"Yeah. Say Vern, has she said yes?"

"I haven't asked her yet."

Charlie puffed out his cheeks. "Well! Well well. All right, Vern. Maybe you oughtn't to count this chicken before she's hatched."

"I know she will say yes."

The two stood a while, shading their eyes and looking across the fields, shifting their feet.

"My brother don't want me to enlist."

"Of course not," Vern said flatly. "It's utter madness."

"Vern, you can't undo what's in your heart. I have to go, Vern. I have once and for all made up my mind. Now why in the wisdom of Heaven, your brother having done the same thing and all, would you think it's madness for me to go?"

Vern swept a hand imploringly. "Because your duty's *here*, Charlie!"

"They'll be all right. They can hold on while we finish up the war. You know Old Abe needs three hundred thousand to do it."

"But not you. Not the last son on a farm."

"What have you got against it, Vern?"

Vernon took off his hat and wiped the brim, stalling.

"Vern, do you feel bad about not going yourself?"

Vernon nodded. "Of course I do. But what I have against your going is that somebody, somewhere, has to stop this. There doesn't have to be a war at all. There wouldn't be a war if everybody would come to their senses and go home, and if the rest of us would *stay* home! Somebody has to listen to reason."

Charlie smiled. "You talking about reason sounds comical just now, Vern. You saying you're going to marry Nancy Parker—made up your mind—haven't asked her—don't know what you're getting into."

"I know very well what I'm doing, Charlie. I am doing exactly what I think men must do now that the country is mad as March hares. Somebody must do what men and women are meant to do. Somebody must carry on— get married, raise a family, see to things at home—and not go off to war!"

They looked at the field of unharvested corn. "Better get back to it. I'm going to get it all in before I go."

Vernon said quietly, "Make you a bargain. I'll ride with you up to Hudson if you'll come back and be my best man."

Charlie held out his hand silently.

They shook hands. "Getting to know the road to the railroad station," Vernon said.

As Vernon walked back toward his horse, Charlie called after him. "Vern!" He walked over, leaving the reins looped on the handles. "Vern, I just want you to know that I do respect and admire your staying here. I know you ain't a coward. Somebody has to do what you are doing, else the whole world *will* go mad."

Vernon nodded. "We each know what we have to do. I know I have to stay here."

"I'll come in Saturday and you can tell me what Miss Parker answers."

But Vernon hadn't asked by Saturday. He was waiting for advice from his brother, and at last two letters came together, the second one very thick. Forrest's army was on the move, and soldiers' letters were not getting out regularly. There had been a great battle in Virginia, another disaster near the old Bull Run battlefield. Vernon frantically unfolded the second letter to see when it had been dated. It was dated after the battle. Then he read the first letter.

August 27, 1862
near Warrenton, Virginia

Dear Brother,

This will be a short letter as there is no telling when we will have to get up and move. I cannot advise whether or not to marry, nor can I advise you as to how to propose to a female. I have, alas, no experience. Simply speak what comes from your heart, if steadfast and true, doing your manly duty, and you will be all right irrespective of the words.

You have been reading in the papers, no doubt, about "Pope's Retreat." Lee, of course, will be the first to bring his two jaws together, and Pope at least has enough sense to fly before the trap springs shut. We have not flown far, and now we have been in near contact with the enemy all week, and it seems every day we are shelled by rebel artillery. One shot hit perfectly in the Sixth as Cutler and Fairchild were brewing coffee—hit the pot and sent everything sky-high. They are not always so funny. An officer has been killed by a shell fragment.

The other regiments were pretty shy at first, trying to dodge the shot and shell, which is useless. We of course had heard it before, at Bull Run. Now they pretty much do as we do: just keep on, and take cover when it seems the sensible thing to do, and when the officers permit it.

Our corps has been joined by one of McClellan's divisions. We are very heartened. They are Reynolds's Division, a well-officered lot, and seasoned, if you can tell from looking. King has been sick, and for a time our division was been put under Reynolds's direction, but now King has resumed command.

Jackson is once more on the loose. His corps of Lee's army must be within a few miles of the old Bull Run battlefield, but nobody knows where. Lee is on the other side of our army, southward somewhere. It is evident that Pope figures to find and attack Jackson before Lee can bring up the rest of the rebel army.

We are camped on the Warrenton Turnpike, which is dry and paved with stones. Tomorrow we will march on this road toward the old Bull Run battlefield, probably—and our guess is that Jackson will be nowhere to be found. We will probably do this until winter.

Give my love to Annabel, and tell Mother and Father that I still haven't found a nice Virginia rebel girl to propose to.

I probably won't write for a while again; this marching tires one so, that all we want to do when we stop is drop down and sleep.

Your Brother Forrest

September 3, 1862
Upton's Hill, near Washington

My Dear Brother,

It is not so bad; Pope has been relieved and McClellan is back in command. The ill-fated army of Pope has been dispersed, and our Brigade is part of the Army of the Potomac.

Could I have written that it is not so bad? Impossible! The last few days have been more bloody and tragic than anything imaginable. This is a letter I do not want anyone to see but you. I hardly have a heart to write it.

You have read of our defeat in the Second Battle of Bull Run. What you will not read of is our battle on August 28, two days before Second Bull Run. We have seen the accounts of it in the papers: "a skirmish," they call it. What wooden-headed fools! Our battle at Gainesville was unimaginable. And no-body knows about it. Perhaps it was fought for nothing. But you must hear of it.

I have a large sheaf of paper, and we are going to be in camp for a few days, so I will set it down while it is still horribly fresh in my mind.

The morning after I last wrote to you we set off up the Warrenton Turnpike, and sometime after midday turned off it down toward Manassas Junction. But we hadn't gone a mile on this road before a halt was ordered. Evidently Jackson was not where Pope had thought he was. Pope's army was now spread out, and there was no new place to concentrate because Jackson had vanished. As far as we knew there was no-one, either friend or enemy, within miles of our Division.

During the halt we received permission to butcher some of the cattle that were being driven along with the division. We were all mightily hungry. We hadn't had anything decent to eat in days; even the miserable hardtack in our haversacks was about gone.

The cattle were being butchered, and some of the men were cooking the beef, when late in the afternoon the order came to step into line and resume march, back the way we had come. Some of the men were so starved that they cut off hunks of the cattle and ate them, raw and warm. It made me lose all appetite.

We came back to the Warrenton Pike. Hatch's and Doubleday's brigades were ahead of us, and Patrick's behind. We have now found out that King was ill again, and nobody was directing the Division as a whole.

It was late afternoon, and we made a leisurely march up the pike. We were all dusty and most of us were still hungry, but we had become accustomed to that. The heat was no longer unbearable.

Early evenings in Virginia in late summertime are very pleasant, as long as it is not too hot. I was drowsing on my feet, noticing a farmhouse up a rise on our left. We had heard cannon fire intermittently all day; there had been some up ahead as usual, but now even that had quieted down.

We marched in column of fours, and our Brigade stretched along the pike about a half mile. Ahead of us was the Sixth, behind came the Seventh and the Nineteenth, then the battery.

There was a woods belonging to that farmhouse, and the turnpike cut through it. We were in that woods with the Sixth just going out of it before us when shells began exploding just ahead in the trees.

Up in front, the Sixth was getting off the road and throwing themselves against a shallow embankment on the left. Colonel O'Connor ordered us to do the same, to shelter ourselves on the ground among the trees and clear the road. A staff officer from the head of the column came flying back along the pike to order up the battery.

Evidently the battery had known what to do, because it was only minutes later that it came careening up the pike, horses pounding, drivers shouting, men riding the caissons behind. The battery's officers galloped alongside. Those brass Napoleons gleamed.

From this moment it is difficult to tell you clearly how things happened. It seemed that the battery had gone into action and was firing a while before we got any orders. But some time—I think it was a short time—after the battery began firing, another staff officer came and then the Colonel had us ordered up into column, and into the woods. General Gibbon then came down the road and he and the Colonel rode to the head of the column.

We began to understand that a rebel battery had opened on us and that our Regiment was being sent to try to drive it off or capture it. We came out of the woods and the Colonel's adjutant ordered us to deploy in line of battle. (The Colonel never shouted orders himself; some kind of throat disease prevented it.)

Ahead of us was an open field sloping upward; we were more than halfway up the slope that led to the farmhouse I had noticed. The farmhouse was a bit left of our line, and our right extended across and in front of the corner of the woods. General Gibbon was watching, and we were all nervous about keeping our line well-dressed on the colors.

The two end companies, Company A and my company, were ordered forward as skirmishers. The Regiment followed us slowly in line of battle, as we went up to the top of the crest. We were fired upon by rebel skirmishers. This we did not expect, because we had thought the rebel battery was probably horse artillery and there was no infantry nearby.

The ridge across the fields from us was barely higher than the one we were on; this ridge was heavily wooded and we could not see into it. Their skirmishers retired back toward those woods, and we pursued.

We saw the Regiment coming behind us over the first rise. We went forward at the double-double quick after the rebel skirmishers and followed them just inside the woods.

Thousands of rebels were in there, in lines of battle three deep. The woods were crowded with gray and butternut. Their battle flags were uncased and they were moving forward through the trees and underbrush.

On both sides of us rebel infantry poured out of the woods as we ran back shouting at the tops of our lungs, "JACKSON! JACKSON!"

Our regiment had rifles at the shoulder, and an officer ordered us to throw ourselves to the ground. An instant later our line tore loose with a volley, which cut the air over our heads. We didn't jump up, because we knew what was coming. Behind us a tremendous fire erupted as the rebels shot back. As both sides reloaded we leapt to our feet and ran.

Taking our places on the extreme right of the line we panted for breath, trying feebly to reload, as the rest of the Regiment fired another volley. Our company was still reloading, so there was little smoke in front of us. I could see then that there was a whole brigade facing us: I saw four or five regimental battle flags; their line stretched much farther than ours on both sides. I was convinced that there were more coming. This might be a whole division. At any rate, our company had found Stonewall Jackson—or perhaps he had found us. We didn't have any idea of exactly what troops we were facing, though we were close enough to hear the shouts of their officers.

They were firing at will now, instead of in volleys, and we began to do the same. The rebels were behind a rail fence. We knelt and loaded and fired with insane energy and speed. All we could see was smoke and the flashes of the rifles aimed at us not seventy-five yards away. At a moment like that you do what you are drilled to do—you load in nine counts as fast as you can and think of nothing else. You are like a lunatic. Suddenly the man on your left lets out a moan; you still fire—then you look. He is face up on the ground. You load. You are in two ranks, and the man over your shoulder fires, and you hardly are aware of it. You finish loading and you raise the rifle and aim and fire. Instantly you take down the rifle butt and reach into the cartridge box, tear the cartridge with your teeth, pour the powder, drop in the minie ball, remove the ramrod, ram, this time not replacing it but sticking it in the ground next to you; you pluck a cap from the box at your waist and put it on the nipple, pull back the hammer as you bring the rifle up, aim, fire.

Doing it again, you hear a sickening thud at your shoulder. Involuntarily you glance back and see a face rushing blood, and you pull another cartridge, and you are a mechanism.

You are aware that now there are troops on your right. It was the good old Seventh filing into line. The roar deepens on the left; the Nineteenth has been ordered to support us and extends past the farm buildings.

Far on the right a crashing volley breaks out. The Sixth has come into line!

"Look! Oh, look!" shouts the man on my right, pointing. The Colonel on his horse is sagging down; he is caught by another man, limp, arms straight down. I know he must be dead. Our Colonel O'Connor!

I am aware of a slithering corkscrew sensation going down my back, and realize that the rebels are running forward with a strange, eerie yell—a high-pitched yipping, a floating "eeeeeeeeee." We shout back the Union Hurrah!, and we are all shouting so loudly that we can hardly hear our officers. The officers are shouting the same things over and over again: "Aim low, boys. Steady, boys! Give 'em the devil, boys!" I realize that the man beside me is cursing, swearing, screaming obscene words—and then I understand that I am the one, and I am cursing in English and Norwegian. I do not know where it comes from. I aim and curse and try to stop my mouth as I fire.

The rebels have come within thirty yards of us. Even in the near darkness now we can see the expressions on their faces.

"Come on then, damn you!" we shout, loading and firing. It is a constant ripping roar, us standing now and firing as they begin to move back a few steps each time they reload.

As they back away we rush forward, not the walking advance we have been taught, but as we have just seen the rebels charge, and a terrible volley from them stops us in our tracks. We back away as we reload, but we stop at our line and do not retreat from it.

They came and they went back and we went forward, three or four times. It was darkening; we could aim only at their musket flashes, brilliant sharp orange in the deep twilight.

They were at a rail fence and we poured our fire at them. Then we realized they were not firing as rapidly.

I tried to calm myself, and found that I was down to the last cartridges. Men were already stooping to take cartridge boxes from the wounded. And suddenly we were going forward again, toward the rail fence, and I saw a man bringing a rebel back; we were right on them, and then going back as a solid line of them came out of the trees. We fell back to our original line.

Then again and again we loaded, waited for a flash to aim at, fired, loaded. Bullets are in the air everywhere, right and left, thsssst, whistling past our ears, searing at our sleeves, the air seemingly filled with them; and now and then next to you the sickening tchug of a rebel bullet finding one of your friends.

On our left we heard the Nineteenth yelling and going forward; we cannot go forward. A terrible storm of fire rises on the left, and the Nineteenth must be moving back, but only to where they were. The Brigade's line is steady.

But the touch of the man at each elbow is gone. There is no-one firing over your shoulder. The line is thin now, only one deep, and not elbow-to-elbow. You kneel or stand to fire, waiting for the flash to aim at; you load, aim, fire.

In the slower but steady fire you notice that the ground is covered in both directions: men lying, writhing; some walk back—many of them clutching their left arms, the one exposed most while firing.

"Forrest!" I look to see the man now next to me; it is Anson Fuller, from home. He holds his right hand toward me: his index finger is gone, shot away, a ragged, red end to his knuckle. "They've shot away my finger, Forrest, but I can shoot yet!"

He holds his rifle with his right hand, and does it all with his left; I watch him as I reload; then he lifts the rifle and with his second finger pulls the trigger, then brings down the rifle and reloads.

I am firing and he shouts again—"Forrest!" He shows me a tear along his left arm, the cloth ripped up and the undershirt ragged and bloody. "They've shot my left arm, but I can shoot at them yet!"

And not long afterward I look and see Anson's head drop to the side; he falls into my arms, shot through the head. I lay him down; I take up the rifle I have dropped.

It is completely dark.

The rebels are stretched in a long line, much longer than ours; they overlap us, the bullets come from angles; they are firing by companies over to our right.

But the fire is slowing. I am exhausted in every muscle. My mouth is dry and unbearably bitter with the taste of powder.

The fire falls off, and dwindles.

Word is given by the few officers behind us that we are to fall back, walking, loading and firing.

We move back slowly, torn from the line of our wounded and dead. We have stood two hours.

I now remember that our brigade gave a cheer, a loud and defiant Union Hurrah, and that the rebels answered with a mighty cheer from thousands of voices. Then it was still; then the buzz of thousands of voices, and the shouts of officers. The rebels stayed where they were, and we moved back to the woods and the pike.

Now we were awakened to the horror of it. During the fight we hadn't heard or seen or felt in the normal way; but now we heard in the darkness the awful moans, screams, pleas for help and for water, from our own men up the slope and from the rebels. It was a weird, terrible chorus. The horror and sorrow of the fight, the finality of its wastefulness, strike to your very heart and soul.

And the body is tired, no—exhausted. I sank down with most of my comrades and slept, right there in the sounds of the dying and wounded.

We lost two thirds of our regiment.

The Brigade as a whole lost 725 men killed, wounded, and missing, and seven of twelve field officers. It has been determined that the Brigade took into battle not many over 1900 men, present and fit for duty. The Sixth, on the right, lost only 75 out of 500; the Seventh lost 160 out of not quite 600; the Nineteenth, in line on our left, lost about half—210 of 425. (One of the fellows has a brother on Gibbon's staff, and so we know the figures.)

But we went in first, and took the first volleys from what we now know was the Stonewall Brigade, and then the rest of the Stonewall Division—and it meant 276 gone out of 430. Company F lost 26 of its 38 men; Company H lost Captain Randolph, killed, and 36 out of 46; and Company G went in with 51 men and came out with 8.

Many of our men were wounded more than once and refused to leave the line. This had helped us, for we were fighting an entire division. We found that two regiments of Doubleday's brigade had come in to help—fighting to the right of the Seventh; but another division of rebels had come in, too. We feel that we did right by our Republic and our State, for there were no skulkers, nobody leaving the line, nobody running away.

We fought the same men we had met last year on the Henry House Hill, and many more besides, and I am sure they came out as badly as we did, if not worse.

And this is what the newspapers call a skirmish. No worse fight than this has been fought in this war. Oh yes, the battle of two days later was larger, with more than 60,000 men on each side, and McClellan went into the Peninsula Campaign with 100,000 men, but nowhere did two or three thousand men stand and face five or six thousand for two hours, face to face, seventy yards apart, with no cover—and stay there even after half the men had fallen.

But Brother, I don't know what it was for. You can see that we had found Jackson, and if King's whole Division had pitched in or stayed afterward and kept the ground we had defended, the rest of our divisions would have come and whipped Jackson before Lee could join him. Instead, King retreated. And Pope wasted the next day. In two days Lee came up with Longstreet's corps, and it was too late for us.

King has been relieved of command, and Pope has been replaced too.

What did we do it for? Some time ago I wrote to you saying that I believed there was a purpose to all this, and that Providence will work the good out of all this horror and evil. But right after a battle you cannot see it. The boys are saying that we were sacrificed for nothing, and our friends' blood was drained for nothing. But somewhere deep in my heart I know that God was there in battle. I do not know where, or how, but if hell is not too deep for God, as Scripture says, then God is on the battlefield. He does not keep us safe—did not keep His own Son safe—but He keeps us in the secret place of the Most High.

I have tears in my clothing and holes in my haversack and hat. I could have been killed there; I was only inches away from it. What plan there is in all this, and why some survive and others don't, I can't say right now.

I don't have the heart to tell you much about the Second Battle of Bull Run. You will have read it in the newspapers by the time you receive this letter. We succeeded in driving the rebels until Longstreet attacked the left of our lines unexpectedly and drove the army back to and almost off Henry House Hill on the old battlefield. But we didn't break, and our brigade was seen by nearly the whole army as it held against an overwhelming attack and retreated in good order. And perhaps the newspapers did not mention that Gibbon's Brigade was the one chosen to form line of battle and let the rest of the army pass through in retreat.

We soldiers do not feel defeated. We fought at least as well as the rebels did. We were outgeneralled.

The newspapers don't know where Gainesville or Groveton are, or what the name of the farm we fought on is, or where Wisconsin is.

The day after our battle with Jackson we had retreated, sorrowing for the friends we had left dead and wounded in the hands of the rebels. We watched as a division approached, marching in excellent order. As they came closer we saw their worn uniforms and their torn flags. Men from the Peninsula! we exclaimed, The Army of the Potomac! Indeed they were part of McClellan's army come to re-enforce us.

Then we looked at our own torn coats and our ragged battle flags: ours were worse than theirs.

It has been days since the battles at Groveton and Bull Run, but I am tired, and a little sick at heart. Little Mac is again in command, and Fairchild, an excellent officer, is in command of our survivors in this Regiment, so things are not all bad. It seems that Lee has gone northward and probably plans on an invasion, and we will have to go up to meet him. But for now we think of our comrades mouldering in Virginia soil, and we think of home.

One last thing I want to tell you, Brother. General Gibbon used to refer to us as his "green troops," but he has been heard to refer to us now as, "the Brigade I have the honor to command."

Your Brother Forrest

When Vernon finished the letters he went out behind the store and walked down to the river. It was warm but not hot. The river shimmered under the afternoon sun; everything looked the way everything always looked. It simply was not possible to understand that Forrest had been in a great, terrible battle—in *two* terrible battles. He had stood inches from death. Rebel bullets had flown next to Forrest. *He could have been killed.* Anson Fuller had been killed right there.

Vernon re-read the letters many times during the next two weeks. The town of Prescott felt a little different. People came into the store to sit and talk as usual but they were nervous and subdued. Father had become strangely strong, or perhaps anxious and energetic rather than strong. He did something he had never done the like of at church: he had actually stood up at the end of the Pastor's prayer. "I think we should pray too for Anson Fuller, and for his family." Then he sat down. The people of the church had speculated all along that Pastor was a Peace Democrat, though he never talked about politics. Now they would find out.

"Anson Fuller?" the Pastor said.

Father stood up again. "He has been killed in the battle at Bull's Run."

"You are mistaken, Nels," Pastor said from the lectern. "All the family knows is that he has been wounded. We will pray for his recovery."

Vernon sat in an agony of chagrin. The Fullers were Methodists, so at least they were not here. They had not heard yet. How could that be? Father stood up quickly. "I apologize for my mistake. Let us pray then for the young man's recovery."

It seemed to Vernon that a hand had reached toward him from Virginia and had touched him directly. Even the government was not as close as he was to that battle.

The people in Prescott, especially those who had sons and brothers and husbands in the Army of the Potomac, waited fearfully during the week of reports concerning the rebel army's invasion of Maryland. Then news came of a terrible battle at Antietam Creek; then a letter arrived. But it was dated before the battle.

September 13, 1862
near Frederick City, Maryland

Dear Brother Vernon,

It has been only two weeks since the great battles in northern Virginia, and the old Regiment is a very small thing in numbers, though we have regained a considerable quantity of our energies. We are hoping that men who have been sick or lightly wounded or detached for hospital or other service will return soon. The whole Brigade is hardly larger than the original recruited strength of any of the regiments. I suppose that we have between 1200 and 1500 men—nothing like the 4,000 we had at the beginning of last winter. We hear that General Gibbon wants Little Mac to give us the next Western regiment that comes to the Army.

Wisconsin is the only State that intends to resupply its present regiments with replacement boys, rather than simply forming new regiments as the other States do, and leaving the present ones to dwindle. The State is to be congratulated for that, because what the others want is excuses to appoint more officers to the new regiments and make political friends by doing so. But I fear we will meet Lee again before any of those new fellows can even be mustered into service, or our wounded comrades come back.

And this time we will meet him in more or less Northern territory. It is certain that Lee has invaded Maryland; we have to find him and try to throw him out. Things do not look well for the Republic at this hour. We read that the rebels have invaded Kentucky in the West; and here the rebels, flushed with victory, have the brashness to cross the Potomac.

When you see the President out on the lawn of the White House in his shirt sleeves, pouring water for worn-out men lying there, then you know "the bottom is out of the tub." For that is what we saw when we returned to Washington after Second Bull Run.

I have no clear memory of what I wrote to you after our battles. The night after Gainesville I was more exhausted than I have ever been in my life. We dropped down to sleep not many minutes after the terrible firing had ceased. A few hours later, probably around midnight, we were awakened. The retreat from that place had little of reality about it, except for the suffering. I would force myself to walk a few yards, then I would fall asleep and drop my rifle; I would pick it up and struggle on a few more yards, then fall asleep again—and so on again and again. One of the poor fellows had a leg broken by a rifle ball, and somehow he dragged himself along, with hardly anyone in condition to help him. He wouldn't allow himself to fall into the hands of the rebels, but I think he died the next day.

We are confident now that McClellan is back. Give us good officers and we can fight the rebels man to man at any time and place—but give us good officers. Thank the heavens McDowell is gone. Our corps commander is Joe Hooker, a good fighter we are told. General Hatch has replaced King at divisional command, but we know almost nothing about him. In our Regiment Lucius Fairchild is officially Colonel now, and the new Major is George Stevens, a very decent and courageous fellow. Our good old Captain Colwell is cheering us up and putting the spirit back into us.

Maryland is a lovely landscape with gently rolling fields, woods, and meadows, and well-kept farms (unlike Virginia). In this part of the State the people are enthusiastic Unionists and have no thought of enlisting in Lee's army as he comes through—which is what he was counting on, but I am certain that he has been disappointed. Here we are cheered as we march through the towns. No secessionist belles screaming hatred at us, no sullen townspeople, no boys throwing rocks. Here the flags wave, the people bring out their loaves and pies and buttermilk, and the girls rush out to kiss us now and then. It is good to be here defending our own North. I feel certain that we cannot fail.

There has been no straggling in the Black Hat Brigade even though we are no longer in the enemy's country. Someone in our regiments started the practice of jeering stragglers from other commands as we pass them, so now we can hardly subject ourselves to the taunts that must assail any of us, in our frock coats and tall black hats, who fall behind among other troops.

We have been singing a new song brought along by the Peninsula boys— "The Battle Cry of Freedom."

> *Yes we'll rally 'round the flag, boys,*
> *Let's rally once again,*
> *Shouting the Battle Cry of Freedom.*

That's pretty much how we feel these days. It seems the rebels are able to beat us every time, but we don't feel beaten. We are as confident now as we ever were, only a bit wiser. Let them come. We shall be ready for them.

I suppose you and Father are running the Store so well by yourselves now that you won't care to see me back. But I'll disappoint you yet, and come back to the old town and family when all this is over and the rebels have come to heel. I've written Mother that I have plenty of socks, but of course she won't believe me. Tell her not to send any more for a while. Tell her we get clapped in the guard tent if we have too many clean socks.

Your Brother Forrest

The only exception to the rule of speaking only English with the children was the Norwegian table grace that Mother had learned from her father, who in turn had learned it from his father, and so on, for who knows

how far back. On September 18 the Mikelsons sat down before a late summer meal of fresh tomatoes, sweet corn, and cold chicken. This time they
all remained silent with heads bowed after the prayer. Vernon looked up at
the steaming corn, then at Mother, Father, and Annabel. They would all be
so alone—so struck—if something had happened to Forrest. Vernon must
protect them; he pitied and loved them so.

The whole country now knew that a battle had been fought in Maryland the day before. People said it was the most terrible battle ever fought
on this continent, perhaps the most terrible in the history of the world. The
armies might be fighting today, too. It was too early for casualty lists.

Mother looked up at Vernon. "Pray for Forrest, Vernie."

"Yes, Mother." He looked down again. *It's no use to pray. What God
wills, happens. It's almost an insult to God and ourselves to think we can beg or
persuade God to change His mind. If God has anything to do with war at all.*

Annabel spoke quietly, "Vernie doesn't believe in prayer, Mother." She
was angry on Forrest's behalf.

Father spoke up now. "What does this mean, Son? Surely you pray."

"I only think that a god who needs our prayers isn't God."

"*We* need the prayers, Vernie," Mother said quietly. "When we pray, it
is not our voice persuading God; it is God's voice persuading us."

"I don't need any persuading."

"Vernon," Father said quietly but sternly.

"I did not mean it disrespectfully. I . . . I don't know how I meant it."

"It is all right," Mother said. "We are all sick with fear for Forrest. Especially Vernie. The rest of us would survive, but I am afraid Vernie would
lose his mind if Forrest has been killed."

"No!" Vernon exclaimed, tears springing into his eyes. "It's not true!"
Not knowing what to do, he pushed his chair back and went out the kitchen
door. He stood on the back steps, gripping the smoothly painted railing.

After a few moments Father came out, quietly opening and closing the
door. He stood alongside Vernon.

"I hope nothing has happened to your brother, Vernon."

Vernon nodded, wiping his eyes with the backs of his hands and
swallowing.

"But if he has been . . . killed . . . then we must be ready, Son."

"What will happen to you, Father, if . . . if . . . . It would kill you."

"I grieved for him all last year. I have made my peace, now. I will be all
right. It is your mother that I am afraid for."

"Yes." Vernon tried to clear his eyes and his thoughts. "We must take
care of Mother."

"Promise me that if anything has happened to Forrest, you will not do anything foolish. You must stay here and help us to survive."

Vern nodded. "I promise." He thought, *I have already pledged to Forrest to hold on here no matter what happens.*

"Now let us go in and eat our dinner." The two quietly went back in.

"I'm sorry," Annabel mumbled, looking down. Vernon rested his hand on her thin shoulder, and sat down. She said, "You are so angry at God about everything."

Vernon looked at his little sister, but found nothing to say. They ate as if waiting for word to come. When they finished, Father murmured thanks absently, *Takk. . . Takk.*

Forrest's name was not on the killed list.

On Sunday, the Lutheran pastor told the congregation that he had gone up to get the list, and no-one in the congregation was on it. His manner had become more subdued, sadder, than before. He was still against the war, he said from the pulpit. The rebel cause was evil, he said, but you cannot change evil. You can change only your response to evil. If you fight evil with evil, evil only grows. But he grieved for the young men, and especially for their families; and he hoped the government won the war soon, before any more of our sons had to die.

He is a good man, after all, Vernon thought. *He has a good heart.* It is a way to do good in this world, being a pastor. Look at these people—sheep without a shepherd.

He thought of Nancy. She would make a wonderful pastor's wife.

He had not yet asked Nancy about marriage. With the news of the past days it had not seemed proper to dwell on private affairs. He believed that private life was exactly what was needed now, especially now; but it did not feel right, and he could not overpower that feeling. He would wait, but not for long. They would both be nineteen this winter—she at the beginning of December. He would ask before the snow flies, and they might marry by Christmas.

He told himself, *I have spent my last Christmas alone.*

*

A letter arrived dated two days before the Battle of Antietam.

September 15, 1862
near Sharpsburg, Maryland

Dear Brother Vernon,

I must write this letter. I wish I could write more pleasant things to you. But to you I must tell the truth, and leave no horrors out. My mind and heart are too full.

    I will write as long as I can, but we expect to be ordered up at any moment. We are resting now and cooking our coffee, which we have wanted for two days. We were fired upon by rebel artillery a few minutes ago; they are in Sharpsburg, the next town. For now we are out of their sight, and our artillery has unlimbered and is entertaining them handsomely. We've been through Boonsborough and Keedysville, and in both towns the people have greeted us on the streets, and in one place an old man stood up on a rock and cheered us, and said he thanked God for us.

    We have need of this encouragement because we have had another battle, our old Brigade has, and we are down below one thousand men now, perhaps as low as 800. Our four regiments each had 1,000 men when we were mustered in back in Madison. How long ago that seems!

    I will tell you about our fight yesterday evening as long as I have time to write. Then I will send this letter back, because I don't think I will have time to write more for a few days, and I don't want to carry this letter with me because it might never get to you. Lee's army is only two miles away, and we all know we are going after them.

    Yesterday afternoon we went through Middletown, west of Frederick City. It's a fine little town and they gave us a splendid welcome, waving flags and cheering and passing out lemonade and pie and other things. They were quite happy to see us, as they knew the rebels were only a few miles away and the citizens could hear the sounds of cannon. We were met by several wounded fellows coming back from the fighting up ahead. We didn't have time to stay; we went on toward the rebels, who were waiting for us in force along a range of low mountains, which the people here lump all together and call South Mountain. It loomed up a couple of miles ahead when we halted to boil water for some coffee.

    No luck that time, because before the water was ready we were told to step into line, and we went on in column of fours. As we marched, the word went through the ranks that the rebels were defending three gaps through the mountain, and the First Corps had been ordered to force all three positions before night fell.

    We were still on the National Road. For a while we left the road, but before long we were ordered to countermarch back to the Road and go straight forward and push the rebels out of Turner's Gap, which stood in front of us. It was our Brigade alone that was ordered to do the work. We began to hear sounds of fighting a couple of miles to our right and to our left as the other divisions of our corps attacked those other two gaps. Why they sent us at Turner's Gap alone I don't know. I would have sent a division, but I'm not a general. The Gap is so narrow that you can't even get a small brigade through it all at once, so maybe that's why they didn't send more.

As we marched beside the nearly ripe corn and the grass in the fields, we looked up ahead. We could see what work lay before us. The road began to rise and the sides of the mountain closed in right and left, meaning that we would have to squeeze through and attack on a front hardly as wide as a regiment. It was some of the roughest country I have ever seen—woods on both sides, narrow and rocky ravines, and stone fences which farther up would conceal plenty of rebels.

We turned aside into a field and waited. It seemed to be about two miles to the very top, to the Gap itself, and nearly all of it was upward. We could see one of our divisions attacking another gap about two miles north of us. It was a beautiful sight—made one think of the "serried ranks of an army terrible with banners"—dark blue lines going forward with bayonets gleaming in the evening sun across the beautiful Maryland fields, artillery batteries behind them shooting silent white puffs of smoke followed by distant thumps. We wished we were with them instead of going up this road alone.

South of us also, though we could not see them, our boys were making an attack; we could see a great cloud of battle smoke rising above the trees, and the crash and boom of musketry and artillery could be heard plainly.

The order came to send one of our little companies forward as skirmishers along the left side of the Road. Then the Brigade was split, half on each side of the Road. (Do not think that the "National Road" is a wide, grand affair; it's barely wide enough for two artillery pieces placed closer together than regulations permit.) The Nineteenth in line of battle was sent up the left side behind our skirmishers, and we formed double column and followed them in support. Across the road the Seventh went first, the Sixth in support. Gibbon was on horseback with the front line ahead of us, shouting "Forward! Forward! Forward!"

Before we had gone a quarter of a mile the way became noticeably uphill. We had hardly begun to labor with the ascent when the rebels opened on us. Every fence, bush, log, and tree up ahead seemed to have a rebel behind it. With their typical craftiness they made use of every bit of cover, and before long their artillery began banging away at us. Our old friend Battery B had put a section on the road and tried to blast the rebels out from behind their fences and thickets.

Then one of the rebel shells, passing over the Nineteenth ahead of us, exploded right in my column. In a flash of fire and smoke and terrific concussion, seven men were knocked down—I should say knocked apart, for that is what happens. I know that artillery doesn't do nearly the damage that musketry does, but one fears artillery more. Its effects, when it strikes accurately, are fearful. The fragments from that single shell tore one man's legs completely away, caught another in the chest laying open his ribs and leaving him a welter of blood, and wounded five others, one of whom lost a foot and another of whom lost a hand up past the wrist. Such a calamity is a severe test of discipline when you are helpless in column of march.

We went about a half mile, when the Seventh halted on the other side of the road. There was a fence ahead of them, and beyond that an open but very narrow field. (How these farmers figure it to be worthwhile to till those narrow, slanted fields I cannot grasp. But the East is crowded, compared to our land. You could compare these fields to the elevations on both sides of the Mississippi at Lake Pepin.)

We could see the difficulty. The woods beyond that field had Johnnies in them thick as sparrows in a cornfield. They opened up on the Seventh—a thunderclap of fire. The 7th couldn't simply stand there; they must retire on the run or go forward. Of course the Seventh climbed the fence and charged the woods. It was a fine sight, that charge, for they went not as our Army usually does, walking with that frail stolidity trained into us, but rushing at them as the rebels do. It must have had its effect on the rebels, for they cleared the woods and ran back uphill.

The Nineteenth was stopped ahead of us, too. There was a farmhouse to our left, and from it and its yard the rebels would have been able to fire into our flank as we passed. We could see (and hear!) Long Sol sending back for that section of Battery B. General Gibbon had moved close behind our regiment in order to direct the brigade. You must not think that he did this out of concern for his safety, for he is very brave and sets a fine example. And no place was safe on that field once the rebel artillery began firing.

In a few minutes the two guns came pounding and jingling up the Road, unlimbered, and punched a few shells into that farmhouse. Then we were able to move forward.

The gorge through which the Road ascended became narrower and narrower. I think we advanced another three-fourths of a mile, driving back the rebel skirmishers and taking fire from uphill. About there we struck their main line. The Nineteenth found not a fence but a stone wall facing them. It was lined with rebels, who fired not only on the Nineteenth but also to their left into the flank of the Seventh across the Road.

Our Regiment, though only a hundred fifty yards back, were still in the role of observers. We saw the Seventh change front, turning its line at an angle in order to fire across the Road at the stone fence. This had ghastly results, *because as soon as they had changed front the woods ahead of them exploded with rebel musketry fire, which now caught the Seventh in the right flank, running down their whole line and taking them virtually from the back. I saw the colors go down, come up, then go down again.*

Thank the heavens that General Gibbon was quick. He sent the Sixth forward past the stricken Seventh, and they went with a rush. Their colonel Bragg ordered the strangest thing I have yet seen, either in battle or on the parade ground. You could hear him shouting, above the musketry: "Deploy column! By the right and left flanks, double quick!" They divided into two bodies, and the one on the right charged up beside the exposed flank of the Seventh and fired a volley into the woods. Immediately they were ordered to lie down, and then the left wing, which had followed them, leapt over them, rushed ahead, fired a volley, and they in turn lay down. Then the first wing, having reloaded, rushed forward, leapt over the others, and volleyed. This was repeated three or four times and flushed the rebels out of the woods. It was wise, because there wasn't room for a whole regimental front anyway, and it couldn't have been more smartly executed.

We were also going forward because the Nineteenth had succeeded in getting around the fence with one of its companies, and suddenly the stone fence became a death trap for the rebels. They were forced to clear out, and a few surrendered. Led by one man of the Nineteenth, a group of them came past us. We didn't have much time to look, but we were surprised by their appearance.

The rebels don't look like us, exactly. Of course they are regular boys just like us, but they were if anything more ragged than we are. A couple of them didn't even have shoes. They wore a mixture of clothing—gray and butternut—and no two of them were dressed alike. They carried almost nothing— that *we noted with envy right away: only a blanket roll looped across their shoulder and under their arm, and a haversack. Their "servants" carry the rest for them. They were thin boys, ragged and dirty; I expect that the last month of campaigning has been worse on them than it has been on us. But those ragged wolves can fight; the guns they had thrown down gleamed as we passed them.*

We were elated and angry with the excitement of fighting. The Nineteenth had done a great share, and they now took a minute's breathing time as we passed through them and advanced up toward the high point of the Gap. Suddenly we had a horrible surprise, for a whole brigade of rebels rose up in front of us on both sides of the Road and poured a withering volley nearly into our faces. This was their main line. It was a whole brigade, five regimental flags, and they were in a nearly impregnable position, firing down at us from behind rocks and trees, and on the right of the Road in front of the Seventh and Sixth from behind yet another stone wall.

We stayed where we were, just as we had done at Gainesville, and fired back. And like Gainesville, it was getting dark and we found ourselves shooting at musket flashes.

Vernon, we lost our brave and true friend, Captain Colwell, who was mortally wounded very close to me. He had just passed behind me, hardly a foot behind me. He had been telling us to remain steady, to aim low. I felt an absence to my right; when I looked around I saw them bending over him, trying to wipe blood from his face. "Two of you carry him farther down," I shouted; "but come right back!" I realized that as I loaded and fired I was weeping.

The fire was as terrible as at Gainesville; we were loading and shooting like madmen. That's what good training will do. I worked like a mechanical device shouting, aiming, firing, loading, aiming, insensible of the steady blazing around me and the boys going down. At first we had been in two lines, the first kneeling and the second rank firing over us. Before long we had but one ragged crowd of men roughly in a line, loading and ramming and triggering in a steady fury.

The firing must have been heavier than at Gainesville because we ran low on ammunition quickly. We were ordered to let the Nineteenth come ahead again through us and keep up the fire as we retired a few rods back to search the cartridge boxes of the poor fellows who were down. I could hardly believe the rate of fire that the Nineteenth was pouring into them. The rebels must have thought they were facing a half dozen regiments instead of two. (I do not say this to boast, Brother. Anyone who has been in this kind of pandemonium understands the horror of it and the almost automatic nature of what you do when you are on the firing line.) We were ordered up again through the Nineteenth, which went in search of ammunition and discarded rifles.

My hands began to pain me and I realized that worse than the near emptiness of my cartridge box was the condition of my rifle, which was terribly hot. It was becoming almost impossible to ram a ball down its muzzle because the fouling had built up inside so thickly. I threw it down and looked for another, but the one I picked up was also hot. Everyone else was looking for another rifle, and all of the serviceable ones already had been found.

I tried as best I could with the one I had. We were told to hold our position with the bayonet if we must.

It was completely dark up there, the sun having gone behind the mountain seemingly a very long time ago. Fire was coming from up to our right, but not at us. We understood from it that either the Sixth or the Seventh had worked their way up behind the left of the rebels and were enfilading them. But nearly as soon as the fire from up there began, it slackened. Because it did not cease altogether, we knew that our boys up there were running out of ammunition just as we were.

At about the same time it was noticeable that fire from the rebels was slackening. They must have been as bad off as we were with regard to ammunition.

Word was passed not long afterward that we were to cease firing and stay in position. The order came from General Gibbon, who had received word that the other passes had been carried and the battle was won. With the mountain gaps on both their left and right gone and our divisions pouring through, the rebels in front of us were done for if they didn't get out.

As our fire dropped to nearly nothing, the rebels in front of the Seventh and Sixth charged them, whooping and shrieking that hideous yell. They must have thought we'd quit firing because we were falling back or had run out of cartridges. But they hadn't got more than thirty yards before the Sixth and Seventh opened on them again, one of our regiments charging with the bayonet even as the rebels came on. The enemy broke off and ran back to where they had started from.

There was a little more firing, but by about 9:00 it was pretty much played out. We hadn't eaten all day, and we had come up and attacked the enemy about as numerous as we, in the finest natural position you could imagine.

We could hear the rebel officers talking, quietly giving orders. They seemed to intend to stay just where they were.

About an hour later the Sixth or Seventh let out three cheers for the old Badger State. We took up the cheer, and the Hoosiers on our side of the Road cheered for their State. There was no response from the rebels. I think one of our officers had decided to try to find out whether the rebels had stayed or had slipped away.

We were then told that another brigade was on its way up the National Road to relieve us, and we were not to go forward. We had no great desire to go forward; we wanted to get a little sleep, but even more, we wanted to find our friends.

Our boys were all over that dark mountainside. You heard their piteous moans and pleas for help—an unceasing chorus of the saddest, most desperate sounds. They wanted water, but there was no water left. There was nothing that could be done for our Captain, whose body lay on the rough ground behind our line. We were sick at heart in our exhaustion, and useless rage mingled with our grief.

You remember Ernest Braddon. He and his sister came to the social at Church last October, and all the fellows vied for her attention? I came upon him lying just downhill from our last position. The sky was light enough so that I could see his face well. I bent over him and he tried to talk to me, moving his mouth but making no sound except the terrible exhalations coming from his throat. A ball had carried away a portion of his windpipe. Poor fellow! He fumbled in his pocket and handed me a sheet of paper, and I assured him I would send it to his mother. It is an unfinished letter; I will enclose it with this, knowing you'll see to it that his family receives it. Do not describe to them what I have written here. They must not know how their poor son suffered. You might use even this to become acquainted with that lovely sister, Vern, if Miss Parker tells you no. See how hardened war makes us? Do not waste any opportunities you have, for life is short—but do so honorably and with regard to her sensibilities at this time.

Even if I had had any water, he could not have gotten it into his stomach. I stayed with him for some time, now and then putting my hand on his head to let him know I was there, until he died. Poor fellow! Had you heard the sound of air rushing in and out of his throat, mingled with blood, you would have required of this country a reason for such sacrifice.

It was a long time before stretcher bearers came up to carry the wounded back down to Middletown. Our dead had to lie where they were.

I am thankful to be alive, Vernon. The slaughter was not so great as at Gainesville—not quite. I think we have lost about a quarter of what we went in with. The Brigade at this moment numbers not much more than 800, I think. Our march today was exhausting after that battle of last night, and more fellows sank down by the roadside. They will catch up with us tonight.

I am sure the rebels suffered less than we did in killed and wounded. But they should have been able to hold off a whole army in that position, and we were very close to having them on the run—nor were we intending to retire.

Colonel Fairchild, who was everywhere along the line last night, is pretty well used up, as is the Nineteenth's Colonel Meredith. Both are suffering physical breakdown, and Allen is temporarily in charge of the Second. I don't know about the Nineteenth.

We lit fires this morning to cook our salt pork and flour. It does not sound like much of a breakfast, but we had not eaten in twenty-four hours. Before we could cook anything the order to fall into column was received. We took up the march, passing our dead comrades lying in all positions imaginable. Ernest will have been buried in that field by now.

When we passed through some troops of the Second Corps we were supposed to have gotten cheered by them. So General Gibbon has told our officers. The Second Corps' commander, General Sumner, is a starchy disciplinarian and disapproves of troops cheering others, so to have that from him means something. I understand that many of the "higher-ups" were able to see our battle yesterday evening. It took place up on the mountain in plain sight of everyone in the rear.

I feel pretty well used-up, and I hope Little Mac gives us a breather before sending us in again. As you can see, I had time to finish this letter after all, and now I'm going to take a little nap.

Your Brother Forrest

P.S. Vern, every day I know less and less about courage. We know what we're willing to die for. Maybe that's it.
This doesn't mean we want *to die. But you must go on with things if I do.*

After noon dinner one sunny September day Vernon went upstairs to lie down, tired from the morning's work—and there was Forrest, sitting in his old chair in a faded blue uniform! A tall black hat rested in his lap. He smiled the most peaceful smile that Vernon had ever seen.

"Forrest!" the younger brother exclaimed dreamily, wanting to step forward to embrace his brother—but Forrest held up a hand in the common Norwegian gesture that wards off impetuous feeling. "It's so good to see you, Brother!" Vernon said breathlessly. "But how is it possible that you're here?"

Forrest smiled in his familiar, aggravatingly patient old way.

"We have been frightened half crazy that you were wounded or worse, Brother!" Vernon whispered. But Forrest seemed to say without words, *I'm all right, you see? I'm fine.*

Vernon turned to dash downstairs to tell *Far* and *Mor* but suddenly felt an overwhelming wave of exhaustion. He dropped down onto his bed for a moment's rest, and fell into a long, deep sleep. When he awoke, he understood that his brother was dead.

*

The family received word that afternoon, and two days later Vernon found Forrest's last letter at the Post Office.

United States Army Field Hospital
Antietam Creek, Maryland
22 September, 1862

My Dear Brother Vernon,

I have lost a leg, Vernon, my right leg. It is gone forever! You must write to Mrs. Emmons of the Sanitary Commission to thank her. You see, she is writing this as I say it. I cannot tell all that I feel, Vernon. I trust our shared years together remove the need for many words.

The wound pains me a great deal. They are worried about the stump. It seems not to be healing properly and there is some kind of poison in it. But do not be afraid for me, Brother; and do not be angry. Do not let my fate soil your heart. These things happen in war, and we must accept them.

I will tell you all I can.

McClellan waited too long. We didn't attack the day I wrote to you, or the next day either. It was thought that the rebels outnumbered us. I don't know. But we beat them; they are gone. On our part of the field they outnumbered us; I am sure of it.

My kind nurse says to rest. I expected to say more.

(continued 23 September)

I am better today, and have more strength to speak. I am comforted to talk with my brother.

They were waiting for us.

We crossed Antietam Creek Tuesday evening in plain sight, all of Hooker's Corps.

We went into bivouac and lay with our muskets loaded. You don't really sleep much. Some fellows say they know they won't survive the battle, and when it happens you remember that they knew. But I didn't know that I would be here now. You think of all kinds of things. You think of home. You think of what you didn't do. Some pray out loud. It drizzled that night. We knew we were going to attack them at earliest light. You are afraid, but you try to ignore your fear. I was afraid of dying, Vernon, but I thought it would be sudden.

Artillery was already firing as we moved forward in our columns. There was a farm and a cornfield ahead of us. The corn was taller than a man, not like at home. The rebels were waiting there.

On our right was a pike with a post-and-rail fence along both sides. The Nineteenth and Seventh and some of the Sixth crossed that road. We went forward on our side.

A shell exploded across the road and it must have carried off fifteen men dead and wounded. The good old Sixth removed them and went on.

They sent us in first, Vernon. Hooker sent us in first. It was an honor. But oh! the price we paid for it. The rest of the First Corps was formed up behind us, but they should have gone forward together with us!

We got to the cornfield and the enemy opened fire. The most terrible fire I have been in. The space was small and at first you couldn't see anything. At least two brigades of Secesh were in there. Their artillery was aimed onto that cornfield too, and you saw arms and other parts of boys flying above the corn.

We stood in the falling cornstalks and exchanged volleys in a hail of bullets. Lieutenant Colonel Allen was shot there and Major Stevens took command.

I don't know how we remained in that cornfield as long as we did. Finally we went forward in a rush and the enemy broke and ran. When we got to a fence at the end of the cornfield we halted, loading and shooting.

The order to charge was shouted and the Regiment climbed the fence and ran forward. In front of the cornfield was open ground, and to our right was a little white church. We went for the church yard with a yell.

The rebels had been running for the woods behind the church, but their officers stopped and re-formed them. They realized that they outnumbered us. They poured a terrible fire into us and we retired back to the cornfield fence.

We stayed there loading and firing as if insane, crying, shouting, laughing. The boys fell right and left while bullets and shells whistled through us.

We charged again and this time the rebels fled headlong, climbing the pike fence or running through the church yard and into the woods.

We got onto the church yard that time. The Seventh and Nineteenth came up beside us. For an instant I looked around at the diminished old Brigade. So few of us left!

The barrel of my rifle was fouled and I saw other fellows having trouble ramming their charges home. We stood hardly a minute trying to regain our strength.

From the woods ahead of us, Vernon, came a solid line of rebels, ten or a dozen battle flags. Two fresh brigades, five or six regiments to the brigade. They came on shrieking that yell and their fire went through us like a saw blade. We were being slaughtered, Vernon! We retreated in order, but it was hard to avoid stepping on the bodies of our own dead and wounded.

The rebel line came on, stretching from the church all the way beyond our left. Going back through the cornfield we stumbled over bodies and tried to load and fire. That field was completely cut down as if harvested. Hardly any cornstalks were left standing.

The boys were scattered through it, trying to ram our hot, clogged rifles and fire. I saw our colors go down. Colors of our other regiments were down, too; then an officer of the Sixth lifted their flag. Because I couldn't see ours, I went to theirs.

The officer was Dawes. More of a soldier I have never seen. An artillery officer ran to us and shouted that the battery needed men to work the guns.

I saw some guns of our Battery B waiting across the Pike. One gun fired a discharge of canister into the cornfield in front of us. Fence rails flew into the air and rebels went down on top of bodies already on the ground.

Major Dawes brought the flag to the guns. I think there were only a couple dozen of us with him. A man pointed back to the caissons, meaning for me to run and get ammunition.

I reached a caisson and saw canister in boxes; I lifted one out and ran back to a gun. Quite a few more of our boys had seen Dawes's flag and now gathered around the Napoleons. General Gibbon himself was there sighting one of the pieces. Mrs. Emmons is saying to slow down, to breathe and talk more slowly. There is plenty of time, she says.

I gave the canister to an infantryman from the Sixth, who shoved it into the muzzle. A man yelled behind me, "Knock off the charge!" but a second man gave a full canister to the same infantryman, who shoved it into the muzzle. I expected the gun to explode but the lanyard was pulled and the gun fired a terrible blast into the rebels coming through the cornfield. Everything in front of us disappeared in smoke. When it cleared the rebels were closing a wide gap in their line. The fanatical rebels!

I ran to the caisson for another load and a hard kick in the back of the leg spun me around. It felt like getting struck with a maul. I was on the ground. The sky pulsed above me.

I think I heard Southern voices. Someone gave me water, but I don't know what happened there finally.

It was night and the field around me seemed to be moving. Constant moaning. Cries and sudden screams. I could not feel my leg, nor could I raise myself up. I moved my left foot and realized that my shoes had been taken off. Let them have them, I said. The rebels were worse off than we were. I cannot tell you how thirsty I was. I still am thirsty.

Mrs. Emmons is telling me to write more tomorrow. I am pretty well done up in describing this. I am quite exhausted and will take this good nurse's advice. She has been very kind to me. She will write to the family when I die. Vern, I know that we will meet again. Think of me as going before you to prepare a place for you, all of you, and we will be together again just as always.

Please leave everything I say in.

I am not afraid to die, Vernon. Only I wish it would come quickly.

(continued 24 September)

They said yesterday I might pull through, but I knew better. Today they say I have gangrene.

You must take care of the Store. Father will be upset and will not think properly. See to it that Annabel and Mother are cared for. That is the most important thing.

I am thinking of those bright orange pumpkins at the Social of last fall. You must go and enjoy things when I am gone. Try not to hate the rebels. They are soldiers, just as we are. It is the civilians that started this war, theirs and ours, and it is they who keep it going. Those who profit by it are at fault.

The Country did a terrible thing in allowing slavery to exist. Two boys from the Regiment visited today and said that the President is going to abolish that abomination. If that had been done years ago we wouldn't be here now!

The boys said our Brigade lost half. We are down to four hundred fifty. We started with four thousand! Men on other duty will come back. The wounded. Boys who get well. I wish I could go back with them! The war will go on. We didn't finish the rebel army.

Boys said we aren't called the Black Hat Brigade now. McClellan has given us a new name. I like the name . . . Take care of Mother . . .

To his Brother Vernon: Your brave brother Forrest became exhausted, and his mind wandered as he dictated this letter. He was unable to say more that I could understand and transcribe. He died in the afternoon. He felt no pain at his death, and his eyes were fixed upon his Blessed Savior at the end. Be assured that he has gone to his Peace.

Ruth Emmons
(Mrs. William Emmons)
Nurse
United States Sanitary Commission

A fortnight later out in the little churchyard, Vernon gripped his stiff black hat. He looked around to try to clear his mind. Ragged branches reached like bones toward the sky. A few high clouds drifted. His father also stood bareheaded. His large farmer's hands held the brim of the black dress hat that he had brought from Norway a lifetime ago. Thin hair wisped in the wind as he looked down. His jaw was square and set—like Vernon's. The two looked alike, everyone said, Nels Mikelson and his silent second son.

Vernon stared at the pine box. It had come all the way from Sharpsburg, Maryland. It had gone to Hagerstown and been put on a train. Then somewhere it had been put on a different train for Chicago. From there, another train had taken it to Milwaukee, Madison, and Hudson. Father and he had brought it here the day before yesterday. A few oak leaves had fallen onto it beside the dry flowers.

This morning at the table, Vernon had said, mostly to himself, "If God is good, why are people so bad?"

"The devil has a say in things, you know—on this earth anyway," his mother said. "But I know that God is good in spite of everything. He gives us love."

"Love is pain," Vernon had replied. "I hate it!"

*

Up in his darkening room, Vernon wrote the first entry in a new daybook. He was not going to write many letters home, leaving a bundle of fading pages for someone to cry over. Now he had nobody to tell the truth to but himself. What he wrote was a sort of prayer, the first he had uttered in nearly a month:

May God punish the rebels and help me kill every one of them.

The Iron Brigade

October 17, 1862
Madison

I have never kept a bound book except ledger accounts for Father, but I intend to do no writing home except Christmas & holidays & at such times as seem to be necessitated by various reasons unforeseen. Therefore I will keep this Journal of my experiences in this War, which I am going to fight in as replacement & revenge for my Brother. I will keep this Journal faithfully but I will talk to no-one about this war until it is over & the rebels are beaten to their knees.

I know what I am getting into. Unlike the boys at home I have been told the truth & spared in no wise the real facts of what battle is like. It is not something the Folks at home should know & in this I am following my Brother's wishes completely, as I swear to do in all things as well as I am able so help me God.

Brother Forrest, I will write this sometimes as if to you, as you wrote to me, because I can't believe you are really Dead. I want think of you as standing over my shoulder reading. I want to believe that somewhere in the light fields of Heaven you can hear the thoughts I direct to you, because it is not possible that such a true & good Brother as you can be lost forever & disappear into nothing. I know this is not what Pastor would approve, because he says there is no resurrection until the Last Day, but I know you, my own Brother, better than he ever did. I have seen you and I know that somewhere you are alive.

I know you but maybe I never understood you. Now I have gone into the Army to live as you lived & find out some of what I didn't understand.

I was not able to get into your Regiment, the 2nd Wisconsin. I went to the Governor's office & they sent me to the Adjutant's office & they sent me to the Assistant Adjutant's office, where I said With the rebels killing our soldiers all over the country I didn't think it would be so god damn hard to enlist. They paid attention to me & in the Assistant's Office I was signed up in the Sixth Wisconsin as a replacement.

There is a group of 18 men who volunteered to go into the Sixth & they have been here in Madison training & I am the 19th.

They said I could either train with these 18 & then wait for assignment, possibly to the Second Wisconsin & possibly not, or go ahead with them next month to join the Sixth. I elected to join the Sixth & signed the paper.

I haven't forgotten what I promised you about not volunteering, but I did it anyway because they are not going to kill one of us in our family without getting shot for it themselves. I have some business to do & I mean to do it.

We have been here these few days being put through the "School of the Soldier," learning about how to stand & how to march quick & double-quick, and how to do the manual of arms & how to do the Load in Nine Counts & how to interpret the drum beats & bugle signals & we go over it again & again & again, all day long, because we have to learn this before they put us on the train. They say we will learn how to march & maneuver with a Company and Regiment when we are in winter quarters and have Company & Regimental drill all day, & I do not look forward to it but I realize I must learn it.

Do you remember how it was at first, when everything was strange and you didn't know why anything was done? Did you ever get angry at having to do it? Today the sergeant who is putting us through the School of the Soldier reprimanded me demeaningly for not having my heels together at attention. Can you imagine the trivialness of such a thing? But of course you can; you had to do it all the time! He said only those who were bow-legged or fat-legged were excused from having their heels together at attention, & that I must be bow-headed or fat-headed not to understand something so simple. He's just a farm boy from near Saukville who was wounded at Shiloh last April and now trains up the new boys & thinks he's bully.

We have learned to fire by file and I wonder what it will be like to have a man thirteen inches behind me firing his rifle over my shoulder, when they give us ammunition.

They have issued us uniforms but no black hats, just the little kepi caps, and I hope I will get a hat like the rest of the Brigade because it will be hard enough to be a new Recruit in the most famous Brigade in the Army of the Potomac. I know they will make fun of us new ones mercilessly & not accept us, but I have determined to show skill & courage or die in front of the enemy, because I intend not to have it said that your brother was a coward or even a poor soldier.

I am beginning to feel wild to get out of here and on the way to the Army, because I fear sooner or later Father will come after me & tell them that I am the only remaining son, etc. The note I left for the family said I was going directly south to Grant's army, where I had already signed up to be in the Fourth Wisconsin. So it will take him a while to find me, and probably they have decided that it is too late & that I am already in, down there in Tennessee or Mississippi; and I can imagine them weeping in grief & I think of it every night & I can hardly sleep sometimes with the thought of it, for I told a lie and have become a grief to Mother and Father and our dear sister, but you understand, Forrest. When there is war, all bets are off. I will write to them from the East.

Many times in the past few days I have wondered what I am doing here, and at night I toss & turn with anxiety & doubt over what I did & how it affects our dear family & how Father will have to do so much more work at the store, but it is a strange and irresistible destiny & I could not resist it any more than a leaf can resist the wind & the only way to prevent me would be to tie me up.

I have filled only a page and a half. Do you remember how you used to make fun of me for my tiny writing in Father's ledger, saying that only the mice and I could read it? Now it is useful, because I want nobody but you & me to read it, and the paper is going to have to last because I didn't bring much money for new daybooks. They have already told us to send most of our things back to our homes. Thanks to you I was prepared for that & didn't bring a trunk with me nor a case of preserves nor the kitchen table.

I did visit Ernest's family.

I don't think I can write to Nancy for a long time, but I am very lonely here & long to talk to her. She said she felt that her brother would not survive, & that is how I felt about you & so we understood each other. This brings tears to my eyes Forrest and I hope you are well and have no hurt nor pain nor grief nor any bad thing now nor evermore. God bless you Forrest.

October 29, 1862
Somewhere in Ohio

It is not easy to write carefully in this jolting train, but I want to record that I am at last bound for the Army & have left the good old State behind, perhaps never to return. It is cool and not dusty today because it has been raining recently, & the harvested fields we are passing smell fresh & wet & remind me of home.

The boys are singing "Aura Lee," a lovely song. "Aura Lee, Aura Lee, maid of golden hair." It reminds me of Nancy, with her lovely golden-red hair, and I hope she is thinking of me. They say that sometimes when you think of a person it is because they are thinking of you. But I am sure she is still grieving for her brother. I must not be so selfish as to imagine she should have me in her thoughts instead, & especially so as I have gone back on my word to her. "Love and light return with thee, and swallows in the spring." I wonder how many springs hence I will return, if ever. Will I come back with empty sleeve or trouser folded up and pinned; & what would I say to her then?

But enough of this gloominess. The overcast skies make me sad & I think too much of home.

November 8, 1862
Bakersville, Maryland
Camp of the First Corps, Army of the Potomac

I have been too busy to write or too lazy, & everything has been too new, so that I hardly know where or what I am & what to think and say in this Journal. But I wrote to the dear family at once.

I am in a vast sea of tents covering the gentle, rolling Maryland hills & fields. They are all white, and in the sun they remind me of the phrase, "I send forth the snow like wool."

An army corps is more immense than I had ever imagined from your letters, Forrest. Regiment after regiment spread out with its tents arranged in company streets, & brigade after brigade, & the great divisions with their headquarters banners. I cannot even see the whole Corps. And we are but one corps of the Army! What a frightening sight it must have been to see Lee's legions in lines of battle with flags flying.

I am in Company B, the Prescott Guards, where I wanted to be, with boys from back home. At first they put me in Company A, the Sauk County Riflemen, but I pleaded with their Captain, and he told me to go wherever I—-—- pleased. It is as if these men are happy to see replacements and think it is about time we came, but they have very little use for us. Perhaps they are withholding their approval & friendship until they see whether we are worthy of being in this Brigade.

I am not discouraged by that. They are Wisconsin men and so am I. General Gibbon has said, "When I go to the Hereafter, let me be together with Wisconsin men."

A new regiment has been added to the Brigade, and the old veterans have mixed feelings about them, too. They say the new men look like fine soldiers, but they are not from Wisconsin or Indiana. They are the 24th Michigan. At least they are a Western regiment like the others. They don't have their black hats yet either. I suppose it shouldn't matter, because we are not called the Black Hat Brigade any more, but it is a way of telling the men from the boys, a few of the veterans say.

There aren't many boys in the 24th Michigan. We new fellows have been over in their camp a number of times lately, because they are new too and do not stiffen their backs to us. I think I have seen thirty of forty of these Michigan men who are around forty years old. In one company there are two brothers—and their father!

You know our officers, Brother. They call Bragg the Little Colonel, and everyone speaks well of him and are proud of him. He is recovering from his wound by running for Congress. The war Democrats back home in Fond du Lac nominated him, & then the Republicans followed suit. The peace Democrats are too strong in that District, but the nomination has been a source of conversation & delight in our Regiment.

You would also be proud to know that our Brigade (how fine it is to be able to say our Brigade, Brother!) was singled out by General McClellan after the Battle of Antietam. (Is it nearly two months since you breathed your last? O, Forrest!) The Commanding General wrote a letter to our Governor & said that this Brigade is equal to the best troops in any army in the world. You would also be pleased to know that the Brigade had no stragglers during the Antietam campaign. I am told that this is unique in all the Army. Not one straggler.

I have not seen the Antietam field, Brother, but I must go and look this Sunday if I can secure permission to do it. I must see where you & the Brigade fought, & where you received the mortal wound. Forrest! Sometimes I do not want to go and see the place. The old soldiers here say they don't want to go back.

Major Dawes is commanding the Regiment in Colonel Bragg's absence. He looks like the model from which the finest of all true soldiers were cut. I would rather have him than anybody for a commander of the Regiment. He is very active in discussing the purpose of the war & we often hear him and the other officers talking in the evening.

Brother, I have thought & thought about why you had to give your earthly life & have not been able to conclude much except that I want to make the damned rebels pay for it. But I heard Major Dawes say that the purpose of the war is to destroy slavery & the southern aristocracy that is supported by it. He said that without the awfulness of the battles fought this year, the North would not have strong enough feelings to make a thorough job of it. I think he's right.

I haven't thought much about slavery. I am here to defend the Union and the freedom it guarantees & I don't know any negro people. But Major Dawes says slavery is the real issue of the war, and the President's Proclamation freeing the slaves brings that to light.

Not everyone in my company is happy about that. Some say they don't want to fight for negroes. But Dawes is right to say that the whole South depends on the slaves & if you destroy slavery you destroy their ability to fight us. And he says we have no free country until all the people in it are free.

Anyway, he thinks the sacrifices of the last six months make it impossible for us to go back to the way things were before & let the South come back into the Union just as they were, slavery & all, with the cause of the trouble not removed.

I have to know that you died for something, Forrest, and that I am living for something. I will take what Dawes says to heart, and make it my reason.

There is one other thing I want to talk about. I know you went through it all, but you know that you & I always were different about things & you were never shocked at people or thought badly of them because they are different from us. But Forrest, how did you preserve your way among these soldiers? Your way was different from mine. I have seen them gamble, which does not disturb me very much; I know some of them visit camp followers, women who are not wholesome company; and there is a great deal of cursing and swearing in the camp. I know these things never worried you very much. But you were naturally good & I am not. I don't know whether I can resist temptation.

You always wondered whether you would be brave in front of the rebels. I worry that I am a rebel myself & what I mean is a rebel against God & I know I will be brave in battle because I am so full of hate & anger but I do not know if I have the kind of bravery that resists temptation. I think a soldier who is not virtuous cannot be as good a soldier as one who is virtuous, & I also think that God withholds His protection from those whose lives are a disgrace. I think if I were ever to give in to great temptations I would become afraid in battle because I would know that I deserve to die. Did you ever think any of these thoughts? I wish you could answer me.

The corporal of our mess is Edgar Abrams. They are farmers just northeast of Prescott, and I think I remember him & his family coming into the Store. He's 27 & is like an old man, but he's been kind to me & makes sure I learn what I have to learn. The other two fellows both had all their messmates killed or wounded in the cornfield at Antietam. I didn't know either one of them before; they have their farms south of Prescott & never come as far up as our Store. Charlie and George Martens are here. It was awful good to see them, even George. We have promised each other to have good old times, if there ever is time. Good old Billy Faust is here, and of course Bods. We are going to make Jeff Davis howl, I tell you, and do some damage. Charlie and George never wanted to be in the same mess, for fear of making it hard on their families if a shell exploded in amongst their file. I wish I could be in the same mess with my Brother.

November 12, 1862
Bloomfield, Virginia

We have been marching all over creation & if this is what it means to be a soldier I think I would rather look into some other occupation. We have not seen a rebel and I thought we were going to take out after Lee & finish them off. But of course Major Dawes says we will never "bag" or "destroy" them, because the Army of Northern Virginia is a splendid army led by some of the best generals, especially Bobby Lee, & if we beat them it will be little by little & over a long, long time, but never all at once. This is discouraging & I hope he is far wrong, but he is the kind of man who does not get wrong ideas very often.

I never was able to go to the cornfield, but the Brigade passed through part of the battlefield a few days ago when we started this march into Virginia. The farmers had been rebuilding their fences but the trees were in splinters all over & there were graves all over & there were wounded men outside many of the houses sitting or lying in the fresh air. I had a very strange feeling there, a heavy feeling, like you have at a funeral. I did not know how these huge army corps could have all fought on that small field; no wonder it was the worst day of fighting in our history.

The fellows in the mess were very quiet & I think wanted to get through there as fast as possible. Even Bodley was quiet.

I wanted to hold onto the place because of you so I took a little of the soil & put it into my pocket. It is as close as we will ever be on this side of Heaven, my Brother.

We have a new commander in the Brigade. General Gibbon has been promoted to command a division, and Colonel Morrow of the 24th Michigan is commanding the Brigade for the time being. I don't understand why a brand new colonel has command, but he is by all accounts an excellent officer, & I never knew General Gibbon. The men say they didn't like him at first because he was a disciplinarian, but eventually they realized Gibbon was fair & that he preferred rewarding good work to punishing bad. This Brigade is officially called the Iron Brigade & the boys give much of the credit to Gibbon. All I know of him is from the letters you sent me. They say that when Colonel Cutler, a Milwaukee man, recovers from his wound & comes back, he will be in command.

All we have gotten in the past week is pork & hardtack. There is plenty of coffee but even though I am of Norwegian descent I do not like coffee, but

I expect I will if not like it then at least drink it before this war is over. Billy spits it out, but the old hands say that will change.

The Michigan men have not liked the food & have complained in chorus now & then, but the other regiments seem to take it as if nothing can be done about it, and I am sure the veterans are right.

It is embarrassing to be a new recruit but I am learning the company drills. All I have to do is follow the others, & I catch on pretty quickly. The other men are hardier, used to marching, but I will die before I fall out of line or complain. We got some new supplies before leaving Maryland, so now I am not quite the only one in the Company with new shoes & clothing. But still no hat.

We are in Virginia & have been marching along in the shadow of the Blue Ridge Mountains for the past few days. It is beautiful country, magnificent & majestic, but I would still take Lake Pepin & the wide Mississippi instead if I could.

November 14, 1862
Warrenton, Virginia

I don't know which to say first, that we have had absolutely nothing to eat for two days, or that General McClellan has been thrown out! As a private soldier, I can't do anything about either one, so I might as well save my strength. I never knew General McClellan except for what you wrote about him, but I used to know food.

On top of this, we had snow the other day. Even in Wisconsin we wouldn't see snow this time of year. Virginia is a peculiarly unpleasant place—too warm for the season & then snow.

General Burnside has replaced Little Mac. I don't know much about him either, except that the fellows say he might be an idiot. What I have heard is that he spent the whole day at Antietam forcing a crossing of Antietam Creek by a bridge, when he could have had his whole corps wade the stream in the morning. So he attacked too late instead of helping you out when you attacked that morning. I don't think I like this general.

But McClellan has made me angry, too, because I came here to fight the rebels not sit in camp & march around. Burnside has been ordered to fight & one way or another we will.

Today Billy, Bodley, and I have been out rabbit hunting. My first military expedition was to hunt rabbits. There is no prohibition against rabbit hunting, so that is what we hunt for, but most of the rest of the world would call the animals we went looking for "sheep."

We found none. This part of Virginia has been shaken out like a rag. There are hardly any decent fences left; all gone for campfires. Pigs, chickens, horses, "rabbits," everything cleaned out. We're not far from the Bull Run battlefield, so I understand why the country is so poor, but it almost makes you want to tell the rebels to keep their miserable country because we don't want it back.

Even pork & hardtack & coffee would be pretty good right now.

Oh what is "the sleep of the brave"? How do you fare, Brother, and where are you? Do you see the dawn as we do? Are you back along our St. Croix and Mississippi?

December 2, 1862
Brooks Station, Virginia

We are not settled comfortably in winter quarters because the public & the newspapers are calling on Burnside to pitch into battle. The boys complain about this, about the bloodthirsty public who don't understand what it is like to campaign in cold weather & rain. But I agree with the ignorant public & want to get at the rebels & thrash them & get this over with.

I like Colonel Cutler because he looks like a fighter. A man that old, with a silver beard & silver hair, doesn't have time to fool about, and I think we would have done well with him. But he's been promoted to command another brigade & our new Brigadier General is Meredith, who was Colonel of the 19th Indiana. I don't know how much I like to have this mostly Wisconsin Brigade in the hands of a Hoosier, but the boys say I talk like a fool. Just so we see something of the rebels before I go mad waiting.

This marching & camping are supremely tedious. It wears on the nerves. The others don't seem to mind it but it drives me crazy. I don't have anything to write in this book.

I found out today that Major Dawes's great grandfather was the man who rode with Paul Revere that night. That is a good omen but what good is a good omen when you don't fight?

Colonel Bragg was beaten soundly for Congress. Our family are Democrats but I hope the Democrats don't take the war away from us before I can settle accounts.

I really have nothing to write about & am not pleased by that.

Can I write to Nancy? Would it be honorable, after breaking my promise?

December 12, 1862
Fredericksburgh, Virginia

I have been under fire now & the agony of it was that we could do nothing.

We have come down to Fredericksburgh & of course all I have been thinking about is your letters describing the town & the people in it. I have no time for the saucy rebel women because we are going to fight a battle here. That much is clear.

We lay across the Rappahannock from Fredericksburgh all day looking at the church spires, nearly as I had imagined them while reading your letters. Our artillery was firing upon the town & beyond the town. About four in the afternoon we were ordered to go down to the river & cross the pontoon bridge, which we did. This was a little south of the town itself.

After we got on the rebel side of the river we marched along the bank & before long the rebels opened up on us with their artillery. They had their batteries on the heights opposite & one by one as we passed them they fired. They are miserable gunners, because they did us no damage except I think one man in the Seventh Wisconsin was wounded or killed. The old boys said I should not be fooled by that bad gunnery, because it was casual & long distance.

At dark we reached a stone house belonging to the Bernard family, and there a very strange thing happened. Two of our lumberjacks began to chop down one of the large old trees in front of the plantation house. The negro servant of the officers of Company C came running up to them. I heard it all. It seems the old negro was raised on this very property where we are lying now. "Boys, what you doin' dar!" he shouted. "You break dat old man's heart if you cut down dat tree! His grandfather planted dat tree!"

Well, they stopped cutting. Until then I never realized how strange this war is. Major Dawes says we are fighting to abolish slavery, but some of our officers have negro servants, just as the rebels do. Then this negro, who is a servant of our officers by his own choice because he wants the rebels to be defeated of course, cries out when his old home is defaced. Of course he loves his old home. But it is the place where he was a slave. He still loves it. It is too complicated.

The boys in the Company don't talk about the rebels as if they were our enemies. Listening to our boys, you'd think the enemies were the civilians at home who made this war and who let us fight it while they make money from it. They say the rebels are only soldiers like us. I don't understand that talk. If the rebels were decent men we wouldn't be out here.

It is very cold tonight, considering we have nothing to make beds with but single blankets and leaves.

I pledge to write tomorrow or day after, whenever the battle is over. If I live, I will write to Nancy.

December 15, 1862
near Fredericksburgh

We are back on the north side of the Rappahannock after three days on the south side & this army has lost the most humiliating & unnecessary battle ever known in the History of the World. Our Brigade was not hit hard, but what we had to go through I hope I don't ever have to go through again. But even worse would have been what the rest of the Army had to do.

There is a small river down from Fredericksburgh & it goes into the Rappahannock I think. This is where we were sent, Doubleday's Division, & we were the far left of the Army of the Potomac. On both sides of this river the rebels had crammed in their artillery, on the hills & in the woods & Jeb Stuart's cavalry was back there too.

On the morning of the 13th after a nearly sleepless night in the cold at the Bernard farm we were ordered to go for the artillery & cavalry on the extreme left. The fog was so thick you couldn't see where you were going.

The whole Brigade marched in column of fours & we could hear booming up ahead but their guns were entirely invisible to us. I told Edgar I wished I could see the devils & their guns & he answered that once again I was talking like a fool because if we could see the rebels they could see us, & now the only reason we didn't have their shells bursting right in among us was that they couldn't see any better than we could. "It's typical for a recruit to be crazy to fight," he said to me, "but you beat all creation for wanting entertainment."

It was a strange march because it was muffled and serious & we were shivering. I have seen that when it is hot & dusty we are pretty sullen & silent on the march, but when it rains everyone is cheerful & joking & there is good singing & talk of whipping the rebs. In the fog it was like a funeral again, but you had to get to the funeral by marching right off the edge of the earth for all we knew.

The fog began to clear after we had been less than a mile out, and pretty soon we could see the open plain in front of us, and ahead was the little river & the hills where the rebel cannon were pounding away. Now they could see us too & I put away what I had thought about the rebel gunners not knowing their business. They had the range on us all right, but their shells weren't made as well as ours because so many of them exploded too soon, while they were halfway between their lines and ours, or they didn't explode at all. The solid shot does little damage but it scares hell out of you.

The 24th Michigan was ordered up to attack a piece of woods where the rebels were posted in advance, shooting at us. You never saw a prettier sight than those Michigan fellows stepping out into line, flags fluttering, orders crisp and obeyed instantly, and then the whole regiment going forward as one man, not a bit of lagging behind or unevenness, first at a walk and then at the quickstep and then at the double-quick. George told me, "That's the way the Iron Brigade charges, all right." I don't know how the 24th knew how to do it.

They cleared out the woods immediately & I think without losing a single man. The rebs skedaddled when they saw the Michigan boys coming like that.

But the rebel artillery on the hills across the little river opened up in earnest then, and Battery B was sent out to the right of the Brigade. They unlimbered in the open & gave the rebels better than they got I think, banging away first rate, but you could see the poor fellows and horses going down now and then because of rebel sharpshooters in front of the 24th Michigan.

The rebel gunners started finding the Michigan men. We could see it all from where we lay, which was in ditches & low spots & anything we could find to make ourselves shrink into the ground. The Battery & the 24th were out in the open. I saw a solid shot take a man's arm off in the 24th. It was as if one second the man stood there & the next his arm was gone & he was thrashing on the ground; & then I saw a man without a head in a flash of blood, which finally was enough to make the Michigan boys hesitate & that part of their line began to waver like a worm. Then we heard their colonel, Morrow, loud and clear over the whole plain. "*Attention, battalion!*" The men snapped into a crisp line again. "*Right dress! Front! Support arms!*" He was taking them through the manual of arms, out in the open in front of the rebel batteries, with shot and shell screaming at them & I tell you I never saw such a sight for discipline and courage & probably never will again.

At first it looked insane, but once again I was told I was talking like a fool. "Morrow knows a regiment can't stand such artillery fire long with nothing to do," George said. So the colonel put them through the drill to take their minds off it. I see now why the boys got to be called Iron.

In a few minutes the 24th went forward again in line of battle and cleared out the sharpshooters. I think several dozen of them went down in the charge. I almost jumped up out of my ditch and ran after them. I & many of our boys cheered at the sight, & I think the 24th Michigan is now officially part of the Iron Brigade in the hearts of the old boys. You wouldn't see better work if you lived to be a thousand.

A while after that we had to form hollow squares to defend against cavalry, which was something I had not seen yet. I followed the others & came out all right. It is a peculiar movement & very complicated. First you have to deploy by companies out of the line of march, or rather by divisions, which is two companies abreast. That is only the beginning.

I heard the command, "Right and left into line, wheel!" & had no idea of what was to happen next. The file closers came out of line & marched to places outside the ranks & stood there. At the same time we were facing left, & then one platoon went to the rear & the next platoon went to the front diagonally. That is about all I remember, because what followed was a maze of companies & platoons marching in parade order in everywhich contrarywise direction, which made perfect sense to everybody it appeared, but none whatsoever to me. Then we did a wheel to the right as the order "Third division, forward, guide right" was given & then *Double quick, march!*" The two companies in front stayed where they were & the rest of us wheeled into line at right angles to them. Then the two companies way to the rear marched forward at right angles to us, the officers and drum & bugle and the colors moved into the center, and sure enough we had a *square* & I don't know how we got it.

At any rate no cavalry with any sense charges squares of good infantry, and Stuart did not charge us in our five regimental squares, so the left of the Union line was secure. The fellows told me that cavalry coming at boxes of infantry would get shot down in bunches, and cavalry don't like to get shot. "Did you ever see a dead cavalryman?" is what they asked me.

"He ain't never seen nothin'," Bodley offered—who hasn't seen a very great deal himself.

We found out that the rebels were holding back most of their artillery south of the town, because only late in the afternoon did they really open up on our corps. They had forty or fifty guns along the hills to our front and right, & then the work of Battery B and the others was cut out for them. We couldn't see the other batteries as well as we could see B, which was still in the open to our right.

We could also see the rebel guns plainly up on the low hills as we flattened ourselves against the ground. The brass Napoleons gleam & give out metallic booms, which you heard after you saw the shooting puff of white smoke with its orange center like a snake's tongue; as soon as you heard the boom the shell itself either screamed over your head or hit the ground with a thud you could feel, or exploded & then you heard the fragments thud somewhere near you as you prayed they wouldn't be tearing your back open. You saw the cannons spring backward as the smoke fired out & at that range it takes about one second for the boom to sound and the shell to plow the ground. The rifled guns are black and have no metallic sound. Howitzers sound hollow. In that one hour I learned all about artillery, all I want to know from that side of the cannons. It was a terrible hour, like being in hell, & despite the cold I realized that my face was sweating & I was getting chilled with sweat all over my body. There's nothing worse than lying in front of artillery you can plainly see firing at you & not be able to do anything except hope the shells don't hit you.

I believed that there is no such thing as random death, but I have changed my mind because during that hour I felt nothing of a Divine plan or order. I only hoped the accidents happening all around me wouldn't chance to happen to me, and though I spent the hour in constant prayer it was a kind of nervous & repetitious prayer more like a crazy man's muttering than a real sensible prayer, and it was habit, rather than talk. I think when you pray Somebody listens, but not when I do. What relation any prayer had to what happened around me I don't know & couldn't feel, because you can't imagine that some puny words of a quivering little soft human being have anything to do with the iron hard shells & shot exploding & plowing over & around you. A few minutes like that entirely explode away all nonsense & all you've got left is a realization that God does what He does & nothing we do has any effect on it & also we have no idea of what God is doing or why. You either forget all your beliefs or you realize that whether you live or die right here & now and whether you escape clean or get hit by an iron ball is nothing in itself. My plan might be to get back home & live fifty years, but that has no relation to what the Maker of the Universe plans. Most of our questions that we used to discuss about God are only based on whether we get our own way or not. If we get what we want then we believe, and if we don't then not, because what matters to us is not God but ourselves.

Of course I didn't think all this out there on the ground, but this is what a journal is for. Out there I thought almost nothing, but I knew that all the Catechism got blown away into the Fredericksburgh wind & all the debates between Lutherans & Presbyterians & Baptists & Catholics & so on are debates about our notions & that's all. What it came down to out there was one whimpering boy with explosions all around him in the hands of an unknowable God. Anybody who thinks he knows more than that hasn't been in the Army.

Battery B was a sight to behold, the way they worked those guns. They fired faster & better than the rebels, who were working around their guns, as Major Dawes put it, "like fiends stirring the infernal fires." Our Battery B blew up a caisson of the rebels for we heard the shuddering explosion & looked up to see the column of smoke, & they also disabled several of the enemy's guns, as we plainly saw because we were so blasted close. But no gun from Battery B was disabled, and no caisson exploded.

When darkness fell we were ordered of all things *forward*, closer to the rebels' guns. Well the enemy I have found is not stupid, and he heard us. We had to move close enough to be in canister range, & sure enough he opened on us.

Again he couldn't see us, so the firing was guesswork. I think they didn't know how close we were, because we hugged the ground & the canister screamed over us, about a foot over us. It didn't do us much harm but it wore you out just to hear it whistling overhead & you didn't dare to raise up. The worst part was hearing the canister balls rattle on the frozen ground, skipping fast enough to smash in a man's skull.

That was the worst night of my life. I was drained & exhausted & starved, but it was even colder that night than the night before & the canister was now & then whistling over our heads. All we had was gum blankets to lie on, and a blanket over. The whole Company lay spoonlike, all on one side at the same time hugged up against each other for warmth. But the side you lay on, resting on the frozen ground, got painful & cold, so the whispered order came, "About face!" & we would all roll over onto the other side in unison and lie that direction for a few minutes at most & then shift again & so on like that hour after hour. There is nothing worse than three or four in the morning like that; despair goes completely through you. But there is nothing to do but lie down, even though you do not sleep or rest, because every so often a rebel gun would fire & you feared if you rose up you would be torn to pieces.

This reminds me of how tired I am so I will get some rest & write more tomorrow.

December 15, 1862
near Fredericksburgh

I have had a little rest and now can rear back and deliver what I think about the great Battle of Fredericksburgh. It is what we all think. To put it as shortly & sweetly as possible, General Burnside is a blundering oaf who hasn't the brains to command a donkey cart much less a great army.

We have had the worst disaster of the war at Fredericksburgh, and countless thousands of the dead & wounded of the Army of the Potomac still lie on frozen ground beyond the town.

We saw much of it that first day as we lay under the rebel batteries. The other divisions & corps of the Army assaulted the rebels, who were strongly set up on the heights overlooking the town. Line after gallant line of our fellows, two, three, & four deep, marched up those heights, straight at the rebel cannon & infantry. The air thumped with the artillery & was filled with the terrible swell of musketry, and we saw those half-mile long lines of blue rise up nearly to the heights like shredded waves, then fall back down, leaving the hard ground first littered, then patched, then blanketed with dead & wounded men. It happened again & again, until we could hardly watch without crying tears of rage.

If it is the President and the public that forced Burnside to attack Lee's army regardless of strategy, then they share the blame, but surely nobody ordered Burnside to be more stupid than any General on record. You can't charge up a ridge in beautiful battle order on anything like even terms and win. Any soldier in the ranks can tell you that, but the generals do not know it yet. The concentrated fire of infantry & artillery can sweep an open field clean & we saw it on the 11th.

For two nights we heard the pitiful and terrible cries & moans & screams & undertone of prayers & delirium of thousands of wounded. It is all because of this blundering fool Burnside. He means no harm; he even tried to decline the command because he knows he is not qualified to command a whole army; that is what we are told. But how does that matter to the ones still out there dying in supreme suffering & agony this moment? Those who put him in command bear the blame & Burnside himself bears blame. But what good does blame do anyone now? We are led like sheep to the slaughter, because someone makes *mistakes*. Anyone who thinks life is fair or sensible from a human point of view is crazy. One little mistake that someone else would not have made or that could have been prevented by some little change in one man's plan has killed thousands & left thousands of homes mourning & weeping & asking Why.

I believe in fighting & maybe even dying for the cause of freedom, but I don't agree to dying for nothing but someone's little mistake, & now that I'm in the Army there's nothing I can do about it. I know now that I might die or be maimed for nothing & to no purpose & that my brother might have been killed by a shot aimed at somebody else.

One should not go to battle before one is 18 because one is too young to make any sense out of it. Where is God in all this? Mother would say we can't know, but I want to know. If my mind is not up to knowing, then I'd like to know why. Where is the sense?

I am happy to write that our own boys were sensible. On the night of the 14th our Second Wisconsin made a truce with the rebels in front of our brigade, so we all were able to get some sleep, and the wounded between the lines were brought in. No higher-up general approved of that truce, I wager, but it made more sense than anything the higher command ever did.

Not that I want to stop fighting, but I want someone to be in command who knows what he is doing & can make use of us rather than waste us like so many corn shucks. The boys are entirely fed up with Burnside & would as soon shoot him as the rebels.

Of course the truce was broken by mistake, when the 24th went out the next morning and fired on the unsuspecting rebels. As George says, the rebs were "irritated" by this and gave us a few licks back & so as a result of another *mistake* more fellows were killed & maimed for nothing.

In the afternoon things settled down again and the truce went back in effect, because one of our fellows challenged a reb to a fistfight & all of us on both sides gathered around to watch. It was one of our fellows from Bad Ax county, a lumberjack, who went out, and I have to say the rebel fought him well. They might not look like much, but they can fight. I guess the fight was a draw, but the two fighters nearly thrashed the everlastings out of each other. I think the graybacks were surprised at the pounding their man got.

George says that fight was like the War. Both sides will simply pound & pound each other & nobody will get the advantage until the side that has the most fellows to get in & die wins. I am willing to stay & pound or die until we are all done, if it means the preservation of the Union and the freedom of every man & woman in this country & the vindication of what my Brother went into the fight for.

After the fistfight we all stood around and traded coffee for Virginia tobacco, which I don't smoke yet but expect I will eventually. Those fellows are a strange lot, the infernal rebels. No two of them are dressed alike, and they look like wild animals, some of them, & they talk a language you can hardly understand & are so profane you can hardly believe it, but they are like regular fellows mostly, except that they hate us & some of them are funny as all get-out. They have a razor wit & a way of phrasing that beats us all hollow, & while we think of them as stupid they seem to outshine all but the best of us, or maybe it was only their attitude toward us, which though friendly was that Yankees are stupid sons of————-, as they say in a casual way, and with our stupid General & our stupid sixty pound knapsacks we are half inclined to agree with them, but they don't know what we are made of & believe me we will stay in & pound them until they come to heel & give up their slaves & their superior ways.

By all accounts the best corps commander in the Army of the Potomac is ours, Reynolds, but he was willing to sacrifice the whole 19th Indiana to get the Corps out. This Brigade is usually the last to leave a field I am told, as I remember from Brother's letter after Second Bull Run, and this time we were supposed to slip back across the river in the dark last night. The 19th was not told of the movement and would have stood their ground ignorantly alone in the morning & been annihilated. But our officers got General Reynolds to give permission to send word among them in the storm because we have more confidence that our men know how to keep quiet & do things properly. It was a great honor to be chosen to safeguard the Army, an honor the fellows of the 19th would not have survived. Battery B was only five hundred yards from the enemy & limbered up & got out with guns fully loaded & primed in case they would be detected. If you believe in Providence then you would believe the storm last night was providential, but I don't think it would convince the rebels of Providence. Where was Providence on the fields of Fredericksburgh?

Brother Forrest, now I am talking to you again. Are you in a place where you can see Providence, and do you now know the answers to the questions we used to ask? I wish I could hear your answers. I believe you are in God's hands & that's about all I got out of Fredericksburgh with.

Christmas Day
Winter Quarters, Belle Plain

Brother wrote to me on Christmas Day, so I have written to my parents & sister. I miss them so. I think I am somehow angry at them but I don't know why. Perhaps because they let Forrest enlist—but they didn't let him, any more than they let me; I only *think* of it that way. I hate and detest the rebels but have had no chance to settle with them yet. I haven't dared write to Nancy yet, but soon I shall.

I almost fear that I won't be able to hate the graybacks as I should. We go to the river on picket duty and send coffee & newspapers & toothbrushes across to them, & they send tobacco which I now smoke, & we talk to them pleasantly. It is hard to think of them as the enemy but we know that when spring comes we will be back at them & they will be the enemy all right. For now it is easier to get angry at the people back home, especially the politicians & businessmen.

I meant to write to Ernest's sister too & have composed a thousand letters to her in my mind, but I don't know what is proper & whether it would be pleasing & am still undecided as to what to say.

We have had old pork and wormy hardtack for Christmas Dinner. This is the surest sign that Burnside is still in command.

Forrest, unlike you I cannot think of home on this Day. Perhaps my mind is too emptied out. I think almost nothing these days. We have built good log houses & I sit in ours & I go on picket duty & I learn the drills & that is about all except cards & idle talking. I still want to get into battle & fight the rebels & make some sense out of this whole thing by doing so.

The Army is pretty well played out & discouraged, though our Brigade is not as bad and we are not about to give up. As one of the fellows says, "Take holt is a good dog but hold on is better."

Belle Plain
January 24, 1863

I have nearly given up trying to keep this journal regularly but I have to write about this or burst. This confounded Fool Burnside has just given us the most wretched & miserable expedition in the History of the World & as if that weren't enough, when we got back in the Dead of Night last night our own log houses had been taken over. But I will go back to the beginning & tell this disgrace with forbearance & cold reason.

On the 20th we were on the march for Who Knows Where, Virginia, no doubt to surprise General Lee who certainly knew exactly what we were doing & where we were going, & had enough sense himself to stay indoors.

At first we welcomed a winter campaign. If this winter is the Union's Valley Forge, then we have use for some stunning campaign such as Washington would have led. Camp life is tedious. Reveille at daybreak, with company roll call; then breakfast; then police call in which the whole camp is swept clean as a dinner table; guard mounting at 8:30 A.M. exactly with inspection, followed by another inspection by the captain in which he even looks us in the face for cleanliness. (The other day notice was given: "Great rejoicing in Company C today: Ford changed his shirt.") Then we have battalion drill until ten o'clock—and then *nothing to do* until *four o'clock*, at which time lessons in military theory for the officers and *still nothing for us*. Finally at 5:30 we have dress parade, and an hour later company drill. At seven the day's official business is over, which means three more hours of nothing until Taps at ten P.M. And the next day the same & the next day the same & next day the same & so on & so on forever and ever world without end Amen.

Burnside's General Order for the march was read to all of us & it sounded confident and optimistic. "The auspicious moment has arrived," he said. So we started out refreshed & happy about the change in routine, until afternoon when it began to rain like hell. There was a freezing, driving wind, or rather a gale, & in an hour we were fighting for our footing, penetrated to the underwear with cold water, & worn out from fighting the terrible wind & softening roads.

We lay down in the rain that night & woke up in heavy, chill rain & mud in the morning, if any slept at all. This state of Virginia is a slab of mud several feet deep that reveals its true nature when in contact with water. Old Burnside ordered the Army forward despite the conditions. We learned that Rappahannock comes from two Indian words: rappa meaning "mud," and hannock meaning "more mud."

It was anything but comical though because we made only about one mile per hour, with horses, mules, caissons, guns, ambulances & wagons getting mired in the mud & the men having to wait for the roads to be cleared or having to pitch in ourselves & try to get the wheels rolling again. We were soaked to the bone & hungry & cold & tired & angry enough to spit tenpenny nails & there we were in the driving rain with mud caking our shoes and sucking them off our feet & using up our last strength to try to heave ambulances and wagons forward (which should have been off our line of march to begin with.) At one point the Commanding General himself slogged past us on the road, that wide-brimmed hat of his covered (unlike our caps and hats) & down over his mutton-chops, and his rubber cape swathing him & his horse chunking up mud; & there was this teamster ahead of us, standing next to his wagon which was sunk nearly to its axles in the quagmire & the mules were floundering desperately up to their knees in mud, and the man stands there lifting his soaking little cap in salute & says, "General, the auspicious moment has arrived."

But I say it was not funny. We camped again that night in pouring rain, lying in the mud too soaked & caked & exhausted & chilled to care about anything any more. Of course there was no possibility of making fires to boil coffee or cook our soaked rations. Hardtack does not relent in water; it merely becomes more mysterious & the nails in it rust. All the next day we remained there at the Rappahannock in the pouring rain & that night lying in the cold rain the men began to shiver & you heard universal coughing & it was a sad, desperate & ominous sound.

That night even Burnside saw the hopelessness of the roads & tossed in his hand & ordered a return to Belle Plain in the morning. He may be just unlucky, but his luck was our luck & we paid for it more heavily than he did. At eight A.M. we started, and it took all day & part of the night to get back. The Regiment's ambulance was full & those who reported sick to the surgeons were entirely out of luck after the first half-dozen. Charlie was unable to carry his knapsack & rifle, he was shaking so & feverish & weak. I tried to carry his knapsack but I couldn't manage it & so settled for his rifle, & George was too done up to carry more than his own things, so it was left in the Virginia mud & Charlie staggered on coughing & crying. But a man from Company D ahead of us had it worse. He asked the surgeon to be let out of line, but the ambulance was full & so he got rid of his knapsack and rifle & tried to stumble along with the column & made it most of the way back to camp, but in the evening he sat down braced against a fence post & died & we passed him slumped there as we made our way along. I have heard this man had not reported for the sick list one single day in his year and a half in the Army. "The race is not to the swift nor the battle to the strong, but time & chance happeneth alike to them all."

And when we got back staggering into our camp among the log cabins we had built, we found they were full of men from another regiment which had taken them over. It was the 55th Ohio. We would have battled them, even in our used-up condition, if they hadn't been as decent a group of fellows as you could want. They gave us the best of their food, welcomed us in with them, & left in the morning. It was no fault of theirs; it had been orders of some blockhead up the line of command that put them there.

And so ended the Mud March of General Burnside & with it I hope his career as commanding General of the Army of the Potomac. This was a splendid Army with good men & we don't deserve a dolt like Burnside. He belongs in a potato patch. I won't write again until we get a new general & he proves he's worth his handful of Virginia mud.

March 16, 1863
Belle Plain

Fighting Joe Hooker has lived up to his promise & these two months since I wrote last have seen the utter transformation of the Army of the Potomac. There is no word of discouragement, there is no complaint, only a determination to get on with the work as soon as the roads are dry & whip the rebels once and for all.

And I am a new man too. I have learned all the drills & know what I am doing & feel like a regular Iron Brigade soldier & I have felt, Brother, that you are by my side although invisible & I believe that you are alive and all right.

The best of all Hooker has done is feed us. No more of the moldy hardtack and rancid pork for every meal. We have had soft bread & onions to keep away the disease & real potatoes & even fresh beef, not to mention ham & dried vegetables & fruit. We are all sleek & bored & impatient—and *I have my hat*. The 24th Michigan got their hats & in the same issue the fourteen of us (there were once 19) who came in last October got ours too.

On our hats we have corps badges showing First Corps, a full moon patch of cloth, in red signifying our First Division. The system of corps badges was Hooker's idea & it has done great things for the morale of the Army. I really believe we have an Army again, the way it was when I came in, with the same feeling.

He gave us furloughs & they have cheered up the men, though coming in as recently as I did I am not eligible & don't mind. I have heard often from the family & they say they are not angry at me & want only my health &

safety & I believe them, but I must be a soldier first before I go home & see them again, which means I wait until the spring & summer campaigns are over. I do miss them & despite everything I wake up at night having dreamt of them & sometimes I do not understand why I am here without them & what for.

I have finally written to Ernie's sister & await a reply. No answer from Nancy yet.

It has been nearly six weeks since Charlie died. His grave is in the regimental cemetery up behind me as I write. George is still listless & I talk to him often because I understand what he is feeling, yet he is not at the place where he can be comforted, only paid attention to & kept active.

We talk about the war often & the idea of Emancipation now usually wins out. We read the newspapers & see that the Country is discouraged & this angers us because we are doing the fighting & we are not discouraged. The Regiment has passed resolutions in favor of Emancipation, in favor of prosecuting the War without compromise until the Southern aristocracy & their despicable Institution are destroyed, in favor of a draft, and against the carping dissenters who are throwing cogs in the wheels of the War for the Union. The Brigade has its own resolutions of similar import & most of us support them fully.

We have a new division commander, Wadsworth, a tough man who seems be stamped from the right mold. Reynolds has moved up to corps command. Cutler has the three regiments that were at Gainesville alongside this Brigade.

With Cutler gone, Bragg is not temporarily but officially in command, and Dawes has been promoted to Lieutenant Colonel. In his place as Major is John Hauser, a native of Switzerland & an old soldier who served with Garibaldi in Italy. He is a fine drill master & of course we enjoy him not only for his soldierly qualities but for his Dutch accent. "You are one damn hert of gooze," he says to us whenever we get something wrong, even the smallest thing. So this "herd of goose" is well-drilled and well-led, & not spoiling for a fight but willing to get it over & done with.

I saw our Regiment's old State flag before it was sent back to Madison for a new one. It was torn and ragged, the most noble thing I have ever seen.

Now we have a new one, and must earn it all over again.

The other day we witnessed a dishonorable discharge. The Brigade was drawn up in a hollow square, and five men were marched into the center, had their heads shorn and shaved & then we formed two long lines through which these men were led at bayonet point, with about 20 drums & fifes playing the "Rogues March," & it may sound funny but it was the most humiliating, shameful spectacle I have ever seen & I have no intention of letting it happen to me for I would rather die first.

We've had two deserters recently, both from the 24th. Colonel Morrow read their sentences with tears in his eyes. He is as noble as he is courageous & intelligent. They were not executed, but a man from the 19th was caught last week for his second desertion & was shot in front of us all. I do not understand what made him desert, unless it was concern for his loved ones at home, for he was the farthest thing from a coward there ever has been. He was marched to his coffin in front of the whole Brigade, and displayed not any shrinking or emotion of any kind. He sat down on his coffin as ordered, calm & collected, & with his own hands opened his shirt & bared the breast that in minutes would be punctured by bullets. A dozen men stood at Present Arms, only one of them with a blank cartridge loaded, & then the prisoner was blindfolded, though we heard him say calmly that it was not necessary to blindfold him. He heard the order to aim, heard the hammers being pulled back—what an awful moment! knowing that in another few seconds he would be propelled away from his family & friends into an unknown. What goes through one's mind? Does one feel the Arms of the Unknown?

We have had a religious revival in camp. These things do not interest me though I don't know why. I feel a strange emptiness when I hear these preachers among us. On Sundays we were sometimes drawn up in forma-tion and marched off to a meeting, though that broke down quickly and more of the fellows were playing cards during that time than listening to a preacher. I usually did neither, though at first I tried the services. Perhaps it is because our Regiment has no regular Chaplain, and we get these preach-ers from other Brigades & localities, that I find them displeasing. They are not the reserved Lutheran pastors but rather the emotional tent-meeting men of the circuit-riding type, which are all right in their own way, but not in Church. They pray in such a way as to make themselves shout or cry, in front of everybody, which seems a strange way to approach the Invisible God who hears the heart, & it strikes me as oddly self-thinking. You are not considered an authentic Christian unless you throw away your pack of cards & cry along with them. I can do without the cards but the other is not for public display, no matter what they call me. Give me, if you have to give me emotions at all, the emotions of the battlefield & not the emotions of bored men in camp.

The Southerners have this kind of religion & right with it they have their slaves. The only differences this religion seems to make are in how the men choose to entertain themselves.

I am fed up with camp life and want the spring campaign to start. If Virginia isn't good for an early spring what is it good for?

I would like to get a letter from Nancy.

March 22, 1863
Still at Belle Plain

It is spring now officially but nothing. The roads are still muddy and it is cool & they say it can snow though I doubt it.

I am bored enough to read this Journal & am surprised I never wrote about our raid in February.

It is too long ago now for me to write about in detail with interest, but I want to record a scene that took place on the plantation of one Dr. Smith.

The Second Regiment and part of the Sixth had marched to the Potomac & embarked on a steamship. Most of the men had never seen a paddle-wheel steamer before, but of course I had. It was a novelty to them, and when we went down a small tributary of the Potomac and the leadsman called out the strange depths to the pilot, such as "Mark twain!" "Three quarter twain!" & "Quarter less twain!" they thought it capital fun.

We landed & went about our business, which was to round up horses & mules & all kinds of provisions & supplies that the rebels might make use of. Upon our return Major Dawes was approached by a negro man & asked whether we were really Lincoln's army, & when assured that we were, he went back to the slave quarters and produced a group of slaves, above three score men & women & children all together, who gathered at the steamship that had brought us from Belle Plain. They carried tied bundles containing everything they had on earth. They were barefoot, ragged some of them, & neatly attired also, & seemed to be in a variety of conditions. I had never seen so many negro people & I stood as close to them as I could and observed them with rapt attention. They have different features from us, as everybody knows, but not so different as the drawings in newspapers suggest. Their families have been in this country much longer than mine has.

Colonel Fairchild of the Second was in command of the expedition & he told Dr. Smith, a distinguished & friendly man, that the slaves were now free to come with us & could not legally be interfered with in any way. The man agreed with no apparent ill-will.

But this Dr. Smith went back up to his plantation house & in some few minutes returned with the most striking lady I have ever looked at. Forrest, you should have seen her. Perhaps now I know what you meant when you described the women of Fredericksburgh. But this remarkable woman was no empty-headed fool & she was truly beautiful & was I suppose in her late twenties. I was not as interested as you would have thought I should have been, Brother; instead I grew indignant, but with the peculiar addition of attraction to this lady.

She pleaded with the negroes for many minutes, even embracing some of them, with whom she had evidently grown up. I think these Southerners are raised with negro children by negro women, and grow up side by side with them until a certain age. They trust their children to the negro women, but do not consider negroes worthy of being literate or free!

She appealed to them to stay, saying that the fate of what she called "free n—" in the North is a terrible one, & I really believed that she meant it for their welfare more than for her own financial security. I do believe she loved those negro people, & she cried herself, plenteously, at the thought of them gone. I do believe the Southerners are fighting for their slaves, but I dare say some of them want to keep their slaves in a different way than we think, perhaps in the way that you want to keep a family together. At least this applies to a few of them.

The slaves wept, too, and embraced this woman, who I am told is Mrs. Brockenbrough, wife of one of General Lee's officers. I dare say there was not one of us whose heart was not pulled by this striking lady, and our discretion would have gone along with it had we not been under responsible officers & been "Lincoln's Army"—and had we been invited by the lady to court her which of course we never would have been. But all along I became more distraught with the confusion I felt in her presence & with the scene that was unfolding, & felt only a wish to talk to Nancy, whose thinking I know and which is not strange & tied up with this deep unusual sickness planted in the soul by slavery.

Several of our men spoke forcefully to the effect that as soon as we left, the negroes would be sold down farther south by these two, Dr. Smith & Mrs. Brockenbrough. I do not know whether it was a fair statement, or the simple truth.

I thought for sure the slaves would stay, the way they all cried and hugged their Mistress, but in the end *not one* stayed behind. And we imagine that these negro people are not intelligent!

This has made me see the War in a new light, as that they, the Southerners, are fighting to preserve their *own* freedom (just as we would), but that *we* are fighting to gain someone *else's*.

And so I would say that if there is a just God we will win, but maybe I have seen enough of this war to refrain from connecting God to it in any way that I can understand; and because I have an idea of what it will take to "win" this war, I do not implicate God in a victory, nor try to predict what such a "victory" will result in. Perhaps God could still be just, though the world be unjust.

Pastor once told me that I am intelligent & should be a theologian someday, but he would be horrified to see that I have become only less sure & more confused & less willing to speak for God.

My thoughts are in the deep mud, as we were when we returned that Sunday when the steamboat stopped at the place below our camp where we had embarked some days before. It was pouring rain as usual, and the march up was another quagmire. On impulse I called out, "Quarter less twain!" In a moment someone came up with the call, "Four and a half!" & another called out, like a leadsman, "Mark twain!" & so on, until finally Jones, in a high, thin, squeaky voice, called out, *"No-o-o-o-o bottom!"* and the men shouted with laughter. I am thought of now as a wit, & perhaps appreciated, but of course it is only a way to relieve the black moods I have had since last fall & I await action if only to escape myself.

I keep hoping that battle will clear things up for me & so am impatient to be in the field.

I could really benefit from a letter from Nancy. I have written to her again.

I feel that writing in this Journal upsets me & destroys my beliefs & that perhaps I should not write so much.

May 3, 1863
near Chancellorsville, Virginia

We are in the midst of Hooker's grand spring campaign & it looks like another washout. The signs of it are plain because we are just sitting here, probably waiting for Lee to attack again when we should be hitting *them*. We are lying in line of battle with nothing to do & I suppose will sit here all morning so I might as well pass the time by recording the recent events.

We had a genuinely "auspicious" beginning back almost a month ago, with a grand review in which Old Abe & Mrs. Abe saw the whole Army pass before them, & I am told the President knew our Brigade, even said it was the only brigade with a Quaker in command. We are famous I suppose. We didn't get much of a look at the President, though he tipped his hat to us. A tall fellow & haggard-looking, & who wouldn't be, with such as he has to think about day & night, & now I guess he's going to have more to think about because Hooker is doing nothing here.

We did see Hooker again, & I must confess that he is so handsome he is almost pretty & I understand why they say his headquarters is full of women. "Fighting Joe" is splendidly brave I am told, but overbearing and haughty. It must be said that he has made us into an army again & dispelled the gloom & pessimism & depression of the winter. We are in condition to meet Lee's rebels at least on equal terms, & are well-equipped & healthy & well-disciplined, but here we sit. If we want the rebels to attack us I am sure they will oblige, "three lines deep and booming," as George says.

It is hard to believe that only the two of us are left in the mess. We buried Edgar Abrams ourselves Friday afternoon but I still cannot imagine it. I also find it hard to believe that I am a corporal now, inexperience & all, but I will endeavor to turn in a good account of myself. I miss Charlie a very great deal; so does Bodley.

On Thursday afternoon we encamped about a mile from the Rappah-annock at a place called the Fitzhugh House, full of grand pines & history, because it used to be owned by the Washington family & I am told it is the place where he threw the dollar across the river, according to legend. The house is weathered & flapping now, & one thinks of the Nation itself, which was once grand & noble, in the days of the great George Washington & the others, but now is dilapidated & I suppose never will be the noble thing it once was, & instead of Washington & Adams & Jefferson we have Hooker & Burnside & Jeff Davis. I don't know about Lincoln yet & suppose it all depends on how the war turns out, but as of today I wouldn't lay any bets.

Fitzhugh House is somewhere below Fredericksburgh, & there was no great enthusiasm among the fellows at being back in that vicinity again. We were instructed that at 2 A.M. in complete silence we were to march down to the river, get into pontoon boats waiting there for us, cross under cover of darkness, surprise the rebels in their rifle pits, & hold a line of battle against the enemy as long as it would take for the engineers to lay a pontoon bridge and the rest of the Corps to get over the river & relieve us. We knew we were to come up through Fredericksburgh & keep Lee busy while the main body of the Army would cross the river at United States Ford, miles upriver, and cut in behind the rebels.

It was a grand plan as usual but when we got to the river bank at 1:30 A.M. in total silence, no boats. At 2 o'clock, the time for the attack, still no boats. We waited in silence on the edge of the river, knowing the rebels were only two hundred yards across the quiet water. We stood like cigar store Indians as the night passed & the water murmured. It was cold & we waited almost another three hours. The sky began to gray, & the sun came up, & then the rebels began to pop away at us through the fog & then the confounded boats came.

The big wagons loaded with pontoon boats were driven down to the river & the rebels had their fun. We waited there in anxiety & excitement & uncertainty & boredom, & to this was added the shameful & annoying confusion caused by the teamsters & horses not used to being under fire. The rebels picked off some of the horses & the rest of them took to rearing out of control, plunging in the traces & generally kicking up a pandemonium with us waiting there.

Our Regiment filed to a stone wall which gave us little cover because it was at the wrong angle, & the 24th fired a volley across the river, perfectly harmless to the rebels no doubt. We lay on our stomachs & fired across the river, but they did more damage to us than we could do to them because we were out in the open on our side of the river while the rebels had good cover & a steep bank, into which they had dug their rifle pits & could fire downward on us & we couldn't even see where they all were even after the fog lifted. The rebels had several regiments there perfectly posted & could have held off a division.

We were too exposed & so were drawn back while a Brooklyn regiment went forward to skirmish with them from behind what little brush & wood existed on the bank. Artillery was unlimbered & began to fire at the rebels, but it was like throwing rocks at flies & the rebels were not willing to be shelled out of there. This continued for about two hours with us watching & it was plain to all that it was useless.

Colonel Bragg was called back & we saw him talking to an officer we thought was General Reynolds, & when the Colonel came back he passed the word that Reynolds had chosen the Sixth to cross the river under the rebel rifles & turn the enemy out. I felt very proud that we had been chosen, but that is because I did not immediately realize what we were in for. The fellows knew, however, & there was low talk about the river getting plenty of Wisconsin blood to color it. Nobody shrank from their duty, but there was no enthusiasm for attacking three or four regiments across an open river & up a steep bank. Edwin said it was the same kind of insanity that always sacrifices the best men, just as Burnside had done in December. But on looking back I think that General Reynolds knew what he was doing & though it was a very long shot he is no fool.

The 24th Michigan was to follow us immediately, and then the rest of the Brigade was to come after. While we held on to the other bank the Division & then the whole Corps would follow when the engineers got the pontoons laid.

Bragg explained all this as usual & so we knew exactly what was expected of us & how to do it. We were to rush to the river in line of battle, deploy into columns of company & go for the boats, one company per boat. Four men who would be best at the oars were to stay up & row, & the rest of the men would lie down on the bottom.

The Captain chose two men immediately, the biggest & strongest, & before he got to the third I spoke out, saying it was not the biggest men but the most experienced who rowed best, and I had rowed boats on the Mississippi & St. Croix rivers since I was a small boy. He hesitated hardly a second & chose me, & another, with a dozen more to take our places when we were shot.

The boys took off their knapsacks & simply dropped them without much thought to where they were left, because it was assumed that not many of us would live long enough to want them again, & the few who did would be dying in rebel prisons this summer.

We formed & Colonel Bragg shouted, "Now for it, boys! By the right of companies to the front! March! *Run!*" & we went forward with a good, strong Badger yell. When we got close to the bank we evolved into columns on the run, never breaking stride, & the men threw themselves into the boat three deep. Several boys were shot in front of us but we four rowers ran in last & found the fellows had lain on the oars, which took some grunting & cursing to get out and into our hands, but we hit the water like paddle wheels.

Then followed the greatest moments of my life. The men were supposed to be down in the boats but everyone was so excited that as many as had room to do it rose up & fired at the rebels, yelling & shouting, & we four really put our backs to it & didn't feel it at all. I saw Bodley standing up on the gunwale of one of the other boats, cheering at the limit of his voice, & the boys were whooping & cheering like Indians.

I saw Edgar taking aim in front of me & the next thing he was leaning forward, blood pouring out of his left temple, & he sank down onto the bottom of the boat. We hit the bank & I jumped out to hold the boat while the fellows leapt into the water up to the waist. The rebels were firing but I didn't see anyone in the company get struck; behind us the 24th Michigan was pouring a steady fire at the rebels & up until we got onto the bank the artillery was pounding away too.

A few of the boys fired shots, & the whole Regiment scrambled onto the steep bank, working their way up using bushes & branches. As the last fellow sprang out of my boat I looked up and saw the rebels running for it up over the bank way above us, & saw our boys working their way up toward the top & I remembered how we had climbed the cliffs of Lake Pepin for eagle eggs year after year, & without getting my rifle out of the boat I splashed to the bank & climbed like going up a ladder.

I was one of the first to the top & saw the butternuts running every which way across level, open fields. I took out after an officer at full speed, not feeling anything of the rowing & climbing I had done & threw myself on him & rolled him over & demanded he surrender & when he began to say he would surrender only to an officer I shouted "Give me your pistol,——you!" & I took it myself & ordered him up & back to our lines. I quickly looked around & took out after another reb & when he saw me with the pistol he threw down his rifle & I motioned him back to the river & went after another.

What I remember next is finally hearing the order to reform & coming back to the trees & dropping down exhausted. Lieutenant Colonel Dawes was there & congratulated me for capturing a half dozen rebels including a second lieutenant & then reprimanded me for not obeying the order to stop pursuit.

All that took place in about fifteen minutes from the time Colonel Bragg gave the order to advance & the singularly magnificent excitement was the highest I have ever known & that grand & glorious quarter hour would have been worth sacrificing a whole lifetime to enjoy. I think I am like some of my Norse ancestors who went berserk in battle, but the other fellows were the same.

The next morning Colonel Bragg promoted me to corporal for bravery & efficiency in the face of the enemy, & because Edwin was dead.

Our march here was infernally hot & it's only the beginning of May. What will it be like here in midsummer? It all would not be so bad if everything were like our fifteen minutes at Fitzhugh Crossing, with no hot marching & missed rations & comrades killed & gone.

Maybe there will be nothing left of Forrest & Edwin & the rest of us except the old songs. But I can't imagine the folks at home singing "Home, Sweet Home" around the piano the same way we sang it here at Chancellorsville last evening, worn out & dirty & then this morning marching into line singing "Rally Round the Flag:"

> We are springing to the call of our brothers gone before,
> Shouting the battle cry of freedom,
> And we'll fill the vacant ranks with a million freemen more,
> Shouting the battle cry of freedom.

This will never be understandable to anyone but us.

What doesn't make sense to us is what Hooker thinks he's doing. There is a rumor that Stonewall Jackson was wounded or killed last night. And all right, the Eleventh Corps was whipped running yesterday, but now the First Corps is here & if I may say so we're worth five of the Eleventh Corps, & what is Hooker doing if not giving up? He is a good commissary & he made us back into the Army we were, but there is a hole in him somewhere.

I get despondent writing this, & pretty much disgusted & impatient. The answer is to quit writing. George is in bad condition.

May 5th, 1863

Sitting under the oilcloth next to George who is nearly dead drunk & I have had a nip myself & feel like writing up the whole war & setting it down for ages to come. Passed out a whiskey ration this morning & this is my first bout & Forrest will I have a headache tomorrow.

But I am writing anyway.

Had to sleep without blankets last night so we would be ready to repel an attack but I say let the *rebels* prepare to repel an attack that handsome rocking horse Hooker has let everything go to smash & it's another flat failure. Hot as hell during the day & then frigid at night. Fog this morning then hot as hell & now it's a ringing Thunder Storm well what else is there to do but have some whiskey & hope Hooker & all the crew in Washington go to h—-. Don't you know Forrest there's a rumor which is self-evidently true that the Army is going to retreat tonight. We haven't been whipped at all but our Generals have.

I have half a mind to give up waiting for a letter from her.

I feel like I've been writing all day.

May 8, 1863
Fitzhugh House Again

So here we are again, the same place we camped last month & nothing to show for it but killed, wounded, & captured. I am embarrassed to think of all the whiskey I drank, & I richly deserved the sick, pounding headache I had the last two days. I feel all right again today & suppose I won't turn down the next whiskey ration if it ever comes.

We got here hungry & wet as river rats & the smell of wet, sweaty wool reminded one of so many dogs & stray cats. But we will be all right again with a few days' rest here under the big pine trees. Father always says there is healthy air in pine trees & I think he is right. There is decent water nearby & in a few days we will be rested & fed & dried out & ready to go back at them again & maybe for nothing again.

I never felt as done up as I did the other evening, head blasting & stomach empty, & covered with mud in the rain & about ready to turn in the whole war for a new one. All of us felt that way but I don't think we looked it. Our Corps passed a couple of divisions waiting by the roadside, and those other divisions cheered when they saw the white banner with the red circle which is our Division, & then gave our Brigade the heaviest cheers I ever heard. We all stepped evenly and smartly, even spiritedly. I looked at the hundreds ahead of me, with their tall black hats and firm step. This Brigade has a stronger habit of mind than the others, & self-respect, & a good sense of shame & we will not allow ourselves to be less than what we resolve to be.

We are determined to make a good camp here, even if for only a day or two, with clean company streets festooned with evergreen branches, & leave the generals to wrack their little brains & the Congress to bring Washington City to a boil.

The Chancellorsville affair was a disaster & I admit their General Lee is a master at knowing how to take advantage of the idiocy of our generals, but let them come at us man to man on even terms, which is to say without the generals, and we will show our mettle, as the Country will see. We are defeated but not discouraged. Or rather Hooker was defeated.

Dawes had left a letter with a surgeon to the effect that the letter would be sent home if Dawes were killed in battle, & the surgeon let the letter be posted by accident, so Dawes's family back home think he's dead. Dawes is anxious but says his mother wouldn't believe he was killed even if he wrote & told her so himself. Likewise with the Army of the Potomac. Let the reports & newspapers say what they might; we aren't killed. Next time let the rebels attack the First Corps instead of the Eleventh, and we'll see.

May 26, 1863
White Oak Church, Virginia

We have arrived back from our Expedition, which was to find the Eighth Illinois Cavalry, which alas got itself lost & if we hadn't gone out to call for it might have got itself injured. The noble cavalrymen from the noble State of Illinois came in all unharmed, just when we had nearly driven ourselves to distraction with worry for them, & they were ever so tired but not hurt, poor boys. They have had such strenuous work, riding around this poor countryside stealing chickens & hogs & robbing starving families hereabouts of their last crusts. Noble fellows! How our hearts swell with pride to know that the Eighth Illinois Cavalry has been abroad in northern Virginia representing our United States, the Republic of Washington & Jefferson, stealing the last wretched plow horses of fatherless families living in one-room shacks, abusing the isolated & helpless starving women, riding through gardens & flowerbeds and breaking & scattering the miserable possessions of women & children left behind by their soldier fathers. We ought to sweep our company streets with those jockeys, but their filthy residue would soil our shoes.

June 7, 1863
Franklin's Crossing, Virginia

Two days under a very warm sun watching the rebels across the river. This is a change. Back at Fitzhugh Crossing we were getting along with the gray-backs capitally. I used the skill I acquired over a long boyhood on the Mississippi & St. Croix rivers to build little boats, complete with sails, for the purpose of exchanging coffee & newspapers for good Southern tobacco. I wish I could talk like those Johnnies. They're ignorant as the day is long, but they can talk so as to make us sound like Dutchmen & rubes, & they may not have been to school but they're sharp as carpet tacks & make you watch your thinking & not say anything they can poke fun at, though they manage to do it anyway.

Roland Eversoll from Prescott was caught sleeping on picket last week. Dawes is for shooting sleeping sentries, but let Eversoll off for being just a scared boy who will never do it again. Eversoll was sweating & shaking, sure he had seen his last daylight & nearly whimpering with fright & shame. Roland Eversoll is nearly two years older than I am.

None of this any more. No trading with the Johnnies & no mercy for sleeping pickets. The mood is different & the Army is different & the rebels across the river act different. They're alert & they look full of fight. We've got A. P. Hill's corps across the river, but the rumors are that the rest of Lee's army has moved out. No-one knows where. But you can sense there is something big on the taps.

The most sensible thing I have heard is that Longstreet's & Ewell's corps have moved up to Manassas again & there will be a Third Bull Run. They've succeeded twice before to make us chase our tails there, & I expect they'll manage it again. It could also be that Lee is on his way to Maryland again. This is not an auspicious time for that to happen, which is exactly what Lee knows.

Our two-year regiments are all going home. In the First Corps alone we've lost 5,000 men and are down to two-thirds strength. Fortunately the Brigade is whole & ready, & we say let them all go. But the Division is only us now and Cutler's Brigade. Cutler's rugged as a wolf. Our Division commander, Wadsworth, is a New Yorker but a good soldier, solid & strong & a fighter, who takes good care of the supplies & such. The two other divisions also have only two brigades each now. We are the First Division of the First Corps, and ours is the First Brigade, & the Sixth Wisconsin is officially the First Regiment. The men in A Company are wearing pretty stiff hats these days.

Reynolds was offered command of the Army but turned it down. There couldn't be a better Commander, but the Corps would lose him & get that stuffed shirt Doubleday from the Third Division. The rebels wouldn't be so saucy if Reynolds were in command of the Army of the Potomac. I don't think he will turn down the promotion when it is offered again, as it will be.

Colonel Bragg is sick & I think will have to be discharged. It is hard to lose him, but we couldn't have a better man than Dawes to take his place. It was Bragg who promoted me officially, but it was on the recommendation of Dawes. We will all do our best for the soldierly, quiet Dawes.

Now the order has come to go back to our Fitzhugh Crossing camp. Will the tomfoolery never end?

June 11, 1863
Fitzhugh Crossing

We came back here & then left again & now are back, all within five days. We're so ready that only the flies dare to attack us, & if we stay this ready in the hot sun day after day all we'll be good for is flies.

I swear the graybacks have gone off to war & all Hooker does is stay ready as a sparrow, & flits back & forth here & there & back & forward and up & down the Rappahannock. The rebels are moving & if Hooker wants to be sure of it all he has to do is ask us here on the river across from their pickets. It's something important & I say they're going North.

I am too blue to write more. Nobody will ever know what this war costs.

June 16, 1863
Centreville, Virginia

I am going to try to write faithfully again because now we know something important is coming & if we live to have children & grandchildren they should know what we ordinary men saw & did during the most momentous times of the Nation. We know now that everything will depend upon the next few weeks, & the soldier's instinct was right. Lee has crossed the Potomac.

There will be another Antietam, or worse, before it is over. If we lose this time it will be the end of the Republic. We are determined to defend our own North, & feel that we cannot be defeated fighting for our own firesides & homes as well as for our liberties and those of the Nation & world.

They say all three of Lee's army corps have crossed. Ewell is at Sharpsburg or beyond, & Hill & Longstreet must be close behind him. Where they will go we do not know. They may turn on Washington or Baltimore, or go on to Philadelphia.

There is great panic in the Government & in the North generally, but not in the Army. Hooker is not our darling any more but it must be said that the Army of the Potomac is moving faster & with more sense of purpose than anyone here has ever known. We are all going up to fight Lee, & we are moving hard & fast.

The past week we have been marching under a fiendish sun and through clouds & clouds of dust. The dust gets into our mouths & lungs & chokes us & there is no way to get away from it. We are all the color of gray chalk, from head to foot, knapsacks & blankets & hats included. Where sweat pours down & mixes with the dust we are caked with cracking mud like pigs. Yesterday when halt was called we slumped down, hungry as we were, & fell asleep though it was still afternoon.

The night before, we camped along the railroad track at Manassas Junction. I asked the fellows where the Gainesville battlefield was, for I knew it was nearby, & what the fight was like. Once again I declined the suggestion that I go visit Forrest's old Company in the Second Regiment.

We had only four hours of sleep along the track before we were ordered back into line.

The Army never has hurried like this. We passed groups & streams of exhausted, choking men in the dust, straggling from the commands in line of march ahead of us. I did not hear one word of serious complaint from anyone in our Brigade on that march nor all week. We would be ashamed to drop out of the march & mix with stragglers, & we know the rebs are brave, desperate, & well-generalled & we are not going to leave it to others boys to meet them alone, for we are determined that we shall throw them back & teach the Southern Chivalry something about Northern valor. If only our generals would learn their business & let us fight on fair terms.

Gen. Wadsworth ordered the headquarters valises thrown out of the ambulance carrying them, & had the knapsacks & rifles of the fellows who were worst off tossed in. I hope he didn't throw out his maps. He is a good man & the men know it & we will stand to our work.

I have tried for over a week to shake off the hypo after Annabel's letter telling me Nancy is to marry Steve Corbin. I don't know what to do. There is nothing I can do. I can't blame her, but I do. I can hardly believe it. My own life is not important now in any case. I feel that this is our Country's most desperate moment & that what each of us does in battle is desperately important. Sometimes I imagine that Forrest is marching along with us.

June 22, 1863

Guilford Station, Virginia

Maybe I was wrong again. We have been here for nearly three days. The Army has halted. Has Lee also halted, or do our generals simply not know where he is?

We needed this rest badly. We have been able to bathe in Broad Run & take care of our filthy clothing & clean our rifles & purge the dust from our haversacks & blankets.

Broad Run meets the Potomac not far from here they say. Must this not mean that Lee is still across the Potomac? Why are we resting here so long?

June 25, 1863
Maryland

Crossed the Potomac around noon. Compared to these green, tidy farms, Virginia was a Sahara. How good it is to be back in the old North again. People along the way come out. Crowds of children in a place called Poolesville, God bless them. The married fellows had tears in their eyes & I remember my living Sister & think of the Sister I never knew.

Orders to resume march.

June 27, 1863
Middletown, Maryland

Halted for the night. In camp within sight of South Mountain. Turner's Gap a few miles west. Remembered Forrest's letter & saw the place. The boys who were there last year told me about everything & looked at the graves of their friends, which are not settled but are covered over with green grass. Could not read most of the rough head boards & it seems when you die on the field you are soon gone without a trace left. My Brother's captain died here & I did not find his grave; perhaps the remains had been sent home, but as I said most of the writing was gone in the weather & sun of a year. The place is still there & the mouldering remains of the good fellows, but soon the memory will be gone entirely & it is earth to earth & dust to dust.

Did not fight a battle at Antietam, for which the fellows are grateful as they shudder to think of it again. Just over the Mt. there at Antietam my Brother breathed his last.

A fellow in Company I lost his mind from heatstroke last week we hear.

These past few days in drizzling rain & mud, a welcome relief from sun & dust. Cheerful & dreary at the same time. Not a long march today.

Men in good spirits though blankets all are wet & we smell like dogs.

There is more to think about but all I can do is lie down & sleep as we will be up & on the march again at dawn.

June 28, 1863
Frederick City, Maryland

Trying to write every day if even only a sentence or two. Never know what will happen though it looks like nothing for a good while yet. But Lee is in Pennsylvania & that is where we are heading & everyone knows what that means.

It is overcast & drizzling all the time, & it is in its way sombre though we are cheery & joking because it is good to march in this. Left this morning & have hurried ever since, though now we are halted & it wasn't a long march.

Hooker is out at last. McClellan is back in command. The old boys are crazy with relief & excitement. I do not know what it means but trust that Little Mac will handle us well; he knows about fighting Lee in the North.

I feel that the rebs are everywhere & nowhere, all at once.

June 30, 1863
Marsh Creek, Pennsylvania

Regiment was first to cross the Pennsylvania line. People all along the way even more enthusiastic than in Maryland. Beautiful, prosperous, green country. Like home but gentler & greener. Beautiful sky today, not hot at all but sun shining in beautiful blue sky. We are on home ground.

Just before crossing the Line some students from a College we passed near Emmitsburg marched along with us for a time. They were all older than I am but they spoke to us as to seasoned old veterans, as of course the fellows are. You could see they were bursting with wonder as to what it is like to be in battle and face guns & bullets. I swear they would have jumped into the column with us, but what use would they have been? When the firing starts they would either run off or stand & get shot uselessly; there is a difference between a soldier and a normal man or woman & I suppose the difference is that you have a different mind, & what is sane in one world is mad in the other. To us they were crazed young fellows & to them we knew something they were afraid they'd never find out. They all wanted to See the Elephant.

I would rather be in a college than here, but I wouldn't want to be one of them.

Our fellows generally did not admit to being afraid, & nobody asked me but I had no fear to admit as I have not been afraid yet. We are a week or thereabouts away from a great battle & I only want to get at it.

We saw the new commander yesterday. It is not McClellan after all but Meade, whom nobody knows much about. He was riding through the drizzle with hat brim down, covered by a poncho, all business & nothing very particular to look at.

Looks like we're going to stay here the rest of the day. Halted here at noon. No signs of moving. Cavalry passing along the road to the next town, Gettysburg, looking for the rebels but we hear they are in Harrisburg, & there is probably nothing to do for a while until the rest of the Army comes up & we go after them & chase them all around the countryside. No rebel cavalry seen for days, so Lee is gone off somewhere again. Next we will hear the rebels are in Philadelphia or behind us near Washington, more likely, & it will be another few days of forced marching to catch up.

Troopers saying the Johnnies are up ahead at Gettysburg in force, but cavalry are nervous & to them a company of cavalry is an army of infantry.

Just been told that the troopers are Buford's men & the same cavalry went past last year saying rebels were around just before the battle at Gaines-ville, & I might as well keep my mouth shut for tomorrow I'll have enough rebels for a lifetime.

July 1; early A.M.

Scribbling in line waiting for the rest of Brigade to form column of march. Writing because might not be time for a while & might be killed. Got up at dawn & cooked coffee & pork with the hardtack. Very quiet almost serious; ammunition passed out as Company prayed. We are going up to Gettys-burg where it is certain the rebels are in large numbers. Nobody knows how many but the boys say the rebels don't attack in little bits.

If I die please send this to NELS MIKELSON, PRESCOTT, WISCON-SIN, whoever finds it. You may read it but please send it; my family would be grateful. I have not written to them much & they deserve something.

Do not know if I will die, but this morning feel strange & have not known this before—have not been in a big battle & it's sudden news that the rebels are in big numbers. Promise to write & thank God if survive day; will do so tonight without fail, Amen.

evening July 1

Gettysburg, Penn.

Know I promised but can't now, will write tomorrow. Alive thank God. So many of the fellows dead; no Brigade left, just a handful here & getting shelled.

later

Slept for a while even with noise & shelling & between alarms but dreams as bad as the fighting. I have barely enough light but will scribble whether it can be read or not. Will write because my mind feels weak & it is better to be doing something. Will probably be dead tomorrow anyway. Rebels will attack at dawn & that will be all for us, but rest of Army will beat them back, damn them, I know it.

Morning marched five or six miles on road.

Weather comfortable, early morning cool & pleasant; very little fog which dissipated soon & gave bright clear day. Fields were green with grass or gold with ripened grain. Orchards looked good for time of year.

Field music was placed in front of regiment as we stepped off, drums & fifes. Regiment hasn't had a Band since last year. Battery B waited alongside road as we passed & we traded compliments, such as "Tell the Johnnies we'll be right along," & we answered they had better stay where they were as the weather in Gettysburg might be unsettling to their delicate sensibilities, & they did cheer us as we passed with rifles gleaming & firm step. Their guns shone brightly in the morning light.

Marched an hour or so before hearing cavalry engaged at Gettysburg a few miles ahead. Marched for another hour or more hearing rattling and thunder, constant & steady though not heavy. Felt rising excitement & put away strange feelings & wanted to get into the fight, which we knew we would do soon unless the rebs broke off before we arrived.

While marching George told me he felt he would not survive the battle & asked me to send letters he insisted on giving me. I laughed though nervously & told him it was nonsense & now wish I hadn't, but I did take the letters, which I still have, though worse for wear. George said, "I know what I'm talking about & have not felt like this before. Vernon I *know* I will not come out of this fight alive." I chided him & reminded him he was a veteran & shouldn't be talking like a girl, & now hope he and God forgive me, but I was just trying to cheer him up as I half believed him. Had heard of such instances being true & now believe.

It was Cutler's turn to lead the Division on the march so we were second. Came very close to the town; remember passing big hill to the right &

then a peach orchard at the roadside. Here we saw the Corps commander Reynolds riding up & Wadsworth with his silver hair & kepi cap riding beside him at a gallop with staff. In a moment the colors were uncased & the baggage dropped. The Brigade Guard joined our Regiment & officers except Dawes dismounted & orders came for face left & quick time across the fields, which we did while loading our rifles & fixing bayonets.

Gens. Reynolds & Wadsworth rode ahead toward the firing & we trotted after. The firing was pretty close, & we saw soon what it was as we ascended a gradual rise running across our front. The Cavalry was in line across yet another rise or ridge which ran parallel to the one we were on, with fields in between. As we reached our rise the order was given to advance by the right & we continued along the ridge toward a big orange brick building with a white cupola. I have since found out it is our own Lutheran seminary.

We were the last regt. in line. A staff officer from Meredith came up & we heard him deliver the order to Lt. Col. Dawes to form line & prepare for action. The other regiments also had been ordered to face left in line of battle & advance on the double-quick. Long Sol rode near the front regt., which was the Second Wisconsin. We all swept down the slope and across the fields & as we did so the cavalry was coming back & remounting, one man holding four horses & the other three scrambling to them. They galloped off through us & around us, going the direction we had come from; it was not a rout of them but clearly a planned retreat now that the Infantry had arrived.

Across the fields we saw a road & beyond it on the next ridge a large Confed. brigade was advancing in line of battle & that was where Cutler deployed, across that road.

Ahead of us our regts. were on the rise taking down a fence & charging, the Second in advance & the other three regts. like stair steps coming after, & then us. Directly across the fields from the Second was a woods & beyond it a big white barn with fences. The Second went into that woods & partly across the pasture adjoining the barn where we could no longer see them. At that moment a staff officer came galloping & told us General Doubleday was in command of the Corps & wanted our Regiment to halt where we were. He didn't say that General Reynolds had been killed but we have since found it out. Reynolds was our best & we lost him at the outset.

The Second had gone ahead into the woods & rebs were in there with two regimental flags flying in line of battle. We saw the Second's Colonel, Fairchild, go down & then be helped up holding his left arm; he came back across the fields & passed through us on his way to the rear, blood all over his arm from the elbow down & covering his hand & across his trouser leg. He has lost the arm I'm sure but no more if lucky.

The woods where the Second charged were thinned & mature & had no underbrush. We could see the Second go right into the smoke from the rebels' rifles. From where we watched it seemed the Second ran over them. Our boys slowed & advanced firing, some of them evidently beyond the woods, extending to the right and around the rebels' flank & about then the Seventh and the Nineteenth struck the rest of the Confed. brigade out to the left of the woods. As these two regts. went forward the 24th on the extreme left crossed the stream and hit the rebels beyond their right, enfilading them. The rebels had our regiments on both their flanks & in front, a thinner line than theirs but made of iron & we could hear the Badger yell from where we were.

Our view became obscured by smoke but it was plain that the rebels were retiring in haste & confusion & before long big groups of butternuts were herded back through us as prisoners. One of them was a rebel general, dressed in fine uniform with gold braid & high collar, in grand contrast to us & also to his own ragamuffins herded back with him. He didn't have his sword & he looked irate but we didn't have time for his feelings as over the road Cutler's brigade was being shot down & forced back.

They had been struck shortly after our Brigade had charged, & I didn't see it, but now you could see the rebel line at an angle on Cutler's flank, enfilading his brigade just as the 24th had done to the rebels in front of us. Cutler's regts. began retiring, as did the battery which had been just across the road.

We were halted facing the ridge & woods where our regts. were engaged, when the order came to face right & in column advance on the double quick. This we did, moving directly to the road. Some officers hastened across the field in front of us carrying what was evidently a body wrapped in a blanket. We know now it was General Reynolds.

Lt. Col. Dawes was riding ahead of us & his horse reared up, then settled back on her haunches. Meanwhile Dawes had been thrown to the ground & it looked as if he had been shot too, but he sprang up. We gave him a cheer. I think the wounding of his horse saved Dawes's life, as not many survived the next few hours, least of all mounted officers.

Cutler's men hurried across our front beyond the road & the battery limbered up and pulled out barely ahead of the rebels. On our side of the road two of Cutler's regts. saw us coming and stayed where they were.

Dawes ordered a deployment by the right flank as we approached the turnpike, & we evolved into line of battle on the double quick, now facing the road. We advanced to the fence along the road & the order was given to fire. We rested our rifles on the top rail. Across the turnpike the rebels were rushing after the part of Cutler's Brigade which had retired, & when we fired we took them in the flank & their whole line shuddered.

It was the first I had fired in battle & my excitement was extreme. I loaded & fired again & everyone was cheering & reloading as the rebels skedaddled back and disappeared. We thought they had retreated entirely & Dawes ordered us up & over the fence. As we did it the rebels appeared out of nowhere & leveled a grievous volley at us, which hit us as we climbed the fence. Fellows pitched into the road & back off the fence & at that moment I heard the sickening fatal thud & there was George dropping forward from the fence onto the road. I knelt and turned him over & he had been shot in the middle of the face & was barely recognizable & instantly dead. I grasped my rifle again & dashed to the fence on the other side of the road & was over it in an instant, but there we stopped.

The rebel fire was like a strong wind. Our fellows were loading & shooting & falling & I shot & reloaded & shot & reloaded entirely unaware of bullets & I felt no sense of danger; I felt like iron or stone, but also I couldn't go forward. The graybacks were down in an embankment behind perfect cover & pouring into us a terrible fire. I was for a few moments next to Jim Kelly from Prescott. He moaned as he was hit & I looked just long enough to see the awful red splash on the left side of his chest, and he sank back against the fence. The terrible thuds of the minie balls struck all over along the fence, & the men were dropping & you had a sense of the regiment getting broken apart & shot down, when the order was shouted "Align on the colors! Close up on the colors!"

In a moment we rushed toward the rebels, who came up over the embankment now as one man & fired. It must have been a hundred fifty yards from the fence to the embankment, & we ran forward in a ragged line. I screamed & shouted as if it would deflect the bullets & kill the enemy. Billy Faust staggered & I slowed to straighten him up, & he was hit again & I had to drop him. I had fallen behind a few steps but caught up just as we reached the embankment, which was a railroad cutting, with rebels in it packed thick as hornets. Their color was to my left & Bodley Jones flew at it & was shot in the breast & then another man lunged down for it & was shot in the face & the man who had jumped down next to him swung his rifle at the head of the rebel who had fired the shot & smashed his skull & there was blood all over him & I was down with the rebels having thrust the bayonet but the rifle was wrenched from my hands & I grappled with the man & then our boys were shouting "Throw down your muskets! Throw down your muskets!" A lieutenant from another of the Regiment's companies was on the ground in front of the rebels' flag but one of our boys was holding it.

Down the line some rebel officers were lifting their swords to Lt. Col. Dawes
& the rebels were throwing down their rifles & raising their arms. Someone
was ordering them to surrender & march down the cut. All of them around
me obeyed the order. I was surprised that we hadn't simply shot them down
right and left in the cut, where they were packed like pigs in a poke. I would
have if I had been up on the embankment instead of down in the cut. I was
terrifically excited; it was a few moments before I realized I was being held
back by two of our own fellows.

The rebels' faces had been wide-eyed & afraid & enraged with a complete loss of self-possession, which I realized only when it was over. We had
been down there clubbing and stabbing & shooting & not knowing what
was happening. You find out what you are when you have suddenly forgotten what you are I guess.

I climbed out of the cut & the rebels were all streaming back to the
far ridge, both on our side of the pike & across it on the other side of the
big white barn. Our regts. had whipped them in the woods & so had we
whipped them where we were. Major Hauser marched perhaps two hundred fifty prisoners out of the railroad cut and back toward the Seminary.

Across those hundred fifty yards to the pike, and in the pike, our boys
lay scattered on the ground, & in the field across the road perhaps hundreds
walked & staggered & crawled back toward the Seminary. Our Regt. was cut
to half & hardly looked like a regiment. The flag was still held up, ragged &
blotted with smoke. The field was clearing & our fellows quickly went among
each other calling out names & I went back to the pike meaning to go back
to George, but on the way I found Eversoll, who had been spared the firing
squad, crying for water, shot in the abdomen & screaming in pain. It was
no use to give him water & he was out of his mind & I could do nothing for
him & was feeling weak & dizzy myself. Farther on I found two men from
our Company. Anderson, from across the River, Stillwater or nearby, had
been shot in the chest; his messmates had propped him up and were trying
to give him water but he had fainted. Then I found Will Bright lying against
the fence, shot in the left thigh & losing blood at an awful rate. I got his
tourniquet from his pocket & tied it & one of his messmates came along &
gave him water & said he couldn't find the other two. Willie was able to talk
but the shot was in the center of the thigh & his messmate looked almost as
pale as he did, & I fear it means amputation at best, but he didn't look good.

I was going back for Bodley and George when we were ordered into
line & this took much time as we had become mixed up & were scattered all
over the pike & field & railroad cut, & then we had to move up toward the
ridge across which the rebels had retreated. They had gone back through another shallow valley & now our whole line, the two brigades of our Division,

was on the ridge with the white barn, across a thin front of about three quarters of a mile or so. It was about noon & we had fought our battle & had defeated an equal or superior force of Lee's army. There must have been a thousand rifles lying in the railroad cut, *& they weren't ours.*

The rebels had left a solid line of skirmishers on the barn ridge, but we cared nothing for them & went forward & pushed them back off it & they backtracked across the shallow valley & I would just as soon have chased them into the creek there, but we halted & the enemy continued to the next ridge. There were rebel batteries on that ridge & they opened on us as soon as we formed line. There was no doubting that they intended to stay where they were until supports came up & then come at us again, but the brigades we had whipped weren't the ones who were going to do it & we were of a mind to stay where we were.

The fellows said again we had been pushed forward in front of the Army & hoped this time we were going to get supports before the rebs came on again with another division or more. I said, We'll lick them again, but when I looked at what was left of us stretched thin on that ridge the heart went out of me a little. We had time to look back toward our friends lying in the valley and on the pike.

The field we had marched over to the ridge was covered with rebel dead & wounded. We had done them worse than they had done us, but we could see columns of them to the west, and where was the Army of the Potomac?

It was here, on this ridge, we said to ourselves. We are the Army of the Potomac. Word was passed that when our Brigade had charged through those woods on our left they had heard the rebels exclaiming, "It's them blackhat fellers agin! That ain't no militia; it's the Army of the Potomac!"

We lay in line of battle until one or two o'clock. We couldn't go back for our friends. Cutler's brigade had re-formed & was back on the rise with us to our right. We were still a quarter-mile from the rest of our Brigade, which was in the woods; in between was the Pennsylvania Junior Bucktail Brigade. The rebs had put a battery just south of the turnpike on the other side of the little river & it sent shells bursting over us hot & heavy, though about half were duds. Their artillery & the constant firing from their heavy line of skirmishers & sharpshooters is what made Dawes order us to our bellies behind the ridge. We had to save what was left for what was coming.

When they came it was in double and triple lines, six or eight brigades wide, & they stretched a mile, overlapping our single line on both flanks. When they stepped out of the woods on the third ridge in that formation we rose up & formed line & waited for the command.

We had a battery up with us—not Battery B, which was back on the Seminary's ridge, but it too was firing at the long rebel lines. The rebels had five or six batteries but ours were better served & the ammunition wasn't full of duds; ours did damage to those lines. But the lines were pretty, if only they weren't coming to kill us. They were nearly straight & even like a great, mile-long bow, with the ends bent forward. It looked like a dress parade, with flags a few paces ahead of the lines. There were many flags.

We had only four half used up brigades & I think one more out to the left of the woods but I couldn't see them, & the rebels were coming at us with twice that many fresh ones. The boys acted like they had seen it before & it didn't scare them, & I knew it was we either stand & fight or we run & I was not going to run. Forrest didn't run & I was no better than he.

Every time one of our shells hit their line they closed up without pause & came on. I was nervous & wanted to run out & fight them & at the same time wanted to be elsewhere watching, & the fellows acted calm but were murmuring whether they knew it or not, "Come on, come on; we'll let you have it presently," & so on. When the word came to fire the whole line it seemed tore off at the same time & the rebs wavered but came on. We reloaded & as I was ramming our Brigade in the woods was already firing again. I whooped for them & our Regiment crashed another volley & I was still not ready.

Then our line was firing at will & the rebels finally stopped advancing. In front of us & Cutler they stayed where they were & fired back. Their whole line was clouded by smoke. The smoke from our rifles drifted up & off the ridge, making the sky, which was mostly sunny, seem faintly overcast. I looked over on the left & saw the rebels trying to cross the stream in front of our Brigade in the woods, but no rebels got across.

To our immediate left the Bucktails were hardest pressed, with three lines of the enemy still coming on. I kept firing but looked too, & saw the Pennsylvanians go forward in a charge; a few minutes later they were coming back but stood their ground & the rebels came on & when I looked again the rebels were back a little but crowding forward with their heavy lines. The flag of the Bucktails was waving front & center, & the rebels were coming on again. When I looked again the Bucktails were charging & for a moment the lines were mixed.

But then the Bucktails were forced back. The rebels were still stalled in front of us & Cutler. The old Brigade was like an iron gate in front of the stream. The rebels in front of us backed off & re-formed. I saw the far right of their line across the stream on the other side of the woods. The old Brigade was flanked on that side & soon would get fired on from the left & rear. Next to us the Bucktails retreated, leaving the ground covered with blue, &

the color bearer was standing in the turnpike holding the flag alone, shaking his fist at the rebels. He went down with the flag an instant later. The rebels now moved through on our left & wheeled so as to fire into the woods.

You could see one of our regiments changing front to fire at the rebels who had forced the Bucktails back. I saw then that there had been another brigade to the left of our Brigade, on the other side of the woods, because they were streaming across the shallow valley toward the Seminary. Now the rebels were getting three sides of a box around the woods & the Iron Brigade was alone. A Penn. regt. advanced to cover their retreat.

The rebels came on in front of us again. This time Cutler's brigade started to withdraw. They were overlapped on their right. The woods was surrounded on three sides by heavy rebel lines firing sheets of musketry, but none of them had crossed the stream in front yet.

Nobody had sent orders to our Regiment, I suppose because we were apart from our Brigade & nobody important knew it. Rebels were past us on both sides now, opening a fire on both flanks & we were in a bottle. The other regts. were withdrawing from the woods, but slowly. You saw them with flags still waving, moving back some paces while loading then facing about & firing as if on the parade ground, with men falling all the time. I saw this on the run, after Dawes gave the order to follow him into the railroad ditch, else we would have been cut down by the rebels on both flanks as if running a gauntlet. The cut gave us cover, but we didn't stop as the rebels had. We kept on toward the Seminary ridge at full speed. The battery that had been next to us galloped back along the pike in the open & the rebels were shooting at them.

I was about last to go into the cut & felt like I wanted to give the rebs one more lick, but followed & we ran like a long string. Not all of the railroad cut was banked up on both sides & as we ran the rebel artillery tried to find us & plowed up wagonloads of dirt which showered us. Several of the men were hit & you had to leap over them.

When we got to the Seminary ridge we were worn out & desperate for water. It was not terribly hot but the air was very humid & you just could not sweat enough.

There was a breastwork of rails & felled trees on the ridge, left by troops that were no longer there. All of us mixed together behind it, Cutler's & the Junior Bucktails, & on the left the old Brigade was still marching up the slope in perfect order, turning & firing & falling, and with them what was left of that brave Penn. regiment, & on the far left waited the brigade that had skedaddled.

We took our stand with Battery B, which was pounding the rebels as they dressed their lines & brought up artillery to the ridge we had left. We had another battery down the line. We all waited as the rebels came on. Even Battery B held fire.

The rebels came on if anything more perfectly than before, with not a ripple in their lines, which stretched not as long as before but way off out of reach of our right & left flanks. From where we knelt behind the rails we could see a mile-long line of rebels coming down at right angles to us from the north. In front of them were masses of our troops falling back & running toward the town. We hadn't known it but another battle had been going on. They were the Eleventh Corps, that had been surprised & routed at Chancellorsville. We were outflanked by a mile on the north. But if the Eleventh was here, maybe more of the Army was coming. Our business was to hold on. Dawes came along the line saying we had to give the Army time to come up & secure the heights on the other side of town. I looked back & saw the heights, including the big hill I had noticed before we left the Emmitsburg Road in the morning, but I didn't see any of our flags on them.

When word came to fire, the artillery let loose as if one arm had pulled all the lanyards together, and a sheet of fire & smoke burst out all along our line. Through the smoke we saw the rebels in scattered groups; our fire had cut into their first line like a scythe & their dead & wounded were down & writhing in an even row. War is the most damnable thing there is. They reformed & we shouted "Come on, Johnnie! Come on!" & they came on.

We put up a steady fire & the rebels halted & returned it. Because they had us on three sides again the bullets seemed to come from everywhere. We could do nothing but face front, & from then on I knew nothing of what was happening north of town. The rebels stopped about half way & then they really began to flail the Battery. Their artillery turned on them too, & the boys in the Battery were in a maelstrom of bullets & shell fragments & solid shot.

They worked the guns like machines as if there was nothing coming at them, firing & sponging & loading & ramming & sighting & firing like clockwork around the guns but at terrific speed & the guns were belching out bursts of flaming double-shotted loads of canister. The rebel infantry in front of them were trying to pick off the gunners but were falling in rows when the lanyards were pulled. Bullets struck & clanged off the shining guns & shot & shell smashed fragments of wheels into the air & horses screamed & plunged. Men running back to the caissons were shot & the orderly sergeant calmly replaced them, giving men double duty; a corporal in front of the gun immediately beside us leaned forward to sight the gun wiping blood from his face, bareheaded, hair flat & streaked with blood; the man with the rammer had to sponge & load by himself, & ram the charge; behind us a caisson blew up with a terrific impact & more horses lay torn & screaming;

& when the man ramming the gun got hit & went down I couldn't stand still any more & ran to the gun & took up the rammer & plunged in the sponge & a man handed me a charge of canister & before I could grab the rammer another man shouted, "Another!" & he knocked off the charge against the wheel of the gun & I took the canister from him & pushed it into the barrel.

I reached for the rammer & as I plunged it down the barrel I saw the section's lieutenant behind the gun, held up by two men. I pulled the rammer, looking at the man, who was shouting directions at me—"Jump back!" he shouted & I did & the corporal pulled the lanyard & the gun bucked & blazed with a deafening crack. The Lieutenant shouted "Sponge!" & I leaped to my feet & grabbed the sponge & he shouted "Water!" & I almost dipped the ramming end into the bucket, turned the stick & then rammed the sponge down the barrel. Bullets seemed to fill the air with that cutting hissing sound & the lieutenant was struck again & still stood up, bleeding from hip & ribs & I saw his foot was turned sideways bleeding with dirty white bone sticking out. "Double canister!"

Behind us horses reared & drivers shouted & cursed & the rebels came on & the lanyards were jerked on ours & the next gun & the rebels were blown to pieces. They came on again with a rush then & I rammed the second charge & the lieutenant shouted "Feed it to 'em, God damn 'em!" as the gun roared & bullets came from the left across us. The Regiment was pulling back. I sponged & pushed in a charge & another & this time the rebels were shouting & bayonets fixed only fifteen yards & some aiming & "Feed it to 'em!" the lieutenant shouted again & the gun blasted right beside me & I was on it immediately with the sponge & pushed in a charge & when I turned for the second charge saw only the corporal was there, the others were pulling back & the caisson was coming & driver waving two men to raise the trail onto the limber & the lieutenant was being carried off & Lieutenant Stewart, the battery commander, was shouting in the brogue we all knew, "Limber up now! You"—he pointed at me, "get out of here! We're getting out of here." I saw the other guns careening away; I rammed the one charge looking at the rebels not ten yards from me. I could see their wide-eyed faces & screaming mouths. "Feed it to 'em, God damn 'em!" I shouted leaping from the muzzle as he pulled the lanyard & the gun blasted the canister & rammer & all & I dashed to help connect the trail. Four men jumped for the limber & the horses were whipped & Stewart & I ran alongside & he jumped on & I picked up a black hat not knowing whether it was mine or not but damned if I was going to leave it for the sons of bitches & then I saw a cavalry carbine as I was running & dropped the hat & picked up the carbine & jumped on. A reb was pulling at me & I swung back with the carbine & kept my grip on a man's hand holding me on.

The horses were whipped to a wild run & now I could see that the rebels following the Eleventh Corps were getting into the town before us. Our Brigade was in formation, not running, the few of them left which looked like a couple of companies & to our left the rebels were running at the gun in a crowd & I used my carbine as a club & we galloped wildly with the gun bouncing & flying & the men throwing their empty pistols & I threw the carbine & held on.

We charged through the streets with bullets hissing around us & striking the limber & flinting off the gun & the second man had to help hold the reins & we drove through the streets & up to the cemetery & held on as all six of the battery's guns galloped up the hill to the brick gate where our fellows were waiting & digging & there was a line of fresh troops waiting & digging earthworks & we knew the rest of the Army was arriving. The rebels were not coming up after us, but on both sides of us boys with First Corps patches were streaming up the hill & into the cemetery & were being directed to re-form. We got off the limber & all three of the men riding on the bench were holding the reins, wounded all three & bleeding & had to be helped down.

It is midmorning & the rebels have not come on here, though the battery has been here all night & morning firing & the rebels hammered us during the night. While I have been writing this shot & shell have been coming from all directions & plowing up graves & smashing headstones, but there has been no attack in earnest & the Army is here & digging in & now we know why the Iron Brigade was where we were. These heights cannot be taken by the rebels & we know it, & we also know they'll try, but this time they will not have us because as long as we stay here it will be no generals only soldier to soldier and we will not be moved. The Brigade has been ordered to the hill behind where I am now, but I am to stay with the Battery until and if some of the men make their way back & the guns can be fully manned.

The 24th Michigan is nearly gone & our fellows are dead on the field or wounded in the hands of the rebels. We did lose the ridge but I swear we gave them twice worse what they gave us. The Army has come up & is here & the rebels had to get us yesterday or not at all & have only their rows of dead & wounded to show for it. The men around me are in better spirits than we were at the beginning of the march yesterday. But I am not. Bodley is gone. Charlie is dead, too. They're all gone, my friends—George and Billy and all my friends. I am alone now.

We got the rebels this time, god damn them. We stopped the superior gentlemen this time. We stopped them dead.

I am exhausted & exhilarated, enraged and full of grief both at once, proud & sick to my stomach. The rebs came on like lions, we fought them like righteous angels, & we all shot each other down like dogs. If the God of our Fathers came to Gettysburg yesterday, he lies dead on the field. He will never trouble nor comfort me again.

Wilderness

July 3
Cemetery, Gettysburg

They're beaten. The fields in front of the Second Corps are covered with
rebel dead & wounded. Their magnificent charge has been repulsed. Our
battery is ordered to cease fire as the rebels have all gone back to the woods
on the Seminary ridge. We have all been shouting at each other not only
because we have thrown them back, but because we are half-deaf from the
last three hours of battle noise & battery fire.

General Meade is riding along the line & everyone cheers mightily. He
is the first general to handle this Army right. From first to last here we have
been put against the rebels on something like fair terms & have punished
them.

There must be three thousand rebels on the fields in front of the Second
Corps line & around that group of trees & along a stone fence surrounding
it. Another two thousand rebels in their gray & butternut rags have been
taken to the rear as prisoners. I saw two of their generals shot down.

We could see everything from up here, just as yesterday's battle was
perfectly visible to us as far as the smoke permitted. It was on our left in
front of the two hills down our line. The rebels came all along our left, &
for a few minutes got up to the place in our center where the attack was
made today. Yesterday it was Longstreet's Corps, we're told. The battle went
on for three hours, until dusk. They got across the road in front of us and
held on, but that's all they got. In the twilight our lines went into the smoke
& we heard Union cheers & with the darkness it was over. Back behind us
our Brigade was sent to re-enforce some trenches when the rebs came up
there in the evening. They came at us here in the cemetery too & got up
among another battery & for some moments we thought they had fooled us
again, but our infantry came back & threw them out with General Meade's
compliments.

Then today at about noon they opened all their batteries on us at once
& it was the most terrible bombardment imaginable & we answered them
in kind & gave better than we took, & I helped serve this Battery's guns. We
lost a caisson blown up & a half dozen men were hit & some horses. Then
the artillery stopped & their infantry came out of the woods a half mile wide
in three lines. We opened on them from here & everywhere, & it's a wonder

any of them got to our infantry line, but thousands of them did, & then it was the wildest confusion you could imagine. We couldn't do anything but watch, & watch we did anxiously, but they had no supports behind them. How did they expect to throw this whole Army off our position, without supporting an attack made by only two or three divisions? Did they think that was all they needed to make the Yankee army run? They learned different, & I daresay the rebs will never make the mistake of underestimating us again. Southern arrogance was dealt a blow today & they had better look upon us as equals as we look upon them. I must say the great General Lee made as bad a blunder today in that attack as ever one of our generals has made, as bad as Burnside did at Fredericksburgh, with less excuse because Lee isn't stupid, just arrogant I guess. We are ordered to go back to the ammunition trains to replenish so I will write more tonight or tomorrow.

July 4, 1863
Gettysburg

Been sent back to the Brigade so I guess I am not an artilleryman after all.

Lee's army is still across those fields, though they've pulled back from in front of the hill & cemetery & town. I thought they would be gone today. Lee wants us to make the same mistake he made yesterday & attack them over the open fields straight ahead, but we are finding that our Meade is no fool. The politicians & newspapers will say Meade just sat here today like McClellan without "destroying" Lee, but they are ignorant. Lee is waiting for us & the rebels are still full of fight, & our army is nearly as used up as the rebels.

I have been told the Second has lost three quarters & so did the Seventh, & some companies are down to three men, & officers are missing everywhere. The rebs have Cols. Fairchild & Morrow. General Meredith was wounded but taken to one of our field hospitals.

Our Regt. lost half almost exactly. Today is Dawes's twenty-fifth birthday.

I went to the 24th Michigan's camp this morning. Their counting shows they lost 80 per cent. There is hardly anything left of them. Their camp looks like a camp of two companies. The Iron Brigade saved the army Wednesday & look what it cost us. We are no more! Who will remember us? They will remember the battles of Thursday & especially they will remember the great Charge of yesterday, but who will remember the Iron Brigade now that it is gone?

Dark this afternoon & pouring rain, as if the windows of heaven have opened to extinguish the fires of hell, & for us & the wounded it means being caught in both—the Fires & the Flood.

I have been wondering today for the first time what we will get if peace is restored & the Union is restored & the Southerners are humbled if that's possible & all the slaves are free. We will never get our old country back. I will never get my Brother and my friends back. Will my old boyish self be restored, and will his old imagined God rise again? It has all been sacrificed.

July 5, 1863
Gettysburg, Penn.

Lee's army is gone & the Army of the Potomac has begun to follow but I am left behind, second in command of a detail from the Regt. to seek out our wounded & to bury our dead, & will rejoin the Regt. when everything is done. Dawes himself chose the detail & I am not happy about it, but the boys say Shut your mouth it's better to stay here helping our friends than to go & fight Lee again, as we are sure will happen before he gets to the Potomac.

Talked to some rebel prisoners this morning & was shocked to hear their hatred for us. Not like the boys we met across the Rappahannock; these were mad & full of contempt for Yankees & claimed they mostly whipped us. I can't understand the Southerner, who one moment is a cordial & gracious & fun-loving boy, & the next in a hundred ways reveals his deep hatred for us & contempt. It is a great misfortune to think you are better than someone else, & here these rebels think they're better than we are & they're not worth a tinker's dam themselves.

The little Brigade formed & marched this morning & I have never seen the like nor have I ever witnessed such an expression of respect & honor, for when they passed other troops they were not cheered; rather the division they passed removed their caps & stood in silence.

Buried many men today. Vast plain of dead bodies & dying fellows & wounded stretching like oceans of wheat with only a few clumps of men here & there to glean them, bending here & there to take them up on stretchers. Have vomited twice from the stench. Haven't been sent to bury First Corps dead. This afternoon we are to go into town to find our fellows in buildings there & make reports. Am too depressed & sick to write more. Am told will get used to this. I hope not.

July 5, evening
Gettysburg, Penn.

I was brought up to believe in God. Person in town directed me to College Lutheran Church on Chambersburg Street as hospital for First Corps wounded & went with two fellows. Town is badly wrecked. Fences gone, houses with shell damage & bullet holes & trampled yards. The church is really called St. Paul's. Hadn't known until July 1st that there are Lutherans here, but find that this is a Lutheran state, with the first Lutheran seminary in America, etc., & there are three Lutheran churches in town.

St. Paul's is a handsome bldg. with a long flight of stairs up, but inside it is sickening. A grand place under other circumstances, large & light, about four times the size of our church at home. But men lay & sat & slumped together on the pews, & boards had been placed across the pew backs to make beds for the men.

It's a First Corps hospital, but not 1st Division. Stayed a few minutes to watch surgeons cut arms & legs, & saw a fellow my age with fingers on both hands badly mashed & some nearly severed, sitting & holding his wrist, leaning with head against pew back. Surgeon came up to him. Surgeon had white shirt rolled up to elbows, with apron & arms to elbows & beyond soaked red with fresh & not fresh blood. Had dark rings under eyes. Lifted the fellow's hands & took knife from apron & with several hard motions on the pew cut off seven fingers & used knife to slide them onto floor. I heard only two of them hit the floor, as the moaning & screaming & crying for help & water was incessant. Had noticed piles of limbs outside of windows & saw orderlies throwing cut arms & legs out the windows. Smell of chloroform & sour blood & festering flesh filled sanctuary. Told to go to Seminary, where we had fought Wednesday, to look for 1st Division wounded.

If we have the evil of Adam inside us & it has to be purged out, then perhaps this is as fine a method as any. If we have been forgiven by Jesus Christ then why do the fellows have to go through this, & why are their arms & legs piled up spoiling in the sun & fellows screaming & stuck to pews with their own blood, & if the idea is to let us chop ourselves up like that fellow's fingers then what is all this talk about Christ's redeeming us? If the idea is to punish us, I can understand it; but what had that fellow done worth chopping his fingers off for? & he was better off than most others in that church.

All I can say is that we must have done something more hideous than we know, to get punished like this. You can talk about sin & redemption all you want, but I didn't see any guilty fellows there unless we are all guilty, nor did I see a kind & forgiving God. What I saw was suffering farther than anybody can deserve or imagine & no God except perhaps a terrible one. Some will say I should thank God that I am alive but I won't, because that would be same as thanking Him that Charlie and Billy and Bodley and all the rest are dead, & my Brother too, & thanking Him that all these men are lying in the hospitals & rotting on the fields. I am sick of the theologians & sick of the tent preachers: they haven't been here & everything they say works fine until you get here. The one thing I can't figure is that my Brother saw all this too, and he still believed. Maybe he never believed in the false god I believed in. If so I want to know that mystery of his.

Went to Seminary & found our wounded spread through all the rooms. Outside was a pile of legs & arms like bleeding meat or like wood, crawling green & black with bottle flies, enough limbs to cover a wagon bottom, piled at the door we went in. Smell there nearly as bad as at the church, mixed with whisky on some doctors' breaths, but who can blame them as they have been working day & night without rest or food. One told me he had been on his feet for 34 hours & his legs were swollen & his hands hardly seemed part of his body. Still he had to cut & saw & tie off arteries. There was a family who lived in that building as caretakers, & they cooked & helped the doctors. Don't know how they stood it. A boy in the family was employed by the drs. in carrying out the cut off legs & arms, & it was he who had thrown them outside.

Found Levi Stedman shot through right lung; Abram Fletcher with leg broken by minie ball & amputated already, seemed not good. Lew Eggleston had a ball in hip, looks bad. Men shot in abdomen in extreme pain & thirst & cry to be taken out of suffering, knowing they are doomed. Some from the Second Wisconsin I took down names & towns: Charles Brandstetter, wound in left side, Co. A.; Cpl. John Christy, right foot off, Co. F.; Cpl. Wm. Ewing, arm off below elbow, Co. C; Jn. Paschke, ball in thigh & soon to be amputated, Co. K; Cpl. Js. Perrine, left arm, Co. I; John Scott, leg, Co. D; Sgt. Spencer Train, left leg broken several places by shell, Co. C. None from Co. B; told there were some but not here.

There was a Cpl. Wm. Barnum of the Seventh, shot in abdomen & in extreme pain; will not survive. Frank Bull of the Seventh I found downstairs in the cellar of the bldg. with about forty others in six inches of water. Four were dead with faces in water & may have drowned. I ran up the stairs & tried to find orderlies to bring them up or put something under them & was promised it would be done. Frank wounded several places, will lose left foot & right leg.

A Thos. Darnell had been wounded in head, & died while I was there. Sgt. George Sain of Co. C, Seventh, lay right next to a dead man; Sain was unconscious himself, wounded in hip & superficially in face. There was a man named John Straight, Seventh, from Westfield in the center of the State somewhere, wounded in the head, with part of skull shot away by shell & brain pulsing, *awake & conscious*, talking to me. Don't see how he can survive long nor how he has until now.

Two hours in barn on farm the Brigade fought on. Asked by surgeons to hold legs & arms down as they sawed. All three of us needed there & worked past when should have started back. Held down limbs & saw skin & flesh & bone cut through as in a butcher shop & thought all along about Forrest, for he was amputated & under these circumstances. What my Brother suffered! Wrote to me from a wilderness of blood & death & screams & pain & exhausted doctors with saws in their hands & blood up to their elbows & chests. Nobody understands this war who hasn't been in its hospitals, not even the fellows in line of battle. The drs. & the wounded have a better idea than we had, & there is no other name for war except suffering, & that is too weak a name. Death & blood & screaming & men dying in inches of water for no other reason than one doctor too few or not getting water or food, are what war is. I know this now & wish I didn't, for I will have to go on fighting it.

Men of the 24th Michigan in that barn & wagon shed & pig sty & uncovered barnyard, lying all over, dozens & dozens. I saw what they had done & how they had stood. Told 75 had been killed outright. Wider spread in age than in our Regt.; saw men from 18 to 42 amputated.

In fairness to Eleventh Corps, saw in bldg. in town a number of them, Germans mostly from Milwaukee, 26th Wisconsin Infantry, 2nd Brigade, 3rd Division. Heard they had upward of 40 killed outright, many wounded, which is even worse than in our Regt., so some of the Eleventh stood & fought & paid the bill.

Regiment has moved & I am under orders of a major from another Brigade. Told we must forward our reports tonight, so must get back to them though they are mainly done.

The woods where the Brigade fought is badly shot up. Many great trees splintered. Everything we do no matter how well-intended is destructive. One hundred fifty thousand men & horses have made this whole place a sewer & a graveyard. Tons & tons of lead & iron lie in the fields, & everywhere you walk you walk on cups & canteens, torn leather, cartridge boxes & ammunition crates, things dug out of the earth & then thrust back in stained & polluted & now poisonous. Not in all my life have I thought of this until today. As Pastor says, surely we are cursed, & so is the earth.

The world does not seem to get better but worse. There has been nothing more diabolical invented than the exploding shell. What mind invented something that only kills—explodes in pieces to kill & mangle? I saw men in that barn who did not look like men, who had faces torn & disfigured, & bodies ripped open with insides exposed & shredded. We pound and chop and shoot each other's bodies, and nothing is a cruder or more blunt denial of our pretentions to civilization and Christianity. Despite anything anybody does or our reasons for doing them, the world only continues to get worse. Worse things will be invented, & no brotherhood nor peace nor unselfishness will reign on earth.

Order repeated to move.

Head swimming with sights of men's faces as I held down their legs that came off in my hands. Air & sky filled with flies, buzzards, etc. I try to think again of what the country will be like once the war is won, & see not the world we have now but a meaner one, & how could it not be, after what we have done here? The civilians do not know what has happened & like fools will not change anything for the better, & too many of us have had parts of our brains & hearts amputated. We could tell them, but they would not listen. The gods & ideas & politics you are willing to kill for are only today's notions & will be replaced by tomorrow's. Men & philosophies die like hogs, though it is only the philosophies that deserve to. The world is at best honor & courage & good faith in the midst of butchery; & nobody knows why.

Even honor & courage & good faith kill.

I am not even twenty-one years old. What will I do if I survive this war & have to go back home?

July 7, 1863
Gettysburg, Penn.

Burying men yesterday & today. A job for skulkers & civilians, not First Corps. Or perhaps: we shot them, we bury them.

A pity I do not have a sweetheart at home to write to, for there is an abundance of sights & smells to report in glad letters detailing my daily occupations & states of mind. Yesterday began to notice things in the trees. Pieces of clothing, sleeves with hands in them, boots attached to pieces of legs. Some of the men reported "missing" are to be found only this way. Saw trunk of a man against a tree, feasted on by birds, thought of politicians & editors & manufacturers, & even my father makes money from this war.

Things you do not see at first you notice when your mind lets them in finally. Severed heads with worms in the eyes. Bodies hit by shell concussions, flattened like cakes against rocks & trees. We bury too shallowly; there is so much to do. Civilians will come along & find bloated black hands reaching up at them through the ground. Will spoil many picnics & be unsettling during Sunday School outings.

July 13, 1863
vicinity of Hagerstown, Maryland

Delightful sojourn in Penn. ended; rejoined Regt. yesterday & am in fighting trim again & ready to kill for United States tariff laws & die for Infant Baptism.

Report is that Lee is crossing Potomac today. Northern press & politicians will shriek that we let Lee "escape" & should have "destroyed" him. It is inconceivable that Meade will not somehow be sacrificed, for he is the only sane & rational man in power. To have attacked Lee with both the rebel flanks anchored on the Potomac would have been the kind of suicide the press enjoys & has come to expect from our generals & ourselves, & to see Lee doing it for once & us refusing the gambit must have been a cruel disappointment. So off with Meade's head! It will come. It is not enough to defeat Lee; we must be refreshed with Northern blood into the bargain, & throw some arms & legs & heads to the wind.

They will not be happy until we get some General of the Apocalypse, someone who will pit blood against blood & keep on until the side with more blood wins. As we have more blood, we shall win. There will no doubt be a parade afterwards.

May 4, 1864
near Wilderness Tavern, Virginia

I have not written for nearly a year.

The Iron Brigade ended last summer, though the five regiments are still brigaded together & are under Cutler; but we have with us a New York battalion of sharpshooters, most despicable of all military occupations, & the Seventh Indiana. We are no longer in the First Corps because the First Corps does not exist; its survivors have been divided up, like garments, & we are now in the Fifth Corps. Fortunately General Wadsworth is still our division commander, as this Fourth Division is now his.

The fall & winter were, when one considers all things, uneventful. The exception was our movement in northern Virginia over the old Bull Run battlefield, which brought us to Gainesville, where my Brother fought. There the Iron Brigade fought its first battle & laid the foundation for Gettysburg.

The bodies of our men buried there were in some cases protruding from the ground; one saw a skeletal sleeve here & there, & bits of skull & uniform. It is beyond shameful that they have been left so. The men were re-buried now. You could see how they fell in line of battle exactly where they fought, not one running away & not one anything less than honorable, & all in a measure heroes.

Two years ago.

I stood where my Brother stood. Would that I had thoughts like his! But I cannot have them. I have been spoiled forever & could not do what he did with the same earnestness & heroism. It is gone & lost forever. Merely two years ago & already the world has ended & become new, but new only in the way a piece of fruit once fresh putrefies in the sun & becomes new but not fresh, poisonous rather, a collapsed velvet of corruption spawning myriads of creeping & flying things that cover the earth & fill the air. So is our world changed & new.

Father wrote that I am bitter because I enlisted for the wrong reasons. But there aren't any right reasons.

Since that day in October I have been thinking, & shall endeavor to do my duty & live up to his example as best I can. I have been putting aside my vile temperament acquired last summer, & shall yet write things for a grandchild to read.

Or perhaps only something to remind me in my old age, lest I forget what I know now.

If I survive.

We have our general now, Grant, who commands the Army though Meade still issues the orders & does the dirty work. I think Grant is the man I prophesied last summer & he will be the wagerer of blood in a sure bet & we soldiers will be the losers.

I am a sergeant now. Was a good soldier in camp.

This journal is a companion I have missed, though still I touch pen to its pages only with doubt & misgivings, because in it I think honestly & can only live the life of a soldier & citizen & Christian if I leave honesty in the inkwell.

But this day should be recorded. We left our camps yesterday & today are near the old Chancellorsville battlefield in a place called The Wilderness. Without doubt we shall fight tomorrow & the old Brigade shall add its ghostly presence & the new brigade shall supply the air with new ghosts.

late afternoon, May 7, 1864
Wilderness

Lying in rifle pits since this morning after two days unbroken hellish fighting. Regt. has lost sixty men. War will go on forever; when we are gone others will take our place & continue.

On the 5th we advanced in the morning through endless woods. Woods not like woods of Gettysburg last summer, but scrub & bushes & second growth of all kinds, impossible to see through. Our Regt. advanced in brigade's second line, regulation hundred yards behind first line, & we couldn't see the first line. Couldn't see them after they stepped off the first twenty paces.

Skirmish firing began in front of us, then artillery from right side of road. Our brigade advanced along our side of road & soon bullets came through snipping branches & zip-zip through undergrowth. We went on ahead not seeing a thing, moving into smoke of the first line. Evident that our first line was driving the enemy. Advanced several hundred yards, though it seemed like a half mile's work.

Heard rebel artillery on other side of road firing at the brigade moving alongside us across the road. After some time of smashing through the undergrowth we got up even with the artillery, still firing off to our right. Knew then that the other brigade had been slowed & that we were alone with nothing to our right but the rebels & their artillery. Went ahead anyway until ordered to stop & rest.

Couldn't see ten yards any direction, except for sweet briars & scrub pine & other Virginia undergrowth. I lay down & after a few minutes realized I could see under the scrub pine branches about forty or fifty yards; saw groups & rows of feet with wrong color trousers in front of us & around to the sides everywhere I looked. I said to nearest Capt. that he should kneel down & look, as I thought we were about to be surrounded by the rebs. Where was the rest of our brigade & how could we be alone & surrounded?

The rebels heard us talking & just as the Capt. ordered "Attention!" they fired into us from front & left, & as soon as these had fired another volley came from our right, the nasty hiss of bullets like hornets everywhere through the underbrush & the sick *thug thug* of them hitting our fellows. Lost John Hedges, a decent man unlike myself who was good-humored & kind & courageous all at the same time & who still believed in the Union & the Country; he was wounded three times at Gettysburg last summer & survived the hospitals & the surgeons only to be shot down in the underbrush of the Wilderness.

The Regt. tried to form but with rebels all around us & almost in among us the formation was not a line but more like a wedge of geese, with the apex forward where I was & the two wings angled off behind. That lasted only a few minutes as we were taken from three directions, so we kept order as best we could & retired back the way we had come, & 1st Sgt. Moore was captured & Charlie Kellogg too; & twenty-five more were shot down & they all were more-or-less random shots, for the rebels couldn't see any better than we could. Their converging fire couldn't miss us. Trying to keep the line together & move us backward, our Capt. Converse was shot through the head.

We went back re-forming to give the pursuing rebels volleys, probably three or four times, & then ran to the rear each time. The rebels were in line of battle & couldn't follow as fast as we could run, but they kept coming on yelling that eerie yell in the smoky woods, & we kept around our flag & turned & fired. After a while we did not hear them & sent a company of skirmishers about a hundred yards forward, & they reported no rebels for the moment. We were absolutely alone.

Our Colonel was gone. Bragg had rejoined the Regt. again, not exactly in good health but wanting to do his duty for the good old flag I guess. He got lost trying to find the front line which was supposed to be ahead of us & came back to us only now, after almost running into the rebel line. He is going to get himself killed with his recklessness some day soon. He said there were none of ours around anywhere, so he ordered us to lie flat while he & Dawes tried to figure out what to do.

From sounds of firing it was plain that we were between the armies & it was decided to try to creep backward to what we hoped were really the Army's lines. Did so, but how we did without getting shot by our own men I do not know. Only the intelligence of Bragg & Dawes probably.

Got to open ground where our Corps was re-forming; made log breastworks. A house is in that part of the field, & we stayed near it until sometime in the afternoon. Found out that because our brigade advanced beyond the one on its right the enemy was able to enfilade & roll up the front line & swept it away to the left & it happened a hundred yards from of us & we didn't even know it, nor did we know the regt. in line to our immediate right were enfiladed & forced back, so that everything around us had been washed away & we were out there like an island in a sea of rebels, but the rebels didn't know it either & this is what the war had become: the War itself. The only thing directing this war is the War, & we humans with our brains & plans & ideas & causes are nothing but what the War uses to keep itself going. Nobody in their right mind would keep the War going now if it were up to them but it is not up to us & nobody could stop it if they tried, until the War eats itself down or wears out. It is a greater force than we, and to the War we are nothing.

In the afternoon we were ordered to the left of the Army's line, about two miles I think, & thrown in with the Second Corps, Hancock's Corps, & again we went forward. It was the same underbrush & scrub pine, but this time with a whole corps & we drove the enemy. I think the rebels had not been up to strength on the 5th & the word is that only yesterday did Longstreet's corps reach their lines & they are what threw us back. But on the 5th we had things pretty much our way. We captured prisoners in the woods & found we had A.P. Hill's corps in front of us & were driving them.

We advanced about two miles & were happy to see the underbrush thinning. Halted at dark & lay down among rebel dead & wounded that our first line of battle had fought & swept over.

Rebels groaned & bled among us & we gave the bastards water & tried to tie up their wounds & I gathered as much clothing as I could from dead rebels & our men & made strips & tried to do what I had seen in the hospitals last summer. One fellow shot in the stomach gasped & cried & said "My God, My God, why hast Thou forsaken me?" So the rebels are wondering, too. This went on into the night; skirmish firing up ahead, artillery off to the right & behind, & smoke in the woods & dying rebels groaning & wounded screaming or begging, & we lying & sitting there among them. Some of our men didn't even lie down but sat against trees & gave up the idea of sleep, but most slept anyway even sitting up; & over & over again, "My God, My God, why hast Thou forsaken me?" I wanted to shoot him to end his suffering & wanted to answer his question, which ran in my brain all night, even after the fellow died.

A very little after dawn we were ordered up again. Wadsworth's Division was formed for a heavy advance in four lines, our Regt. being in the second line. We drove the enemy again easily. There was some halting, & then we knew something was wrong. We were now in oak forest with no underbrush, so we could see well enough & the officers should have been able to see, but the dispositions for the advance had been made back in the underbrush & so the blunder now coming to fruition was that the Second Corps had been advancing at an angle toward our Division, & now the two were coming together obliquely & mixing together & a halt had to be called to separate the commands & straighten the lines & re-orient the direction of attack.

The rebels seem to have a devilish kind of luck or sense of timing & this is just when Longstreet's Corps came into the battle. The Brigade gave it to them at first when they came at us across a small farm cleared from the woods, but we got flanked & then it was everyone for himself.

We poured back through the oaks on the run, dashing for the underbrush we had come out of earlier, the rebels hotly pursuing & firing. The whole mass of the Division's front lines crowded back everywhere, streaming & running, hundreds of yards left & right of our Regt. all through the woods, in full rout.

The line originally behind ours had already reached the underbrush & disappeared into it, when from out of the undergrowth emerged a mounted officer carrying a national flag, a fresh regiment behind him. It was General Wadsworth himself, his silver-white hair visible under the usual kepi cap, gripping the staff of the flag & shouting in his loud voice, "Rally, men! Rally 'round the flag!" It was a gallant sight. Our Regt. stopped along with other fellows & turned & we all went forward, Wadsworth out ahead, his splendid horse prancing into the oaks & the General was shot immediately, knocked from his horse & the flag hit the ground.

The little charge was enough to check the enemy, who seemed to be changing front to attack the Second Corps to our left. We fell back in good order.

Slept on our arms last night, cartridge boxes on our belts, expecting a night attack. Firing went on here & there all night, skirmish fire from men lying down & firing low under the growth. To get up was fatal, as both sides had learned how to shoot in the underbrush.

This shooting ignited many fires in the dry leaves & brush, & around us the woods began to blaze & smoke, with lurid red flickering light, musket fire & the *zip zip* of the minie ball, the evil witching mournful whine of the spent bullet, & all around in front of us bleeding boys lay in the creeping fires. The fresh memory is a vision from Hell itself; I slept not at all last night, only this morning after we moved. When the fires reached a man he screamed & screamed.

I am lying down as I write this & would like to go to sleep again. We have a new division commander, & likewise we have a new Regt. commander, Dawes, our usual one, though this time I think it will be a permanent change, for Bragg is not on sick leave but was finally promoted to command a brigade. It is always like this in the Army—the commanders change & the units change & the old Brigade is gone forever & how many were lost in the underbrush & the fires? I think our Regt. lost sixty men in the last two days. Today we will be ordered forward again, for it doesn't matter to Grant whether we lose or win in the Wilderness. This I am beginning to understand. All that matters is bleeding the enemy. Why didn't anyone see this before? Being humane is inhumane: that's the War's logic. I believe McClellan & Meade saw it & refused it & only prolonged the cruelty, but now the War has someone who will hammer out the sentence. Grant is the War's perfect executive officer, & we are its ants, its bees, its fuel. I saw its greedy eyes & brain pulsing in the woods last night, to the music of our screams.

May 8, 1864
somewhere near Spotsylvania Court House

Now behind another log breastwork.

Marched all night to get here. Dead tired. Enemy had got here first & constructed earth works on hill in front of us full of artillery. Hillside covered with small cedars with low & sharp branches.

Rebel line is miles long & this is the strongest point I would imagine, & I could not help laughing when heard we were ordered to attack the hill.

Went forward in usual gallant style & before we got out into the open our skirmishers came back running from the right, shouting the enemy was himself advancing & that the brigade which was to support us on the right was nowhere to be seen & sure enough soon we found the brigade to our left was also not up yet, so there we were again, in the usual position, which was alone. To the right & rear we heard firing & shouting, which of course meant the enemy had got in our rear.

What is there to write? Always the same now. Turned & broke away just as the rebels came out of the cedars & underbrush in our former front, now our rear. Lt. Pruyn, who started out as a private back when my brother enrolled, must have got sick of running & sick of the rebels, or it was just time for him to stand, so he was shot; we saw him spun & thrown to hands & knees alone behind us; he rose up & staggered toward us & reached the timber & fell forward. The boys who got to him first said he was dead; I knew that, had seen it as he fell.

Dawes rallied us again around the flag & when the rebels came on we volleyed & fired & they had enough of that in a few minutes & so that was all for now, except for burying Lieutenant Pruyn. Company A buried him, Lt. Huntington digging the grave under some pine trees in our rear. Wrapped his body in a blanket, laid him in the hole, not a deep one, covered him quickly & got back to the line. Never know; rebels might be coming again; might be ordered to attack again; might be ordered to march again; only the War knows.

June 8, 1864
Washington

Only a month has passed since last writing, & a great divide has been crossed. I can't go back to the war & I can't go back to regular life either. Unless my requests were not honored, my family (strange term now!) think I am gallantly leading charges & being terrible on the enemies of the Republic, when I am here in a hospital & can't even get up to make water.

I grieve to be away from the Company & it is an unbearable thought in spite of everything that I cannot go back to them & see them. How I want to be able merely to talk to them again, to sit in a camp with them or even stand with them on the firing line, for even a few moments! But such a request cannot be granted. Never! I will never see them all together again. The thought is unbearable & an agony worse than anything I feel in my face & leg & breast or have ever felt. To have your comrades taken from you one by one in battle seems kind by comparison. Now I must imagine them still alive, still digging earthworks & advancing together & sitting in the rain, for so they are & I am forever gone from them. Forever. Better to have died.

They are my family. The people at home will know nothing, will understand nothing & must be told exactly nothing. The fellows in the hospital here know enough, but they are not the Sixth Wisconsin nor the old Brigade, know nothing of the Seminary on the first of July last summer, know nothing of Battery B on the pike, know nothing.

Many times I thought we were there again. Many times on the green Pennsylvania hills, & then I would be digging graves again & would wake up. Waking is torture & sleeping is torment. I should be happy not to have been killed, yet no-one has been able to explain to me *why* I should be happy & why I should not complain. It is the soldierly thing to do, not to complain.

And soldier I am. Now I understand what the "U. S." on our belts & cartridge boxes means. We are the property of U. S. Grant. Should he require an attack of us, we attack; should he wish us to camp, we camp; should he require of us a leg below the knee, we rapidly comply; should he want us to retain a bit of a shell in our chest, we do our duty. Our lives please? Without hesitation. We obey orders. We are soldiers.

I have been thinking about this man Grant these past weeks. The newspapers say the fighting goes on day after day without ceasing, & every day more wounded & dead & more men crippled for the rest of their lives who can't expect to run or marry or even walk properly. Grant is not the equal of Hooker or McClellan or Meade as a tactician; he is a grand strategist and works with the arithmetic. He simply won't retreat, even when he hasn't beaten the enemy. But the careful generals have cost even more. War's logic! What is such logic but insanity? War is insanity! The Government sends Grant more of his property & he grinds ahead & what Dawes calls the Carnival of Blood goes on.

Even though I don't believe in fairy tales I would like to be St. Peter at the Gate of Heaven when these fellows come to apply—Burnside, Stanton, Halleck, Jeff. Davis, Stonewall Jackson—& be the one to tell them to find other accommodations.

That is enough for just now. Will write more later.

Will not date these, as I am not exactly sure of the dates. About June 9 or 10, in the hospital. Washington.

Carried outside this noon. Hot as hell. Asked to be carried back in. Left outside; at least there is a breeze.

I have determined to describe my last battle. There will be no grandchildren to read this, but perhaps it can solace me in my solitary old age. Once I was a young man. Once I was a soldier.

No-one will want to read this; I am too poisoned.

The morning after Lieutenant Pruyn was killed we slept long, having marched or stayed awake night after night since crossing the Rapidan. At nine or ten we woke to the sound of firing in front. We had our rifles leaning against the logs we lay behind, bayonets fixed, & a man from another company fired toward the hill in our front. He was standing back behind the logs & his bullet struck a bayonet & split, one of the pieces flying back & hitting someone in Co. A in the cheek, spinning him like a top. Even the ludicrous events are deadly; the man was not killed but will not kiss a girl for some time either, or eat. (At this moment he is probably back on the firing line, or dead in the ground somewhere in northern Virginia.)

The rebels were higher than we were & their skirmishers were all over the hillside. Some of their sharpshooters were in trees shooting downward at us. To keep your head above the logs for more than a second or two was suicide. At first you could wait for the puff of smoke & then grab a root fast enough for the bullet to miss you; but after a few hours the firing became too steady & we stayed down as much as possible. We got a few of the green-suited U.S. Sharpshooters in our lines to try to rid the front of the rebels; they had globe sights & could have hit squirrels at five hundred yards. Two of these brave sharpshooters were wounded in the face trying to punish the rebels so exit Sharpshooters, continue Sixth Wisconsin.

There was an open stretch between our breastwork and the base of the hill where the trees started & whenever we got a group of volunteers to try Indian fighting with the rebel skirmishers, several of them always got shot running across the open space. The Seventh Wisconsin has some genuine Indians & they cut some pine branches to conceal themselves once they reached the trees & dashed out with war-whoops, but even some of them were shot crossing that field.

On the second or third day an assault was ordered. We went forward & in less than an hour came back. The rebels swept the hillside with artillery & musketry, & though we got some way up the hill we couldn't stay there & had to retire. I think it was the next day we were ordered to form up again. Another regiment near us refused to advance. We held them in contempt, the way anybody with brains is held in contempt. We went forward & Dawes directed us up toward the left flank of the hill. We got up to within two hundred feet of the enemy's works & that was all. Spent a couple of hours there pinned to the hillside, air over our heads full of bullets. I was lying behind a small pine & saw a corps commander, Warren, with his bright gold sash & as he went by Dawes, Dawes grabbed the sash & jerked the General to the ground, saving the fool's life for better or worse.

The underbrush up there became ignited too, & a Captain of the Second Wisconsin was shot & lay above that regt.'s line. From where I was I could see an officer of the Second crawling back & forth to get suspenders from his men, & then crawled as close as he could to the body of the Captain & tried to loop the end of the suspender rope onto a foot, but could not stay there & I do not know how he escaped being shot in the head, but after trying for some time he crawled back down, I would say weeping & angry. We retreated back down the hill shortly after that.

We tried another assault the same day or the next day. It was sheer stupidity to try to capture that hill, the strongest point in the rebel line, & the officers who ordered it rather than the men who tried to take it should have been shot.

So day after day, for four days, constant firing & sniping & assaults, hour after hour, morning & evening & all day, & there we lost some of our strongest survivors, men who had good hearts and had fought steadily for the Regiment & were true fellows. For nothing.

On the morning of the 12th we were ordered forward again, & again we went & again we were shot back. Like true U. S. men we went forward & stood up to the fire & were shot down; & more men were killed as compared to wounded here than usual, an interesting piece of information which unfortunately cannot be savored by those whom it directly affected. If Burnside or Hooker had tried this they would have been cashiered after a couple of days, but Grant does it & he is not replaced, either because they are tired of making changes & have no idea of who to drag out of the barrel to make our commander, or because Grant & the President work by the same arithmetic. It is clear that the rebels are going to lose this war now, finally, for we are taking many prisoners & we are not retreating, so the fault is more that of Jeff. Davis & his crew, or of Lee, or of the rebels in general for keeping this Carnival going. I hate and despise the idea of having to win the war not on generalship but on the carcasses of soldiers. We always knew we were the strength of the army, but does it seem Just & Holy to spend all that strength & life because we can't get generals who know anything except how to accept slaughter?

I'm sure after these battles Grant is upset, & Lincoln is upset, & the Country is upset; & we're dead.

That evening we were ordered away from our logs & sent to reenforce the left, to the angle in the rebel line which had been captured during the morning. We thought we had been in hell up to now, but it was not until we went to that angle that we really entered Hell.

Five days & nights fighting & a night march & the two days in the Wilderness had exhausted us. It was a new Army, full of conscripts & strange regiments, with new commanders, & now it was a new War, or rather the War it had been all along, War as it really is. No more campaigning & maneuvering & weeks in camp & on the march & re-organizing & drilling. Constant fighting, constant killing, constant suffering & constant death. We were too tired to fight but it didn't matter.

We arrived in the dark to the scene of pandemonium. Flashes of musketry & artillery constantly lit the smoky, desolated place with red, orange & yellow, giving ghostly, machine-like profiles of the two lines not forty yards from each other, firing & aiming among the dead & wounded.

We rushed forward to the log breastwork which had been taken from the enemy. Mud rose halfway to our knees & we slipped against dead bodies. The rebels in their second line kept down except for quick shots as long as we maintained our fire. But if we paused to form for an attack they jumped up & poured a volley into us.

So all night we crowded against that log barrier, & then we went forward to the enemy's line with a rush & thrust bayonets between their logs as they did the same, & men lunged over the top to shoot in other men's faces, & it went on & on, hour after hour, with bayonets & point-blank fire & clubbed muskets & howling & the wounded screaming & begging, & muskets & cannon crashing so that it constantly sounded like a house falling down, rending & crashing. A strange nightmare fury possessed everyone; it was rage against the War & we died of it. Sometimes a man would jump up, crazed, & stand at the top of the breastwork & fire his rifle down & if still alive he would take rifles we handed up to him until he was shot dead. I saw it several times: each man was riddled with bullets & thrust through with bayonets.

When we fell back to the first captured line we could not rest. I fired my forty rounds, then forty more, then more as I could gather it. It was not the manic, rapid firing of last summer at Gettysburg, but it went on hour after hour, steady, careful, deadly. We aimed at the head logs the rebels had put on short blocks on top of their trench, enabling them to thrust their rifles through without having to expose their heads over the tops of the logs. Our fire chewed up those logs & no doubt murdered many a rebel peering at us for our musket flashes, & there was a tree behind their trench that was there when we first charged, but which toward morning wasn't there any more, having been severed by countless of our bullets. Behind us the trees were smashed & coated with flattened lead. Dead men & horses between the lines lost their shapes, riddled & chipped with bullets until flat & distorted. If believing could save us from hell, then I would believe with all my might, but I have believed & still been in hell. I don't know of a heaven that could make up for this.

I volunteered with five others to go back to the ammunition trains to get more cartridges. We dashed off & two were shot immediately & only two of us got to the ammunition wagons. The other man & I took on an eighty-pound box of ammunition each & started back through the darkness & flashes, & waded & slipped through the mud & stepped on & over dead bodies & the half-covered wounded, & amid the hissing of bullets a searing flash exploded in front of me all white light with concussion like a barn hitting me throwing me into the air backward. After some time I felt for the ammunition box & couldn't reach it & couldn't move my left arm & the right leg began to throb but I couldn't raise myself up to look at it, & so I lay in the mud & then I had the idea to take off my cartridge box to place it under my head to keep my face out of the mud & couldn't feel the box; then I felt along the front of my body & felt only my own flesh. I understood a shell had exploded in front of me & had torn my uniform to shreds, & I felt along my chest & found an oozing hole low down the ribs on the left side. I felt my mouth for blood but couldn't determine whether there was any.

Perhaps I became a beggar, raising a hand for water & feebly & deliriously crying. I cannot describe the despair that washed over me & the feeling of being had & the regret for not having avoided & prevented what had happened to me, which still had not happened an hour ago & still had been avoidable, & the pain of the fire in my side & the pounding throb in my leg.

My face was lacerated by shell fragments but I shall grow a beard & it will not all be seen. I have scars on my chest & arms, but they will not be seen. The fragment under my rib will stay there the rest of my life but will not be seen. But my leg is shattered.

It is now the end of July. I have lost interest in the war & do not want to hear about it. They say our troops refused to obey Grant's order to attack at Cold Harbor. Good. Let it end there. But it will not. Grant will keep everything in the meat grinder & will win the war & will be the Country's hero. Why not even elect him President? Dead men don't vote.

War itself is President. It is a monstrous thing to go to war, & War itself is the punishment & the retribution.

I think my Brother died in some kind of peace. He gave his life for something, for God & Liberty & Justice & Union & Home. But I have had the feeling since Gettysburg that the rest have given their lives for Nothing.

What will be won from this War? It is only loss, our Honor & Liberty gone forever. The Country is gone & neither side, North nor South, will ever get it back.

April 16, 1865.

The President is dead! Shot by an actor—Lincoln dead! Lee surrendered a week ago, & now our President Abraham Lincoln, who meant only good, is shot & is dead! I do not recognize this country any more. It is not the country that Forrest went to war to save. Or maybe it's the same age-old place, where the good die and heaven is silent.

I might not recognize this country, but I recognize the God behind it all. It is the raging, jealous God of the Old Testament who punishes people left & right for god knows what—the Great Southerner, jealous of his rights. Volatile as prairie fire: you never know what he's going to do next & there's always something to be afraid of. You can never be good enough, you can never be right, because you haven't any idea what is going to set him off next. Why does He let a good & honest man die? It's the same thing over & over—Forrest, the innocent Savior Jesus who went about doing good, and now our suffering president—sacrificed by God, by the Great Slave-driver. It is that Great Overseer that I went out to fight. But maybe this world is too much of a nightmare not to be illusory. What if the God who orders death and the Savior who suffers death are one and the same, and seeing them as two is an illusion?

April 17.

I walk with a single crutch now, and in years to come it will be a cane—for *all* the years to come! I ought to consider myself lucky. How many tens of thousands are maimed worse than I am: blind, lame, armless, whole legs gone forever, faces scarred and burned so even their families can't face them. No one will ever look them in the eye again.

Can God look them in the eye? Will God face Abraham Lincoln? How can God face Jesus Christ? Or will we discover that God was in the mystic Nazarene all along, and was lying with the wounded and the dead on our fields of battle?

Already I am finding that the world is essentially lonely. I would rather have God down here beside me than up in the sky protecting me.

I have read and re-read Mr. Lincoln's Second Inaugural Address. He believed that God brought "this terrible war" on both north and south for our crimes against another race, that *every drop of blood drawn by the slave driver's lash is paid by one drawn by the sword*. He believes in the god of the old priests and Pharisees, but he speaks and acts and dies like Jesus.

I have never been so unnerved as I am by the death of our good President—not by battle, not in the hospital surrounded by men dying in the stink of infection & crying out in pain.

I am a Grant man now. I see that Lee lost more men than we did—including his whole army, & that Grant lost fewer men succeeding than all our previous generals lost failing. But it has been loss, loss, & loss. Now the loss of the last good, honest man, Abraham Lincoln. I hope there is more to all this loss than meets the eye.

July 1, 1913
Gettysburg

After 50 years these pages are brittle & yellow. I have not kept these day-books out of sentimentality. From the beginning I knew it and lo, it has come to pass: the War we fought has been made into a different war. It has been replaced by a noble struggle over nothing in particular, a kind of exhibition of Southern pluck and Northern industry.

During these three days the United Confederate Veterans & the Grand Army of the Republic are sharing an encampment on the old battlefield, the fiftieth anniversary re-union. I am surrounded by white beards like mine.

These men have chosen to forget. I hear it in their talk. It is now the grand and glorious war that civilians imagined all along. Our sorrow has changed and become a lament for lost youth rather than grief for the early dead.

For fifteen years after the War there were no veterans organizations. Nobody wanted to talk about the War because the people we came home to either could not or would not understand the real War. But as our youth passed to middle age, and our vigor & powers faded, we dreamed again of our former strength, of our once firm step & clear eyes, which for us happened to be a time of war. Never mind what it was; we must have it back, for anything is better than watching the decline of life & hope. We wanted back the unrecallable years of possibilities, of the promise of love & happiness, of intimations of great & noteworthy accomplishments.

So there was a twenty-fifth anniversary encampment. I did not go. I was Editor of the Madison Herald, still owned the store back home, was active in State politics & busy supporting Battling Bob LaFollette, & would not be bothered by sentimentality when great & noteworthy accomplishments still awaited.

Now I am a tired, prematurely old man whose knee and ribs pain him whenever it is damp & cold, still writing angrily on occasion for the *Herald*, living back home in Prescott, Wisconsin. No-one waits for me. My only surviving sister lived and died a farmer's wife in North Dakota. I have no excuse not to look at my past again. So I have taken Forrest's letters and my old daybooks out of the trunk where they had lain undisturbed, mostly, for nearly fifty years, and I have come here for a last look at what I lost. The retired newspaperman must write one more editorial on the War, make one last literary attempt at the truth.

Seeing how we old survivors are honored here for what has become an imaginary war has troubled me. It causes me to change my mind about burying this journal & your letters, Forrest. I am going to leave these for someone to find & publish, and perhaps to fill in what you & I haven't written. I want those who come after us to know something of what was committed and suffered. May the Past come alive for those who otherwise would be doomed to repeat it.

The field looks different now. There are more trees. The woods where the Brigade fought is studded with big trunks dying of lead poisoning. They are emblems of my heart, but, being stronger, they weathered many years before succumbing to the violation that is war. Many new trees are coming up. The Department of the Interior is not cutting them back as would have been the case had the woods remained a woodlot. The undergrowth now resembles more the maze & tangle of the Wilderness than what existed here fifty years ago. Perhaps it is fitting.

A trolley now runs between the town & Devil's Den. It goes along the Emmitsburg Road, upon which we marched that morning; today you can ride past our scores of white tents full of veterans Blue & Gray. Two days from now men of the Philadelphia Brigade & Pickett's Division Association will meet & shake hands over the stone wall where I saw them fight and kill fifty years ago. There are good feelings & respect among us all, Blue & Gray; they are the understanding of men who shared a youth together, never mind how we felt then.

It is well if the War aroused nobility and courage; unfortunately, the younger generations have grown up believing the lie that says the War was primarily nobility and courage. As if we maddened boys were filled with stout-hearted feelings of duty and honor and patriotism. From the civilians who start it to the soldiers who fight it, war is primarily hate and fear, as far as feelings go, and it is primarily and always killing, as far as behavior goes. If battle inspired unselfishness in some of us and devotion to our comrades, it was in spite of war not because of it; or it was War, the indiscriminate mocker, mocking itself.

A mild but unrelenting presence tugs at me. Perhaps it is my imagination of the Brother who will always remain a young man in my mind's eye. It forces me to confess that I do not understand Forrest and the thousands like him. For him, the War was not fear or hatred. I did not know malice in him before he went off to fight, did not read it in his letters, do not feel it in this strange, kind, imaginary reproach. His goodness will survive whatever truth I tell. That goodness will make of this War a story whose mythical truth transcends the facts and whose light will inspire this country and the world down to the last generation to tell it. I do not understand that goodness or where it comes from, but here I can feel its power. The fields are radiant with it and it overwhelms me with its lucent force. It is alien alike to my bitterness and to the imaginary war the country is making out of the old battles. If this is hallowed ground, it is so because of the invisible light which survives the rage, stupidity, chaos, and murder that seemed to overwhelm it, and purifies them instead. That is my brother's immortality. That is the harvest of sacrifice.

July 2, 1913

I see hundreds of Grand Army veterans shaking hands and talking to those murdering old buzzards from the South, as if they were only some rival baseball or ninepins team instead of the rebels who started the War and would have torn up the United States—rebels who killed our friends and were glad to do it—and who killed my Brother. Those gentlemen still despise the Negro and underneath their smiles and homey drawls and country charm they still despise us too, and we are just the stupid fools they think we are if we don't know it. But I feel a deep-down suspicion that unless I forgive them, my Brother's sacrifice somehow will not apply to me, and I will die as I have lived until now: bitter and unhappy, and alone.

It will not be easy. These old rebels failed to break the United States and failed to keep their "servants" but not for lack of trying, and in other respects they seem to have won the War. Or at least they have succeeded in pretending they never lost it. Southerners, storytellers from way back, have made the War into a moral victory of sorts for themselves—people who fought for one of the most immoral causes in history. Starting with General Lee at Appomattox, they say not that they were beaten, but that they were "compelled to yield to overwhelming numbers and resources," as if we hadn't defeated them by marching and fighting and dying and persisting and believing, but merely had out-populated and out-manufactured them. At the same time they glory over shining moments like those here at Gettysburg when they could have won the War—and fail to mention the inconsistency. They have sold the country this bill of goods. Worse still, they have sold the country the idea that the war was not fought by a slave society willing to destroy the world's last best hope of free government in order to retain their human "property." It is a lie that would make my Brother's death meaningless. Their "tyrannical principle," as Mr. Lincoln termed it, must be admitted and repudiated, or else it will be all the easier for selfish tyranny

& ignorant crowds to dominate and brutalize their fellow human beings in times to come. Truth versus falsehood is the great and perpetual civil war, the outcome of which will determine the future, if any, of humanity. The unreconstructed Confederacy would like to rule another race, and I would like to remark to them that all of us are equal in the heart of God; but I am a bad preacher because I have learned here that all are not equal in my own heart.

Yet sometimes I have almost as much difficulty hating these old Southerners as my former comrades have. I drank coffee with four good old rebels this morning and in spite of everything I know, I found them to be no worse than myself and a good deal more likeable. They used the term "damnyankee" like they never learned it's comprised of two separate words, which I found amusing in a persuasive sort of way until I realized, *They mean me.* It was a little similar to my first time under fire: when I heard the bullets I realized *They mean me.* As tactfulness is a disease I have never had, I observed that they weren't worth the damn that they damn us Yankees with. Politely they excused themselves, and left me at the table alone. I should have become ennobled by fighting for a noble cause; I should share the magnanimity of Lincoln. But Lincoln died before the lies came. In any event, it was my Brother who fought for Liberty & Justice; I cannot claim that nobility. I entered the war out of hate and I have lived on hate ever since.

In order to be reconciled with these old children of pride, it seems I have to do it on their terms, which means submitting to their story of the War. I respectfully decline. A person has to believe in something, so in the face of Southern affability & apparent decency I will continue to believe my brother's truth, and try to remember what he fought and died for.

There are not many men of the Iron Brigade here, except in the ground.

I visited their graves. They are buried under long stone markers arrayed by State in concave lines as if part of an advance, or waiting in a grassy amphitheater listening perhaps for the awakening Bugle of the Last Judgement, or musing on Mr. Lincoln's speech. But the world will little note nor long remember why they did what they did here unless we the maimed & embittered relics constantly remind it.

We Grand Army veterans sit at long tables for our last messes together, drinking coffee out of large & shiny tin cups, eating heavy portions of fresh bread, pie, & ice cream. Some trust there will be a reunion in heaven, and banquets worthy of an immortal host. Most nights I don't believe there's a heaven but I sure hope there's a hell. The fact is, we will all be gone in a few years.

I would like to pray fire and brimstone down upon these old rebels' arrogant heads that are filled with murderous rights and hypocritical ideas of freedom. Yet somehow I feel that to pray for them, blessing or curse, would be to pray for myself.

I haven't prayed for many years. When I think of prayer I think of Mother and Forrest in church next to each other looking like Mother and Son, one a copy of the other: "Mother, behold your son; son, behold your mother." That picture comes back to me across the decades: the son a sacrifice, the mother his suffering image on earth; both the images of a suffering God, in whose suffering image we are all made. Now that my own death and its inevitable suffering approach like a rebel line of battle, I see that the dream god of youth must die, and the nightmare god of raging humankind must perish. Wounded One, share with me sour water from this pierced canteen. Crucified God, have mercy!

July 3, 1913

Farewell to these green hills & fields! May they return to their innocent beauty and become again what they were before we killed & died here. Meanwhile let the place be a monument to the nobility, savagery, & folly of the human race.

Disembarking from the train a couple of days ago I was helped by a colored porter, into whose palm some of us pressed dimes & quarters as he handed us our portmanteaux. The puzzle & the hopelessness of it all stared me in the face. Certainly it is better to be free than to be a slave, but is this is all we can offer a free Colored man? There will never be a Colored president of the United States. How useless it has all been! Human nature remains human nature, and as Sherman said, "you cannot refine it." Our national sin is race-prejudice. It was here at the very beginning and it is still here now. The War didn't end or redeem the crime of race rule, but once upon a time the boys in blue said No.

I heard one of those old rebels at another table affably drawl something about "self-righteous Yankees." I suppose he might be correct, in which case I represent another kind of lie. Maybe our national sin is just plain hate, like every other country's national sin. If that is so, I am as guilty as any of them & probably more so, because the fact that my Brother would have forgiven these pleasant and likeable old graybacks doesn't mean that I do.

Europe is on the brink of a cataclysmic war into which every soul on earth will be drawn, yet all that Americans can find to talk about is prohibiting liquor, retaining the gold standard, preventing trade unionism, & finding ways to make more money.

The present-day creed is really the ancient belief that there need be no limits to desire or the means of its attainment. It is born in us. But when my

Brother fought, there was at least the notion of *duty*, an outmoded notion but Forrest lived by it & died by it, & it is the one distinguishing feature that separates beasts from heroes. But because of the condition of this world nothing is uncontaminated, & even men of duty do incalculable damage without knowing or intending it.

I stumped through the Soldier's Cemetery again this morning. Some of the best friends I ever had are there. Billy Faust is there: the body of a young man, what is left of it, is in the ground up there. And Bodley Jones is there, whose spirits used to lift and sustain my own. What Lincoln said, not in that cemetery but at his second inauguration—that the War might have been needed to pay our national debt of guilt—it could be correct. But I think the purging that came from bleeding was matched by the stain that comes from killing. We and those who live after us are both freed and contaminated by our War. No human being and no nation is independent of the ambiguities of the human heart, but there are differences among people. Those who did their duty without malice worked whatever redemption that came out of the war. The rest of us contaminated this hallowed ground.

We live in the rubble of the past & build it monuments, for the present is even worse. The War goes on for us, the living. I am not my Brother. I am an unreconstructed Yankee and the War is still alive in me. It destroyed me and all I had & gave me nothing in return. If I am embittered, it is because war is bitter. The questions and sacrileges remain. But what the war gave the world is proof that representative democracy can work; that government of the people by the people ourselves can be strong enough to suppress rebellions against majority rule. Slavery started the war, but the war's main issue was whether an elective majority can remain sovereign. Neither kings, queens, nor tyrants are sovereign here: the majority of the people is our sovereign—and if a minority rebels against an election result by violent means, it must be put down or else elective government vanishes. This, the war proved, to the benefit of humankind.

There are mangled bodies in the ground all over these acres, & the air seems to be filled yet with bullets, screams, & curses. In some way incomprehensible to me, my Brother did not become all this. He stared it in the face & went on being brave & good & true.

I and my cane went for a long walk indeed, with only scenes of the past for company. I strolled to the old woods and fields west of the Seminary, where no veterans sit at long tables eating ice cream and no long barracks tents are pitched; for people have forgotten what happened there in those long & narrow fields and in those park-like woods and around the big barn that still stands near the Chambersburg Pike.

It was beautiful and quiet. The fields are as they were that morning, fresh and fragrant & not trampled; not littered with men and pieces of men, knapsacks and muskets and caps and wide-brimmed Confederate hats. All is peace now, and the grass of the fields undulates dreamily—fields in motion not with marching men, not with men crawling & writhing, but lapping like waves of the St. Croix back home, never the same from one moment to the next, here butternut shades of maturing grain and there streaming hues of grassy blades that lift on warm summer wind. What a flowing field of beauty! How the woods on the low ridge whisper! Here are not the pounding flash of cannons nor the ragged volleys of musketry, nor the vast moan of battle rage & agony—but peace, and quiet, and timeless calm like the stillness between stars.

For Gettysburg now is like one glass photographic plate laid upon another. One is the eternal stillness and beauty of the painterly hand of creation; and the other is the nightmare of vivid memory, in which I see woods filled with bleeding soldiers and fields streaming with lines of men shelled into pieces. Is this not the way of the whole world? Soft rains of spring & overflowing fruits of harvest, gleaming blue rivers & a great broad peace over all—and human suffering laid upon it like the photographic plate of another world. Beautiful & horrible beyond imagination. It is a picture that baffles the mind.

As dusk fell today I sat on a camp chair outside this large tent, drowsing from my exertions during the morning & afternoon. In my misty state what appeared to be an old Confederate stood before me, battered campaign hat & silvery moustache dim in the twilight of my ruminations. The man—whether speaking or simply communicating in thought—said *Forgive!* It was a plea and a demand. I thought, perhaps aloud, *Am I God? Who am I to forgive?* And with a familiar & aggravatingly patient expression he seemed to say *Who are you not to forgive?*

As the figure seemed to move away or dissolve I experienced the peculiar sensation I had felt when my brother appeared to me long ago, in September of 1862. The thought of him transmitted an electrical shock of realization: perhaps this is how Forrest would look if he were alive today. Are these old rebels also my brothers? Perhaps it is my own hatred that I cannot forgive; and in not forgiving them I am failing to forgive myself.

The War has left me with a pale and distorted similitude of wisdom—half romantic and half ironic. Very well. If I must stump after my brother on only one good leg, let it be so. I am coming, Brother, following your youthful & elastic step the best I can, into that nation of promise and that world of light.